Going Up

Also by Peter Hunt

THE MAPS OF TIME
A STEP OFF THE PATH
BACKTRACK

SUE AND THE HONEY MACHINE
FAY COW AND THE MISSING MILK
(Blackbirds)

PETER HUNT

GOING UP

*For Aileen
with all good wishes from the
author*

Peter Hunt

Horsley 1993.

Julia MacRae Books

A DIVISION OF WALKER BOOKS

I would like to thank UCCA for permission
to use the page outline of their University
Admissions Form but I would like to point
out that the University appearing in this
novel is a place of fiction, and is not
modelled on any single real-life institution.

P.H.

© 1989 Peter Hunt
All rights reserved
First published in Great Britain 1989
by Julia MacRae Books
A division of Walker Books Ltd
87 Vauxhall Walk
London SE11 5HJ

British Library Cataloguing in Publication Data
Hunt, Peter
Going up
I. Title
823'.914 [F] PZ7
0 86203 323 3

Printed and bound in Great Britain by
Billings and Sons Ltd, Worcester
Typeset by Graphicraft Typesetters Ltd, Hong Kong.

CONTENTS

—————————●—————————

APPLYING

I think of the prizes that were ours for the taking
and wonder when the choices got made
we don't remember making.
– Liz Lochhead

"Best years of your life," said Tom's father.
"What are?" Tom said.
"School," his father said.
Tom looked at him. "In that case, I may as well do myself in now."

Chapter One
SUE

Jojo parked the horse beside the gate into the back garden, hitching the reins over the gatepost. Behind her was the field and the woods and the countryside. In front, the fence and the garden with the swing they were too old for, and the garage with Daddy's Volvo Estate and, upstairs, a hesitant sound of tapping. Jojo grinned, patted the horse on its nose, and went up the path to the side door.

She pulled her boots off on the boot-puller Sue had bought her for her fifteenth birthday, last week, and went in and through the kitchen, hung her hard hat on the bannister knob and went upstairs. She opened Sue's bedroom door, quietly.

Sue was sitting at her desk, with the computer screen looking blank and green, and a pen in her hand.

Jojo said, "Can you help me with the animal? It needs raking."

Sue rose slightly into the air and put her arm over the papers in front of her.

"Go away."

Jojo came across the room and looked ostentatiously over Sue's shoulder. "Why? What'cha doing?"

"Playing the bagpipes, what does it look like?"

"Ooh," Jojo said. "You're doing joined-up writing. Very good."

Sue said, "Go back to your horsie, O insignificant one. Actually, I'm applying for university."

Jojo came round the chair and looked at the long, folded form. "I hope they let you have one," she said, absently, reading it. "'Fill in your preferences. Four places only.' Which do you prefer?"

"How should I know," Sue said, a touch fraughtly. "I mean, it's not just places, is it? It's people, air, worms. Infrastructures. Look." She reached forward to the window-sill where there was a neat row of small books. "University prospectuses." Sue opened them and flicked pictures at Jojo and dropped them onto the floor. "All these places. New ones and old ones. By the sea. Up mountains. In fields. Back-streets. How do I know?"

"I'm reading a book," Jojo said helpfully, "where all these refugees come to a place where there's a line of buses, and each one's marked with a different country, Italy, France, Sweden... And they have to decide what to be for the rest of their lives."

Sue nodded, staring at a picture of a lecturer, lecturing, in a lecture room.

"It's terrifying. If I go to London, think of all the people I'll never meet in Bristol. I might miss the perfect person." She looked at Jojo. "Not getting too deep for you, am I?"

"Get on with it," Jojo said. "What's the first question?"

"'Personal Details'."

"Tell them to mind their own business."

"'Sex'."

"Yes."

"Daddy's right about you," Sue said. "What shall I put down for this? 'Further information. (a) Practical experience; study abroad...interests (intellectual, social, and other).'"

"Everything," Jojo said. "Make it up. I bet they'll be impressed. Lot of dry old lecturers."

"I'll draft it first," Sue said, and turned to the keyboard.

I am interested in travel and I have lived near Paris and visited Florence, Italy, and Israel, where I visited sites of biblical interest. I help with the local 'talking newspaper' for

the blind. I have been in several theatrical productions
including 'Hamlet' and 'Rosencrantz and...

"How do you spell it?"
"Not like that."

...Guildenstern are Dead.' I enjoy

"I wouldn't tell them that, if I were you."
"Won't your horse be missing you?"

riding, swimming, walking, cycling, tennis, squash and
sailing. I have contributed to the school magazine, and I help
to run the Botanical and Biological Society. I enjoy reading

"Barbara Cartland, Jeffrey Archer, Stephen King..."

(especially Jane Austen, Doris Lessing, and Mervyn Peake). I
enjoy visiting art galleries, playing guitar and piano, and
singing.

"Do you think that's enough?"
Jojo looked critically at the screen. "They'll probably
give you *two* universities," she said. "I never knew you were
so talented. I'll look on you with new respect."
"Any would do," Sue said. "Now push off while I write
it out proper."
Jojo retreated, bowing, and thumped away down the
stairs. Sue sucked the end of her ballpoint for a minute,
seeing ivy-covered towers and glass-fronted libraries and
hearing northern accents and southern accents. She looked at
the video screen.
"There's only one thing to do," she said to it, very
quietly. "Panic." But her hand was very steady as she began to
write.

Chapter Two
TOM

While, about a hundred miles away almost due south, Tom, having failed to catch anything in the stream at the bottom of the valley and having failed to think of anything much to put on the university application form, came up the field and climbed the wall into the yard of the village shop.

There was a precarious-looking corrugated iron lean-to shed, the white shop-van and an old and rusting Ford. Its engine was hanging from two unhealthy-looking ropes from the shed beams. Tom patted the car on its bonnet and let himself into the back door of the shop. He met his father, the shopkeeper, in the corridor, trying to manoeuvre a large crate of bottles among the stacks of cornflakes.

"Haven't you gone yet?"

"Sorry," Tom said. "This time next year."

"Pity. I sold your bed when you were out."

Tom, having lived with this sense of humour for seventeen years, didn't smile. He propped his fishing rod in among the boxes and followed his father into the shop.

It was crammed with everything, almost, you could want to buy, up to the windows that looked out onto the narrow village green which was hemmed with stone houses. His father took up his standard shopkeeper's position behind the counter.

"What've you been doing, then?"

"Filling in forms." Tom took a long envelope from inside his anorak, and passed it over, resignedly. His father slid out the form.

5 Further Information. (a) Practical experience; study abroad...interests (intellectual, social, and other).

I have an old car which I am working on, although I don't really enjoy mechanics. I helped to renovate some warehouses for use as a community centre, which was rather better. I read, paint (mostly watercolour) and fish. (I'm sorry if this sounds unimpressive.)

His father folded the form with great care and slid it back into the envelope.

"I see. Well, I'd better buy your bed back, quick."

Tom picked up a bar of chocolate from the counter and then put it down again. "Has a refreshing touch of honesty, don't you think?" he said.

"It has a refreshing touch of the smarty-pants."

Tom shook his head. "No, you should see what the others write. Done this, done that. Read everything, been everywhere. They have to write small to get it all in. Makes you wonder how they have time to go to school. The universities can't be as thick as that."

His father sucked his teeth briefly.

"What do you do with it now?"

"It says: 'Pass it on to your head teacher or other referee.'"

Confidential statement by referee (first read pages 5-6 overleaf)

Referee's name _____ Ms Anne Henderson

Post/occupation/relationship _____ Headteacher

Address _____

		Type of school or college	6th Form College
		Number on roll	Full-time
			Part-time
Telephone (including STD code)		Number in Sixth Form (upper plus lower) or equivalent group	
		Number normally proceeding to university each year	

This form will be photographed and smaller copies made: please type with a good black ribbon or write in black ink on this side of the form only, within the frame. Typing is very much preferred. No continuation sheets can be accepted.

Name of candidate *(block capitals or type)* _____ Susan Annette Marriot

Susan is a very able student, well liked by her peers. Although her background is not particularly academic (her father is an Estate Agent), she is under some pressure to succeed because her younger sister is very gifted.

In her last school, her results showed talent on both the science and humanities sides, and her decision to take Biology Maths and English reflects her good academic range. She is a steady and conscientious worker, rather than a high-flier, but we would confidently expect the following grades:

BIOLOGY - B, ENGLISH - B/C, MATHS - C.

Her decision to take Biology at University is fully supported by her teachers. She has been particularly interested in Ecology and her laboratory work is meticulous. In English, she has been more interested in analysis and in narrative, rather than in poetry, which again reflects her rather more scientifically-orientated mind. Her background work is always thorough. In Mathematics she is a solid worker.

As a member of the College Council, she has shown herself to be helpful and responsible. She is very self-confident (one might say, self-contained) and inclined to be dogmatic in discussion. She helped to found her school Pony Club, (she is a competent rider), and has been active in the choir, the squash club, and the travel society (which she also helped to found). She has stayed abroad (in France) on an exchange visit, and helped to organise a trip to the Holy Land last summer. She came to us with good languages.

Susan should perform well at interview, although she can be rather quiet, (this seems to be because she makes thoughtful judgments). She is a sound worker, and all her teachers confidently expect her to take a good degree. I recommend her to you as a good all-rounder.

Sections 6 and 7 checked	Yes/No

Signed _____ Anne Henderson

Applicant's fee enclosed	Yes/No

Date _____

ree's name ___M.J.C. Wadcock___

/occupation/relationship ___Deputy Headmaster___

'ess ___

Telephone
(including STD code)

Type of school or college	Comprehensive	
Number on'roll	Full-time	
	Part-time	
Number in Sixth Form (upper plus lower) or equivalent group		
Number normally proceeding to university each year		

form will be photographed and smaller copies made: please type with a good black ribbon or write in black ink.on this of the form only, within the frame. Typing is very much preferred. No continuation sheets can be accepted.

Thomas Sebastian Rowlands

ne of candidate (block capitals or type) ___

Tom Rowlands joined the school in the fifth year, and has settled well. His work was not very good to begin with, probably because his family had moved around the country a good deal, but over the last year he has developed his natural talents.

ART: Predicted grade, A. Tom is stronger on creative and graphic work than on historical or theoretical areas, but he is well motivated and is working hard, and he is expected to do very well. He has won the school Art and Design Prize twice.

ENGLISH: C. Tom is a rather diffident and shy person,and is reluctant to form or express an opinion about the books he has read. This is a pity, because he is intelligent and creative, and his writing style is lucid.

MATHEMATICS: C. Now that Tom has decided upon a career in Architecture, he has become somewhat more motivated in his mathematical studies. However, his concentration does tend to wander. If he can overcome this, which seems probable, he should do well.

We recommend Tom as a student whose combination of talents should make him a successful and creative Architect. He is overcoming some difficulties in his background. His father gave up his job as nuclear-power engineer, on a matter of principle, and he is now a small shop-keeper in a nearby village. He has not encouraged his son to go into higher education, and this may well have affected Tom's motivation.

Tom is a solitary character, although he gets on well with his contemporaries. He has taken part in school sports, and played Rugby for his House (although without distinction), but he appears to be gifted mechanically, with an interest in cars.

He may need to be drawn out at interview, and may seem to be shy, but we would rate him as a worthwhile student, worthy of encouragement.

ions 6 and 7 checked	Yes/No

licant's fee enclosed	Yes/No

Signed ___M.J.C. Wadcock___

Date ___

GOING UP

Autumn's bright moon
However far I walked, still afar off
In an unknown sky
– Kaga no Chiyo (1701–1775)

I was nineteen years old, still soft at the edges, but with a
confident belief in good fortune. I carried a small rolled-up
tent, a violin, a blanket, a change of clothes, a tin of treacle
biscuits, and some cheese. I was excited, vain-glorious,
knowing I had far to go; but not, as yet, how far. As I left
home that morning and walked away from the sleeping
village, it never occurred to me that others had done this
before me.
– Laurie Lee

The place, as we approached, seemed more and more
To have an eddy's force, and sucked us in
More eagerly at every step we took.
– Wordsworth (The Prelude)

Chapter Three
FROM THE COLLECTED LETTERS OF S. A. MARRIOT (1)

Monday, September 28th, this year

Dear Jojo,

Well, I promised to write a lot, so I may as well start now.

I'm still at 'ome, in the bedroom what's going to be your bedroom, when you stop lazing around. I'm sitting on my trunk because the only thing that isn't packed yet is the computer, which is lucky because I'd find it very hard to type inside the packing case. (And I hereby apologise for accusing you of eating that bag of toffees four years ago. I've just found them behind the bookcase. I've left them under your pillow; they're a nice green colour.)

I've cleared all the old books out of the bookcase, especially the ones with Princesses in. They haven't seemed the same since you asked what they did with the rotting corpses of the dragons the Princes kept dragging in. Anyway, most of them had the sign of the fifth-year feminist league disapproval stamped on them. I think they ought to go because they never mention the plumbing; must have been pretty disgusting to be the Lady of Shalott after a week or two, and anyway, everything's so black and white it's silly. I think I stopped being Romantic when Mummy told me about her wedding day. Did you ever hear that? How she got a grain of rice in her eye walking out of the church gate and concussed herself on the car door, and Dad was sick all night with food poisoning. Still, I was reading one of your High School bodice-rippers just now. All the heroes are *so* plastic. Dark hair, white teeth, glowing eyes. I just want to meet one with relatively few spots and no groping. Maybe the next doctor you get will be dishy.

Anyway, I stuck them all in box on the landing. You nearly had Dad in hospital with you. I think he just exaggerated how far he fell.

I hope you think this is funny. Dad came in and said, "Try to make it funny." He must be joking. I bet you're just dying for a good laugh. (How are you going to read this, anyway? I suppose they'll stick it to the ceiling and give you a telescope.) I've been right through all the problem novels, about getting anorexia and divorced and athlete's foot, but I can't find anything for people flat on their backs in hospital.

Anyway, I don't want to complain, but it was a pretty silly day to fall off your horsie. I'm supposed to be getting all the attention, you know, poor waif leaving home for the big cruel wicked world, with all those nasty men. I've tried to talk the parents out of it, but it looks as if they're going to drive me down there so I don't fall off the train.

I went and groomed Smudge from fetlock to matlock or whatever. Bow to stern. (I was going to rename him Swine, but I suppose it wasn't his fault he stepped on you. Silly place to be lying, under his hoof, if you ask me.) He looks OK, that is, he doesn't look in the least bit sorry, and your friend Becca, who *does* look like a Shetland Pony with glasses, is going to look after him for a couple of days until you're up.

I'm going to have a bath now; it'll probably be the last comfortable one I'll have until Christmas. Can't say I'm looking forward to all the tiled shower-stalls. (Actually, it's all a mixture of exciting and scary, like the first time you go up in an aeroplane. That's why they call it going up, Mum says, but Dad says that universities have got altogether too high an opinion of themselves and it should be called 'going along', so boo to them.)

So it's off to the big wide world. I'll write the exact minute I get there, if I'm not carried off by a Prince or a

Dragon, or fall into degenerate student ways on the first evening (you never know your luck).

So, kindly stop mucking around and get up soon and come to see me (and don't take on if the mama blubs all over you, it does her good, the poor old thing).

Lots of love and kissis,

Senior Sister xxxxxx

Chapter Four
LEAVING

Dear Mr Rowlands,

I have now received your acceptance of a place at this University. You will be required to register on Wednesday, September 30th, in the Main Hall of the Old College Building. Please bring with you the enclosed forms and three passport-sized photographs.

After registration, you will be required to register with your Department or School, which will be sending you the relevant details.

The Students' Union has organised a 'Freshers' Fayre' for the weekend from Thursday until Sunday. Lectures will begin on Monday, 5th October.

I enclose a map, and confirmation from the Accommodation Officer.

Yours sincerely,

4. Leaving

Dear Mr Rowlands,

May I offer my congratulations on your acceptance into the School of Architecture. I enclose a syllabus and reading list, together with registration forms specifically for the School. Registration will be on Wednesday, September 30th, in the Wright Building (Room 212). Please register with the University itself BEFORE coming to the School; the Registry should by now have sent you the forms. Please bring the enclosed forms, together with two passport-sized photographs.
Lectures begin on Monday, 5th October. You will be issued with timetables and other details at Registration.

Yours sincerely,

Going Up

```
ACCOMMODATION OFFICE
_____
                                        LODGINGS
  r T. S. Rowlands                      FLAT
M..........................
                                        H̶O̶U̶S̶E̶
Accommodation has been arranged for you at
    54 West Park Street                  R̶E̶S̶I̶D̶E̶N̶C̶E̶
    .................................

on the basis of      b̶e̶d̶-̶a̶n̶d̶-̶b̶r̶e̶a̶k̶f̶a̶s̶t̶

                     bed, breakfast and dinner

                     f̶u̶l̶l̶-̶b̶o̶a̶r̶d̶

                     s̶e̶l̶f̶-̶e̶a̶t̶i̶n̶g̶

Please confirm your acceptance and time of arrival with

      Mrs W. Evans
      ...................................

      Above address. Tel: 895682
at    ...................................
```

The morning of the day he left home for university, Tom woke up and decided to panic.

Oh God. Please don't make me go to university. It'll be even worse than school. Can't I do fast forward until it's over?

He sat up and looked at his packed room. Yesterday, he'd taken down all his posters with half an idea of rolling them up neatly and taking them along, but the corners stayed on the walls with the tape, and he'd flexed his elbows and rammed the thick paper V shapes into the wastebin.

He got out of bed, stepped over the old cornflakes carton which held his collection of books, and put his face against the window.

Suppose I don't go? Suppose I just give it up now and get a nice mindless job on a farm? My mother would kill me, that's why. And anyway, what farm would have me?

That line of thought didn't seem to be very helpful.

And then there's going to be girls: females. His stomach, which already didn't seem to be particularly attached to his

18

body, filled up with ice-cubes again. He was getting rather used to the feeling. Never know what to do with girls.

He put on the unpacked clothes and went downstairs. His father, who seemed to spend his life in the back corridor stacking crates, was in the back corridor, stacking crates. If he says "Haven't you gone yet?" Tom thought, I won't have to worry about university. I'll be in jail for Dad-slaughter.

"We decided not to sell your bed after all," his father said.

Tom stopped and looked at him, cautiously.

"Very difficult to let your room if it doesn't have a bed." He went out into the yard.

Tom looked round for an offensive weapon. Living with a humorist, he thought, gets very wearing. At least that's one advantage of university. In the kitchen, his mother was washing the dog in the sink. She looked round at him.

"Your grandfather used to say he never worried about what was going to happen tomorrow. He'd just say, 'Well, they can't shoot me. Whatever happens, they can't shoot me.'" Tom took the cornflakes packet from the shelf and his mother turned the dog over amid a certain amount of soap. "Always said that." She paused, as if contemplating the deficiencies of her father's conversation. Tom stopped pouring cornflakes in mid-pour. The dog lay still, apparently waiting. "He said it on his way over to France during the D-day landings in 1944."

Tom forced himself to say, "What happened?"

"They shot him," his mother said. Tom rested his head on the table. "Being so cheerful as keeps me going." She went on with the dog and said to it, "What's the biggest problem?"

Tom didn't have to consider. "Being at the bottom of the heap again," he said. He took some sultanas from his secret store and added them to the cornflakes. "When I was in the first year at school, I thought I'd be in control when I got to the sixth-form. Then when I got there, I wasn't, and now I'm going to be a 'fresher' at university. Lowest of the low."

"That does sound sort of at the bottom of the heap." His mother hauled the dog out by the scruff of its neck, took three steps to her right and threw it out of the door into the yard. It shook itself thoroughly, spraying the side of Tom's car. "That'll be a pound for a quarter of a car wash. Well, you can smile, anyway." She began to run the water out of the sink. "There must be some positives. Not having to take the dog for walks."

Tom didn't have to think about this, either. "No more Rugby," he said. "If you ever see me on a Rugby pitch again, you can have me certified. You did burn the boots, didn't you?"

"I gave them to the deserving poor."

"Nobody's poor enough to deserve Rugby boots."

Tom ate his cornflakes and sultanas, thinking things that he couldn't quite say. Like, from tomorrow, I can't be forced to do anything again, and that includes being cold to the bone and hacked and cut at games. There'll be no more being reviled for not coming first; no more being bullied by thugs and getting no sympathy because they're smaller than me; no more being laughed at because you like the wrong book, or do unmacho things like painting; and no more of not being able to understand the subjunctive or how to make a dovetail joint.

"What are you going to miss?" his mother said. "Present company excepted. You can take the dog if you like."

"Well, I won't miss anyone from school," Tom said. Especially, he thought, the crew he went for a drink with yesterday. Three people he had nothing in common with except that they'd all sat in the same classrooms for two years, and now they were all going to university. One of them was going to Oxford, and so the three that weren't were a bit uneasily rude to him. They drank pints of beer in a pub beside a canal (all except Tom, who was driving), and one of them took a glass home as a jolly souvenir and they all said goodbye in loud voices. Tom was glad to be rid of them.

"Well, I don't blame you," his mother said. "You can choose who you like from now on."

Tom washed up his bowl and took a mug of coffee out into the yard. It was a misty, autumnal day, full of sadness and endings. Or, he thought, rather reluctantly, beginnings.

He walked across to the car, which was almost ready to go; the result of hours of oily, gruesome effort. He sat on the bonnet and looked down into the valley where there was a line of mist over the stream.

He thought, there are a few things that I couldn't say at all. No more not being allowed into pubs, never having any money, and not being able to choose the clothes I really want. Or the haircut. Or the foul smell of chalk and kids, and school dinners which make the floorboards smell of old carrots. Or gym. Or cycling to school in winter when it was so cold that I would have cried if the tear ducts hadn't been frozen solid. He looked at the car and smiled. No more of that, anyway.

Then he stopped smiling and took a long breath and went up to his room and brought down his box of books, and his holdall, and his suitcase, and two carrier-bags of provisions, and his squash racket, and another carrier bag full of everything he'd forgotten, and an armful of coats and anoraks. His father looked out from the shop counter.

"Anyone would think you're leaving home. Was it something we said?" He came out into the yard with a book and balanced it on top of Tom's last armful.

"Aunt Lynn thought you'd need this." Tom tried to look down his nose at the title. "It's called *Student Cooking*, though I don't know why you'd want to cook a student. Times must be hard." He held the passenger door open, and Tom tipped the coats into the back seat. He went on cheerfully, "I survived *my* student days on a diet of fish and chips and meat pies and beer. And look at me." Tom straightened up and looked at him.

"I'll learn it by heart," he said.

"If it's any help," his father said, with a seriousness that upset Tom more than the millionth joke, "everyone feels like that. Scared stiff and can't wait to go in the same breath."

It seemed very odd, not having to go back to school and Tom, trying not to think about all the saying goodbye that had just gone on, drove very carefully out of the village and down the very familiar road to the town. Everyone seemed to be going about their normal business and no-one turned and stared or waved or anything. He began to get the uncomfortable feeling that he was invisible and then that turned into a rather good feeling and he pulled up nearly opposite the school gates, turned the engine off, and watched the last of the pupils going in.

Tom leaned on the steering wheel, and waited until the place had gone quiet. It was a curious sort of revenge to think that the teachers were still in there and that he was out here, with a car (even if it wasn't much of a car), and a new world to go to.

He turned the key and there was a dull clunk from under the bonnet. Tom's stomach froze and he turned the ignition key back and forward again. Clunk. He thought, if the car won't start, here of all places, I'll curl up and die. No, I'll chop it up, and then I'll curl up and die. They must all be watching out of the school windows.

Not being able to swallow, he tried again, and this time the engine turned and fired. He let it rev for a moment. Simple, really: the battery's a bit low; not enough power to throw the starter-motor in. He found that he was talking to himself and he let the clutch in and pulled out into the traffic and headed south, out of the town, holding the wheel tightly to stop his hand shaking.

The town slowly dwindled away into scruffy suburbs and petrol stations and, as Tom drove past the delimit signs feeling as though things were OK after all and the engine was warmed up nicely, a sniff of smoke started to come from under the dashboard, and then it got thicker, and the engine cut out abruptly.

With a small squeak, Tom pulled over and ran the car up onto a piece of pavement that had been left over from the town. Lorries crushed by. The smoke didn't seem about to set the whole car on fire, so Tom got upside-down in the driver's seat and looked under. Somewhere in the wiring loom, there were sparks. Tom briefly considered screaming or bursting into tears (at least nobody would see him), or simply putting a match into the petrol tank and ending it all. The day, which had seemed rather fresh and clear, now seemed dismal and cold and sad.

He forced himself to do something, which meant pulling the burned wires apart and then twisting them together (amid sparks) whereupon the ignition came on again. He drove on rather nervously, and after about two miles, the engine cut out again.

With a mixture of relief and black despair, Tom twisted the wires again, and turned back towards home. Perhaps he wasn't meant to go at all. It was all a sign from the gods. The wires got progressively shorter, but he only had to stop three times (not, fortunately, outside the school) before he and the Ford, which by now he hated comprehensively, perspired into the shop yard.

He thought, perhaps I can mend it without anyone noticing – but his father was standing in the doorway with an expressionless face.

Tom put his lips together and got out of the car but, for some curious reason, his father was in an efficient and unwitty mood. He didn't say anything about Tom not being sixty miles away; he just got the big toolbox out of the workshop and together they traced the wiring fault to the ignition switch. There was a silent agreement that they didn't have the time or money to buy a new one, so the whole thing was by-passed, and Tom set out again with the only car in the world with a large brass Victorian light-switch bolted to the underside of the dashboard.

"At least you don't have to worry about losing the key," his father said.

"Try again."

"Good luck."

This time, clear of the town and heading south, with the mist evaporated into the late September thin blue sky, Tom began to feel just a little bit great about things. He chose a route which avoided the motorways and drove along quiet roads, and there was no sign of smoke from the dashboard although the temperature gauge did tend to creep rather unnervingly towards the red bit.

And, in the mid-afternoon, he came to the crest of a hill and there was a vista of sloping fields and a town and, beyond it, the sea out to the horizon. Tom steered the Ford into a lay-by (leaving the engine running), and opened the door and stood up on the sill. On each side the smooth hills skirted the sea.

Down there, not only a town, but a future. Not a very profound thought, he thought, but he still stood there, trying to remember what it looked like, first time.

So this is a landlady. It must be a joke, surely.

Tom stood in the small hallway, inside the stained-glass front door of 54 West Park Street, and felt ill. There was a hall-stand with glass and curved wood and umbrella racks, and a dispiriting smell of old jam, and a square woman, who obviously didn't like him. She could have been old or young and she had a peculiar smile that didn't seem to have anything to do with him. For some reason, Tom felt terribly guilty as well as about eleven years old.

"I'll show you to your room," she said. Tom wondered slightly whether to grab his bags and run, but before he could do anything decisive he was walking up the steep stairs which wound back on themselves and had thin bannisters which were presumably stronger than they looked. "One of the other students is here already. You'd like to meet him." It sounded like an order.

Tom, who was wondering whether he should have brought some bags up with him, stopped beside her on the first landing. She knocked on a door and it opened and a fold of hair-oil and soap and medicine-loaded air fell out at them like an atmospheric mattress. There was a very precise figure with a hand outstretched.

"Hello. I'm Anthony B. Thompson."

For a good three seconds, Tom looked at the hand, thinking, this isn't fair. I have to get a weirdo, first crack out of the box. Things have got to get better. Then he shook the hand and said, "Hi, I'm Tom, nice to meet you," and the precise figure beamed at him and said, "That remains to be seen," and shut the door.

Perhaps I won't wait for my bags, Tom thought, but Mrs Evans was standing, half-inside the bathroom, indicating what seemed to be a broom-cupboard with a sliding door.

"You said you wanted a single room," she said, as if pre-empting any criticism. Tom looked into the room. There was a bed, a wardrobe with the veneer standing off the wood, a single-bar electric fire with a grey slot-meter, and a window onto a blank yard. So this is education.

"The other two will be here this evening," she said to the back of Tom's neck. "Evening meal at six, breakfast at eight, and don't use too much hot water because it isn't on the slot."

She went away and Tom stepped into the room and switched on the light, which had the effect of making him think he'd gone blind. The pink wallpaper seemed to absorb light. The room smelled of sweet dampness.

He went to the window. Outside there was a small grey yard. Tom rested his head against the cold glass and said, without allowing any sound to come out: I want to go home, please. Now.

Out in the late paling afternoon, having dumped his bags on the bed and slid the door behind him, Tom walked down narrow sidestreets and came out, almost with surprise, on the seafront, and thought, if you've always lived with hills and houses, it's funny to find one side of the world taken away.

The street opened onto a wide road with an even wider pavement on the far side, and then white pipe-railings and then the sea, which was grey, out and out to a vague horizon, and there was a splendid smell. Tom stopped and breathed. Ah, well. Perhaps I'll survive after all.

He crossed the road and looked over what were, on closer inspection, white and rust-streaked railings, down to the beach. The sea swashed against the pebbles and swashed out again, and Tom felt the sea and the sound being very big and calm and calming. He looked round, and the promenade seemed like a huge, ironic parade of Christmas cakes, and he felt on his own, and ready to be something after all.

Further along, the sideshows and the rides in a small pleasure-patch had been shut down for the winter. There was a lot of painted concrete and sand which had drifted into corners; big Victorian houses stalked along the bay and great green and brown bulks of headlands came out of the sea at each end.

Towards the far end from where he was standing, there was more activity; cars were stopping and turning. Tom walked along the promenade. There was a dead-end and a turning-area, and Tom sat on the white railings that ended the promenade, with a two metre drop onto the pebbles behind him, and watched.

The large building with the big central doors and the windows going up and up under slightly sea-eaten Victorian convolutions, was quite obviously a Hall of Residence, and, to judge by the proportions of the sexes going into it, very largely a Hall of Residence for females.

There were no very posh cars; there was the occasional aging Range Rover, but they were mostly 1.6 litre middle-

range cars, driven, perhaps, by middle managers or shop-
keepers. They stopped and out got mothers from the
passenger seats, and sometimes from the back; occasionally
wild women with wild daughters. But mostly there were
fathers who looked like fathers, and the daughters looked like
daughters and sat in the back seat. Tom turned his face away
so that it would look to the passing observer as though he
were looking up the hill, but he kept his eyes on the rituals.
The doorway had ornate stone carving over it and lights in
iron brackets on each side.

The cars stopped; one person said that they weren't
supposed to park there because it was a turning area, and the
other said, ignore it. Then somebody, usually the male,
opened the hatchback or the boot and lifted out two cases and
a couple of supermarket carrier bags, sometimes with a poster
rolled up; even, once, a complete saddle. Then they all
walked, rather hesitantly and laden with bags and shoulder
bags and cases and rackets, through the open doorway of the
Hall and, ten minutes later, the mother and father would
emerge, often dabbing noses, and get into the 1.6 and roll
away.

Being sisterless, Tom had only formed a provisional
attitude towards girls, females, women. The girls at school
were generally self-contained, very off-putting and inaccessible, and comprehensively de-sexed by having to wear
green blankets. Then there were the females on the top
shelves of magazine racks, who bore so little resemblance to
anything imaginable in real life that Tom wondered why real
women made a fuss about them. And then there were these.

The girls crossing the prom were inaccessible, and aloof,
and very much older than him, but, significantly, they were
not wearing green blankets. Some miraculous metamorphosis seemed to have come over them during the summer.
There was no trace of them ever having been 'schoolgirls',
whereas Tom still felt the mark of the regulation blazer and
shoes clearly stamped on him.

But, he decided, this was a day for positive facing of such terrors, so he got off the rail and went for a nonchalant walk, (which began as a hobble because all the blood seemed to have run into his feet), through the thick of it.

The latest arrival was an almost-new Volvo Estate and, as Tom came alongside, the father, fighting a large cabin-trunk, had got it stuck on the lip of the rear door and was clearly trying to decide whether to sacrifice his knee-caps or his fingertips. Tom mumbled helpfully and got a hand under one side of the trunk and they hoisted it clear and over the pavement and into the entrance hall.

Tom thought, this must be a record. Ten minutes and I'm in the girls' Hall. He looked round quickly. There was a porter's lodge and a high corridor, rather like school, leading through into a large assembly room. There were wide stairs going up.

"Thanks a lot," said the man.

"That's OK," Tom said.

He edged his way out, past the mother and daughter coming in with shoulder-bags and parcels. The man followed him out and started to drag a carton containing a computer from the Volvo. Tom offered to help, but the man said, "It's OK, it's just bulky."

Tom stepped away and then strolled back down the promenade, rather wishing that he'd brought the map with him. Not knowing quite where the University was made the afternoon a little aimless.

The early evening settled around him with a coldness and smokiness in the air which was both exciting and lonely.

He stopped and looked out at the sea. "What worries me," he said to a seagull which was sitting on the rail, flicking its feathers, "is that I don't *know* anything."

The eating room at Mrs Evans's house was the back room of the two. The front room was stuffed with what seemed to be several three-piece suites and gave the impression of not having any air in it. Beyond the eating room was a glass door leading into forbidden territory, a kitchen, and, beyond it, presumably the Evans's living area. It didn't seem to be very big. A stocky figure, assumed to be Mr Evans, could occasionally be glimpsed. Otherwise, there was a dining table and chairs, the table permanently covered by a plastic cloth, an armchair and a dead, tiled fireplace. The smell of jam was pervasive.

At six o'clock, the appointed mealtime (although it fitted fairly neatly between any late-day mealtimes that Tom was familiar with), he came downstairs, having been waiting in his room for half an hour rather unsure of what to do.

Anthony B. was sitting at a table set for four and each place had a plate between the knives and forks. Each plate had two tomato-halves, and a thin circular slice of a pink substance. Anthony B. was sitting to attention, apparently in rapt anticipation. Tom felt as though he had lost the use of his brain. Anthony B. looked around.

"I trust you had a pleasant walk."

"Yes, fine, thanks," Tom said, his eyes on the plates.

"Looks good, doesn't it?" Anthony B. said. Tom was at a loss for a moment. He nearly said, "You can't be serious," but he sat down and thought, I know how they make this stuff. They steam-strip carcasses and mix it with a slurry of bones and eyeballs: mechanically recovered meat. Yeugh.

But he didn't say any of that, largely because he thought that he might throw up if he opened his mouth. His father, who had a fairly un-husbandly view of his wife's cooking, had once said, after a particularly soggy serving of Brussels sprouts: "One day, you'll learn to appreciate cooking like this. Once you get out there, you'll soon learn not to be fussy." Not that he was right about either thing, so far. But, Tom thought, if Anthony B. actually thinks this is good, it gives you a new perspective on the way other people eat. More education.

Mrs Evans wobbled unsmilingly in from the kitchen and

glanced witheringly at the empty chairs. She was carrying a bowl of chips.

"Ah, chips," A.B. said, displaying a penchant for stating the blindingly obvious. "Can't go wrong with chips."

Tom looked at them and thought, you're wrong there, A.B. They were quite distinctively chip-shop chips; not home-cooked chunks like his mother produced, nor yet the slim, golden, evenly-graded hamburger-chain chips. They were faintly grey and smelled of disinfectant.

A. B. shovelled chips onto his plate. Tom, whose spirits had returned to zero, spooned some of them onto the round of pink animal sludge, which began to dissolve slightly. Tom stared at his plate, thinking that this must be the most desolate place in the whole space-time continuum.

The door from the hall opened. Tom looked up. What appeared to be one of the less advanced species of ape was looking in at the door. It was dressed in jeans and a blue-striped black shirt and a leather jacket. It contemplated A. B., Tom, the luncheon meat, and Mrs Evans comprehensively, then showed its yellow teeth and retreated, shaking its head. The front door banged shut.

Mrs Evans regarded the door with her pale eyes.

"If he doesn't want them, you may as well have the rest," she said. She went back into the kitchen.

"That's number three," A. B. said cheerfully. "His name's Vince. Looks as though we'll get plenty to eat, doesn't it?"

Tom closed his eyes, but when he opened them it was all still there. He pushed back his chair, hardly daring to look at A. B., went out into the hall, took his coat from the hanger and went into the street, closing the front door very carefully behind him and almost expecting Mrs Evans to come running after him, waving a bowl of chips. He wanted to shout: "You can't expect me to live there for three years." Not even for three days.

He walked in the general direction of the sea, and the

smell of disinfected chips came up to him and it was so fatty in the air that there were almost floating smuts. He stopped breathing and walked past the chip shop. The next shop was a newsagent and tobacconist and Vince the Ape came out. He gestured at the chip shop.

"Amazing place," he said. "If you ask for a pie, they drop it into the fat and fry it." He stood and scratched his stomach. There was a smell of old tobacco smoke that nearly outweighed the smell of grease. "Horse fat," he said decisively. He looked at Tom. "There's a good kebab house two streets over. If old Fanny Evans is going to feed us that rubbish, we'd best look out. Fancy a pint?"

"No, thanks," Tom said. "Maybe I'll try the kebab house."

"Suit yourself," said the Ape. "See you around."

Tom watched him walk into the cold evening and then walked round the block to where he'd parked his car and got in. He sat, holding the steering wheel, and wondering where there was to drive, but there wasn't anywhere. But at least the car was a bit of home and a bit of himself. It had cost him his savings from four summers of helping on the farm, and delivering milk, and working at the petrol station, and serving in the shop, and it was his. He patted the steering wheel.

"Well, we're here," he said. "This is it."

Chapter Five

FROM THE COLLECTED LETTERS OF
S. A. MARRIOT (2)

———————————————●———————————————

Tuesday, September 29th
Dothegirls Hall

Dear Jojo,

Well, I promised you a blow-by-blow account, or rather a
flop-by-flop account (don't expect it to last more than a day).
The parents have just driven off along the promenade
(really, a prom), and I'm sitting in this room up in the attics of
St Angela's Hall of Residence which for years was apparently
just for us Women (you see, elevated to womanhood in one
day). Actually, it's been co-ed for years now, but they keep
the men decently out of the way, down the other end in
cages and we're allowed to go and feed them every now and
then, or something. (I thought you'd be interested in that,
first of all.)

I'm not going to complain because I suppose this is
better than lazing around on my back looking at the ceiling,
so you're still winning on points. But you didn't miss anything
with the trip down here.

I mean, you'd think I'd never been away from home
before, the way the mama was going on. I thought she was
actually going to come in and help me unpack and tuck me
up in bed. She had a thermos and some sandwiches in her
basket, but I pointed out that they probably have food, even
this far south, so she took them away. They're no doubt
destined for her secret box, along with our first locks of hair,
your first tooth, the remains of the first fence you rode

through, and all the rest of it. Maybe I should have taken them now I come to think about it. She looked a bit miz.

When they left, I felt just the same way I felt when we gave away the hamsters. This hamster's hutch is about five metres square and decorated (well, I say decorated, m'dear) in a sort of pale brown (beege) and there's a little notice stuck on the back of the door with THE RULES. One of them is, don't stick posters on the wall because it pulls the paint off, and all over the wall there are little square plaster-patches where ancestral occupants have pulled the paint off. I think this constitutes what Dad would call a precedent.

Anyway, it all went pretty smoothly, considering. Dad didn't get lost, and nothing went wrong with the glove box, so Mama didn't have the vapours, and we had lunch at an hotel as a treat, and Daddy only complained twice, so you can see, it was all normal. Then on, on, and we ended up at this Victorian pile. It's on the seafront at one end of the prom, and looks like a badly iced wedding cake (about your standard). There's a wide road and very wide pavement with what is either a bandstand for a very small band, or a circular bus-shelter for circular bus queues. Then there's some white railings, with k-nobbles, and a beach with big pebbles (the kind that when you lie on it, it feels as if you're all shoulder-blades and backbone). Then there's a lot of grey stuff sloshing around. Informed opinion has it that this is the SEA, and there are *les bateaux* on it to prove it. It's either very restful or very depressing, and just between you and me, it's touch and go which it is, just at this minute.

Anyway, there were lots of other mummies and daddies delivering lots of other little women, which generally made me feel like a complete idiot (or idiette, if you prefer). I knew that stupid trunk was too big. Daddy slid it out of the Volvo and got it caught on the back of the boot. Some passing native had to help him into the entrance hall with it, which didn't please him too much. As We Know We Marriots

Do Not Ask For Help Unless It Is Absolutely Imperative, Do
We Susan. Then the three of us got it up the 87 steps to my
room (Daddy will tell you it was 287, ignore him) and then
they sniffed around and looked at the loos which are of the
limbo-dancer type, and Daddy showered me with money
(well, drizzled), and Mama shed a tear, and off they went.
(Actually, Jo, don't tell anyone, but I did just feel a little bit
hollow in the region of the knicker elastic. Maybe going to
all of those other places just put off the feeling that I was
really leaving. I know I could just get on the bus and come
back – but I can't really.)

So, after they'd gone, I chose one of the wardrobes and
started to unpack. It's funny, you'd expect the wardrobes to
smell of something, but they don't. I chose the right-hand bed
with the feet facing the windows. (They're dormers, with a
window seat, so in three years I'll be able to let down my
hair for the princes to climb up.)

Then there's two desks. This one is JUST big enough for
the computer, and I can sit on the bed with the keyboard, so
that's OK. (The beds are covered with green seaweed baked
into a kind of waffle, and the bed is a lot less than a metre
wide, and the pillow is made of pebbles. I should have
followed Grandfather's advice.)

Still, the clothes look pretty OK (including the ones I stole
from you. Oops, didn't I mention...) I can see them from
here because the wardrobe door fell off while I was sliding it
shut. I took your advice about the riding boots and the crop
and put them right at the back of the wardrobe so that
visiting men won't get the wrong idea, and I've stuck up a
couple of posters to make the place look more homely. (And
so I've broken the rules already!)

I've just been interrupted by a Bright Spot. She's called
Joy and she's a sub-warden, which means she's supposed to
look after us. She's only about two years older than I am and
she said that she didn't think she'd really be doing much
looking after and she grinned a lot, so she's an asset. I think

she meant being nice – I mean, it wasn't just an act.

Well, that's 40 minutes, and that's yer lot for the minute. There's supposed to be Tea In The Dining Hall now, which sounds pretty grim, and then I suppose my room-mate will turn up. She's supposed to be allocated by computer, so I'm expecting the worst. (Sunday afternoon here feels just like Sunday afternoon there, I can tell you, and this place is rather like a hospital.)

Love,
S

PS at 11:30 pm in the night

Tea was pAthetic. The dining hall is just like any old school hall you've ever seen, all polished floor and beams, and the ghosts of dances in 1952. (You can tell it's late!) At the back they've built on a Club Room, which is nearly but not quite a bar. They'd dug out a tea urn and there were loaves of bread and boiled-sweet jam and lots of mummies and daddies in suits, and everyone looked either frightened to death or bored stiff, so I brought my plateful up here and went for an explore.

At the end of the corridor, next to the loos, there's a utility room with cupboards and kettles and ironing boards and things. I met Zoe, who lives across the landing. Her room-mate has a severe case of daddy-itis, so Zoe had escaped to make coffee. She's definitely one of us. The first thing she said was, "Just think what it'll be like up here with 50 pairs of knickers hanging up to dry." Cheered me up no end. Then there was somebody from down the corridor called Annie who looks reasonable, too. So we might survive. Annie took us into her room and showed us what her mother had bought her, clothes-wise. We think we'll use it as fancy-dress. My dear, why do they do this to us? At least our mama admits she's got lousy taste.

And you're wondering what my room-mate's like, aren't you? Well, so am I . She's called Liz and she banged her way in about 6, carrying a pile of brown-paper bags and dumped them on the bed. She's got what Mama would call Per-sonality: comes over big, you know. First thing she said was, "God, what a dump." The bags were full of the weirdest. My education begins here, I think. (Mind you, I may have to write to ask you what some of the words she uses mean.) She had a shower, weirded herself up, and zoomed out again. I think she thought that I was next thing down from a nun. Mum would think she's on drugs. Mind you, she thinks the next-door cat is on drugs. Probably true, actually.

The rest of us had supper, which was OK and served by a huge woman called Mrs Lamb and all her little lambkins, who were very jolly. Calories figured a lot.

When it gets dark the rooms get a bit crypt-like. The screen gives out more light than the lights, and the bedside light is a fifties museum piece, with a sort of chrome pipe which falls over. (I'm rambling. It's the exhaustion of the intellectual life.)

I thought I'd just tap you a note until Liz comes in, but she doesn't show any signs of it, so I'm awa' to my bed.

More bulletins soon. Get good quick.
S

Chapter Six
HOW TOM SURVIVED THE FIRST DAY

———————————•———————————

Tom pulled on his green waxed jacket and put pens, and a map of the campus, and the envelope full of forms, and passport photos of some complete stranger, and the front door key into the poacher's pocket, and went down the stairs, trying not to breathe.

On the whole, it seemed as though he'd been trying not to breathe since last night. Coming out of the cinema, rather depressed by the high blood-factor, he'd met Vince, who seemed to take a strange ape-like liking to him. He dragged him into a corner pub, the likes of which Tom would never have had the nerve to go into, and bought him a pint, and tried to start a conversation about Rugby Football and then another about chess, neither of which Tom knew anything about and, by the end of it, didn't want to. Vince did, however, fit into the category of human company and that was what Tom needed.

Then, in the morning, he discovered that sharing a bathroom with complete strangers is not for the fastidious, and although he had an idea that germs didn't generally leap, fully armed, from the plug-holes of sinks, he found that he was remarkably sensitive to the least bit of grease or hair.

But that paled into insignificance beside Mrs Evans's eggs and bacon. Having been brought up on fried eggs that were fluffy and crisp on the outside and runny on the inside, Tom only just recognised what was lying on his plate as being of the same species. It was flat, pure white, with a pale, solid yolk surrounded by transparent jelly. The bacon was slightly purple, coarse, with thick rind.

A. B. was reading *The Times*, and was on to the toast. He nodded vaguely. Tom sat down, cut a piece of bacon with some difficulty, tried to chew it (it tasted like salt cod), removed it from his mouth, placed it on his plate, stood up, and went back upstairs to pack his jacket. Vince's snores came down from the next landing. His room-mate hadn't arrived yet. Tom wondered whether the house could be any worse.

But, outside, it was different.

It was a high day, all blues and greys, and at the end of the street Tom could see over the houses to the hills. It was, he thought, a bit like climbing a cliff. Absolutely exhilarating, as his mother would have said, and enough to scare the trainers off you. He waited until there were no obvious students around and got the map out.

I can only assume, he thought after a moment or two, that stress numbs the brain. According to the map, the Old College Building seemed to be three hundred metres out to sea and the rest of the University (marked helpfully in red) was either in a park or scattered about odd corners of the town.

Tom worked from street-corner to street-corner, and then there were quite a few obvious students about in new coats and scarves, all going purposefully in the same direction. Tom, wishing he were going purposefully in *any* direction, joined the general flow and came into a leafy square with something that looked like an Edwardian Town Hall, with a car-park barrier and benches, and old beech trees.

The first thing that really cheered him up was that everyone seemed to be having difficulties. There were parents' cars gridlocked around the square because the car-park needed a magic card to make the barrier work.

"I think I'd die of embarrassment," a girl said, standing next to him. Tom resisted the temptation to leap away. She was holding a stack of folders against her coat. "Poor things," and it had to be said that there were occupants of the rear seats quite clearly dying of embarrassment. Tom couldn't think of anything to say and the girl smiled and went off towards the building. Tom followed.

Stress also makes you short-sighted. Tom went up to the large glass doors and pulled. They clunked. He then pushed. They clunked again. At that point, sweating, and being watched by several people inside, he noticed the sign just in front of his eyes: PLEASE USE OTHER DOOR.

Inside, having tried to make himself invisible purely by mental effort, and, having failed, he stood back from the jostle and tried to apply his intelligence to finding any more signs. If I can't even get into the place, he thought, it doesn't look good for the rest of the career. There was a row of tables against one wall, with four people sitting with stacks of cards and file indexes and four terminals. Stretching around the walls was a queue.

Tom walked very carefully along it, not wanting to ask, and stood at the end. The queue shuffled forward. Tom shuffled as well, wondering if he'd managed to read the instructions wrongly and sure that he wouldn't have enough photographs. They can't shoot you; but on the other hand they can laugh at you or send you to the back of the queue again. I wonder if this is the right university?

He made a massive effort to be rational and started to look around. The students were all sizes and ages. There was a woman, a bit younger than his mother, in front of him. She turned round, and was quite unmotherly.

"Amazing how you have to queue everywhere," she said.

"Amazing," said Tom.

"I almost expect to have to pay at the till when we get to the end."

There was a pause. Tom said, "What year are you in?" It seemed like a neutral way to fill the gap, but Tom was a little nervous in case it wasn't protocol to ask questions like that.

"First, same as you," the woman said. "Retarded." She

laughed. "I thought it was about time that I caught up with my education. The people at work bought me a Mickey Mouse pencil case."

Tom arrived at a table. He handed over forms, which were rubber-stamped and his name was typed into the terminal. The man glanced down the form.

"You're down for a first," he said.

Tom looked at him. Was this his father in disguise? Only his father would never have worn a shirt and tie. The man typed again. "Anyone who fills in the form without making a mistake gets a first."

"What happens if you spell your name wrong?" said the woman. She was being signed in at the next table.

"Third," said the man.

A new language, Tom thought. There was more stamping. People were talking all around them.

"Is that it?" the woman said. "I thought some magic pall would fall over me. Sort of academic halo." She stowed forms in a sack she was carrying. "I haven't seen a single gown yet. Or a bicycle. I thought that's what universities had."

"Not this kind," somebody said behind her. "We're yer masses."

"Poor but honest," the woman said. She looked down at the last piece of paper in her hand. "But now I'm a member of the University. I even have a number. On to the next queue." She moved away. Tom was distracted by the thought that he might not actually ever see her again.

"I'm afraid your grant won't be here for a day or two," said the man, cheerfully. "Call in at the Bursary next Monday." How Tom was supposed to survive until then didn't seem to be his business. The thought of finding the Bursary, new forms, and another queue seemed to freeze his brain again.

Tom shuffled up his forms. The man looked up. "Welcome to the University. It's wonderful, really."

Tom nodded, trying to simulate an enthusiastic response, and walked out of an arched doorway, over a hard grey floor, and there was the campus; a park with what looked like the architectural history of the last fifty years stuck around it.

Tom stood to one side of the doorway and breathed in, and thought, wait a minute, this is easy. If I'm going to be a great architect, I could start now. Maybe I should take notes. There was a grey pseudo-stone thing, with concrete window-liners, circa 1950, and a plain square glass-faced tower, circa 1960, and a sort of demented aluminium and smoked-glass geometric shape tacked onto the end of a refurbished Victorian monster-terrace.

There were signposts stuck into the grass. Tom followed them to a building that seemed to have been built of Lego. This one had a sign mounted on a block of stone: HUMANITIES AND ENVIRONMENTAL STUDIES.

Tom studied the doors carefully as he went up the steps, and managed to get one to open, first time. In the foyer, there was a certain amount of milling around which was rather comforting. Everyone else looked lost.

The first corridor had a black sign: DEPARTMENT OF ENGLISH. Tom looked along it at the blank doors and the people. The woman in the queue was coming towards him. She smiled a vague sort of greeting.

"Very disappointing," she said.

"Why?" said Tom, feeling rather relieved to have replied coherently to somebody at last.

"I sort of assumed that English students would be more poetic than that," the woman said. "Come to think of it, I even thought that the staff would be sort of demi-gods with flashing eyes and floating hair."

"They're not, then?"

"Haven't seen one yet. I could be in the Town Hall rates department. Maybe I am." She searched in her sack. "At least it's not like the Students' Union. Have you seen it? It seems to be entirely lined with black rubber. Great for fetishists." She went away, leaving Tom feeling just a touch out of his depth.

Feeling a need for positive action, Tom found a sign which said ARCHITECTURE and opened the door that it pointed at. He was in an unplastered short corridor with mops in metal cans standing against the wall, three broken desks, and seven standard-sized manual typewriters. Tom started to sweat, which hadn't much to do with the waxed jacket, and backed out into the main corridor. He looked at his watch, which, for a wonder was (a) on his wrist, and (b) still working. All it did was convince him that he was going to be late for something.

A porter came up behind him.

"Got a problem?"

"It doesn't look a lot like the School of Architecture," Tom said, nervously.

As usual when he tried to say anything that was not a solid-gold cliché, the reaction was much the same as if he had suddenly started to speak Swahili. The porter looked at him with deep suspicion.

Tom said, "Which way is Architecture, please?" and then said it again, and the porter, with his finger, pointed the way.

Tom went down more wide steps, where the light came in from high, square windows and there were free-standing notice-boards headed, at last, SCHOOL OF ARCHITECTURE. He stopped and searched through several lists before realising that they were last year's examination results and old tutorial rotas. There didn't seem to be many architects about, only a smell of wax and sunshine and some architectural models.

Then a girl came along the corridor; not a schoolgirl; a person. Tom suddenly felt terribly well-pressed and clean.

The girl paused. "Is this the School of Architecture?"

Tom waved his arm expansively. "That's right. I think it's all along there."

"Oh, thanks so much. I thought I'd never find it."

"No problem," Tom said, senior by thirty seconds. The girl smiled rather uncertainly and Tom let her get through the first set of swing doors before he followed.

Tom sat in the end cubicle of the ♂s, thinking, there that wasn't so bad. The staff and the other students weren't exactly demi-gods, but they looked intelligent and interested and interesting, and he no longer felt quite like a fraud. He opened the green folder he had been given which had timetables and booklists and complex messages from the Students' Union, notably: 'Freshers' Fayre Tomorrow'.

There were other messages around, carefully inscribed on the metal walls. At school the graffiti had consisted mostly of improbable anatomical information. Here, it was more philosophical. Pointing to the paper-dispenser was a neat arrow:

SOCIOLOGY DEGREES: PLEASE TAKE ONE

and, further down:

PETALS ON A WET, BLACK BOUGH

and, underneath that, mystifyingly, a single

£

At the bottom of the door was a small, neat, and very unencouraging observation:

Does it have to be like this?

Tom went into the Students' Union Bookshop, a bright airy clean well-lighted place. He took a wire basket and walked rather dreamily among the new files and pads and books, thinking how nice it was and how he would somehow have to scoop the knowledge from the books and slip it onto the paper. He resisted the temptation to buy a stapler and some multicoloured paperclips, or a jar of small plastic clothes pegs, and became alternately cheered and depressed by the new feel of the books and the heaviness of things he didn't know inside them.

In the end, he bought three matching ring-binders with the University Crest, a rather magnificent affair of wings and shields stamped in gold on the front, and some file paper and a University scarf; after all, it was October nearly, and his mother would like it. Wearing the scarf and carrying the binders in front of him, he went across to the Students' Union, very carefully making sure that his new ID card was to hand, but nobody asked to see it.

Tom got into a corner of the entrance hall, out of the way of all the purposeful people, and consulted the STUDENTS' UNION HANDBOOK, which rather looked as though it had been printed by hand.

THIS IS YOUR UNION
– *and you're welcome to it!*

This sumptuous scrumptious building was thrown up (if you'll excuse the expression) (all right, erected) a mere five years ago, even though it looks a lot older and we're not surprised. But for your delectation (look it up) we have no less (and no more) than THREE *bars, the* BALCONY, *the* DREGS *(thank you, Mossy), and the* WIGAN PEER *(this is supposed to be a dead subtle joke by the Engl. Dept. and we're open to suggestions, even clean ones, for another name).*

When you've inspected those, you might feel in need of some sustenance, so there is the REFEC *with a sandwich bar (there's that magic word again) which is open all day from 10:00 to 19:30. (If your watch just goes up to 12, tough.)*

6. How Tom Survived the First Day

For the jolly healthy hearties we've just built on five squash courts (see under SPORTS HALL for the really sporty stuff) with showers (so will Ev please use them this year before steaming into the bars). And the peace de resistance (another joke) is the great enormous fantastical GREAT HALL where many a night you will be thrilled to the greatest bands in the Universe (well, the ones that ENTS can afford after taking their drinking fees out of the fund), but, sorry all (especially Dave), there will be NO intoxicating liquors (i.e. booze) allowed into the Hall after what happened last year. (You missed it? You were lucky. Only the strong survived.)

On the tip-top floor is the business end and the Union Offices with the incredibly humble office of our handsome beautiful brainy incorruptible PRESIDENT Sal (on whom closing time never sets) and her gorgeous ASSISTANT PRESSIE (well done, Jeff, the bribes worked) and all the genius-type writers of gems like this 'ere and the offices of the GREATEST STUDENT NEWSPAPER as ever is, APATHY, the twice-monthly or whenever-we-can-do-it fantasmagorical voice of the downtrodden student body, of which you are one.

We've been asked to point out that some students may not be alcoholics or athletes. We think this is unlikely, but we should say that the bars stock non-alcoholic goodies, there is a reading-room on the top floor for anyone who needs to WORK (sorry, four-letter word), the all-denominations Chaplaincy joint office is on the third floor, and there is a QUIET ROOM for contemplation and such along the hall from the WIGAN PEER.

Tom shook his head. This seemed to be written in some sort of code. He slid the book into his poacher's pocket and looked around. Everyone seemed to be going somewhere and doing something and there was a lot of laughing going on. He went up the rubber stairs and followed the signs to the Balcony Bar.

There were four other people there, leaning on the bar with their backs towards the wall of long windows which opened out onto the concrete balcony. There was a smell of old beer and cigarettes which reminded him of sitting outside the village pub and thinking how grown-up it smelt inside. He paused in the doorway, wondering if he should have grown out of such adolescent ideas, but it wasn't clear how he was supposed to do that, so he went in.

The barman, who seemed to have his mind elsewhere, came along the bar and Tom ordered a pint of real ale on the general assumption that to order anything else would brand him as a wimp with the rest of the world. He thought, rather defensively, I am now grown-up; I can have a drink at lunchtime if I want to, and he took his glass outside into the day and propped his folders against the concrete balustrade by his foot and looked out over the University and the town.

Below him were patches of grass worn into brown paths, and there were trees with benches around them and between the buildings and out over the town was the line of the sea with the shapes of ships moving across it. People were walking in intricate patterns.

Tom held his glass up to the sky to look through it, to see if there was any floating sludge.

"I once saw a bloke do that in a pub," a voice said, conversationally, "and the landlord chucked him out for insulting his barkeeping." There was a male, slightly older than him (but then everyone was slightly older than him), with a copy of Dostoevsky's *The Idiot* uncomfortably stuffed into the back pocket of his jeans, resting his beer glass on the balustrade. He was wearing a sweater that must have been found at the bottom of a very disreputable dustbin. He looked down.

"Have you noticed that there are two types of people

down there?" Tom looked. "And they're both wearing uniforms." Tom glanced at him. He didn't seem to be making a point about any of this; it was merely academic conversation. "There's the ones who are doing everything right. They walk in the right direction, they have college folders with crests on and they wear scarves." He didn't seem to be making a point about this either. "Then there's the other lot. They walk in the *wrong* direction, they do everything just slightly not right, and they're scruffbags. They wouldn't be seen dead with a folder with a crest on it." Tom moved his leg slightly to hide his folders.

"Maybe they can't afford them," Tom said. "Clothes and folders."

"The ones who can't afford anything are the ones still wearing their school trousers." He paused slightly. "The name's Alf," he went on. "Want another?"

"No thanks," Tom said. "Hardly started." Alf went back inside. Tom considered. Should he unwind the scarf and let it float down off the balcony or should he tie it round the nearest stanchion and hang himself from it? Presumably, he thought, the only way not to signal something would be to curl up and die, but that wouldn't work, either. People could tell you weren't going to play squash. At least he was the only person on the balcony, looking down on everyone.

He left his glass on the balcony ledge where it wouldn't fall off and brain somebody, picked up his files, and walked quietly past Alf's ordering back and into the GENTS.

In the mirror was an angular person, looking rather fresh and new, with a fresh and new college scarf. Tom took it off and looked at it. This might, he said to his reflection silently, be a mistake, but I can always change my mind. If you look at people who look grown-up, you can see that they've *designed* themselves, and it's about time I started. The scarf was very soft and bright and new, but it was, after all, exactly what A. B. would wear. That was the deciding factor. Tom folded it very carefully, slid his files together, and put the whole lot into his poacher's pocket. It made him look like a lop-sided pregnant bullfrog. But not like A. B.

He came out of the GENTS. "Have a look round," the people in the School of Architecture had said. "Make yourself at home. See you on Monday." All that freedom, all of a sudden. It occurred to him, standing in the corridor, that he'd already forgotten what school was like. Unfortunately, he also seemed to have forgotten anything that he'd learned there, as well.

He walked back to the balcony. Alf was now talking to somebody else and nodded at him. Tom looked out over the campus, the University, the town, the world. Bit of an anticlimax, really, he thought. I expected to be slaving away over a book by now. Back at home, the shop would be closing for the lunch-break. He took another drink, and then took his glass back into the bar and left it, half-full, on a table, and went out into the town.

He had a hamburger for lunch in the sort of hamburger chain that hadn't reached his own town, and bought a postcard to send home.

In the main Post Office, with its vast hectares of polished floor, he joined one of the queues behind a man in a raincoat. They shuffled forward, Tom writing the postcard on his palm.

> 'So far, so good. The natives have strange eating habits. Don't sell bed. T.'

The man in front of him reached the counter, and said: "*Poste restante*, please."

The girl in the glass cage hesitated slightly. Tom looked over the man's shoulder. She seemed to be rather worried, although rather nice to look at as well.

The man said, "*Poste Restante*. Letters waiting. There might be a letter waiting for me."

The girl slid off her stool without quite saying, 'I know what *Poste Restante* means,' and said, "What name?" as she turned with her hand up towards a rack on the wall.

The man said, "Mr X."

Tom tried to look over his shoulder at his face, but couldn't quite do it. The girl turned back, slightly.

"How do you spell that?"

Tom was beginning to wonder how strong the beer had been.

"X," said the man, patiently.

Suddenly Tom needed to get out into the day before he laughed or choked, or whatever this feeling was. So this is the outside world.

Tom spent half the afternoon walking. Back at the Union, which seemed like one still point in a turning world, groups were forming for tours of the University. As he seemed fated never to get in at the beginning of things, Tom joined the back of a group. There was a tall female leading the party but, when she spoke, her voice merely echoed up and became a vague vacuum in the rest of the voices and the high ceiling, so none the wiser Tom tagged along as the group straggled past tall buildings and squat buildings, with a small homily outside each one which simply drifted away into the air. It was chillier now and the air seemed to smell faintly of burning leaves.

They walked along the anonymous corridors of the Mathematics Department and looked at rooms full of terminals and a large lecture theatre and smelt a lot of wax. It reminded Tom of School Open Days. When they came out, the party had to turn back on itself rather like a sock being pulled inside out. Tom, who hadn't moved, was now walking beside the guide. She had an air of confidence and inaccessibility that, as far as Tom was concerned, seemed to reside by birth in all females. She was older than him. All girls unless they were actually in nappies tended to seem older than him. This one especially.

She, however, seemed disposed to be civil. "I'm Trish," she said.

"Tom," said Tom. They stopped outside the Sports Hall.

Trish said, "I suggest you all go in and have a look round, and we'll start again in half an hour." She sat down on the steps. Tom had been listening to her accent.

"Where are you from?" he said. Trish looked at him carefully.

"Why?"

That was clearly the wrong thing. Tom mumbled again. "I just thought you sound as though you come from where I live." Now it was said, it sounded pretty trivial. Trish was still looking at him.

"You don't do that, you know," she said. "It's like you don't ask what people's fathers do, or anything like that." Tom looked at the steps, as if he were being told off by the Headmaster. Trish clearly had some sympathy for him. She said: "I think it's because we're all evens, starting. It doesn't matter where we come from or who our parents are." Tom managed to look at her. "It's not like Oxbridge where you have old school ties. Most of the schools people here come from have never seen a tie." She smiled at him; a really very nice smile. "Well, that's not true. But you get all sorts of everybody here, and we're all doing our own thing ourselves, and where we came from doesn't matter."

Tom spent so much time thinking about the implications of this that, later on, when they were working across a wide cul-de-sac of stately Edwardian redbrick houses with blank windows, Tom sat down on a slatted bench under a huge Turkey oak and let Trish's crocodile crocodile away.

The day was hovering between half-warm and half-misty-crisp. The bench had varnish lifting transparently off, where it had not been quite dry when it was varnished. Tom looked round the empty road, and took out a packet of cigarettes from the bottom of his poacher's pocket. He unwrapped it carefully. Just one won't hurt, as an experiment.

There was a slight wind; just about enough to blow out the match, and Tom breathed a sulphurous singe smell up his nose and under his tongue. That didn't seem quite right. He tried again, pulling a match off the match-book which took so much concentration that he put the wrong end of the cigarette between his lips and lit the filter. A disgusting smell of burning fibre hit the back of his throat. Tom screwed up his face and choked and spat the cigarette out. He opened his eyes, saw a pair of black shoes and, sticking out of the top of them, somebody in a black skirt, and a long way above that a clerical collar and above that a face which, remarkably, combined mildness and threat.

Tom put his heel on the cigarette, feeling somewhat at a disadvantage.

"Hi," said the face.

"Hi."

"Why don't you come in, it's warmer inside."

Tom tried not to look positively unfriendly, but he thought, that's how witch doctors get away with it; you dress up in black so you must know something the rest of us don't.

He stood up and looked past the priest, and there was a neat white-painted sign beside the front door opposite the tree:

STUDENT CHRISTIAN UNION

Tom went cold and then hot and cold again. All this time he'd been sitting under observation from those blank windows, probably picking his nose unconsciously, let alone failing to do something that he wasn't supposed to be doing anyway. The last thing he wanted to do was to go in and be patronised by the people in there, who would undoubtedly be mostly girls who would be tall and plain and spotty with glasses, and all the men would be overweight or one-legged. Either way they'd be wearing jeans that didn't fit if they were meant to or did fit if they weren't meant to.

"Come and have a coffee. No obligation to buy."

Tom said, "Fine," and followed, wondering why he was letting himself in for more of this rubbish. He hoped he wouldn't be forced to express an honest opinion, like he didn't go for all this Lord King Master business in these democratic days, and that Jesus may have been a good guy and a guru and all, but you wouldn't catch him dressing up in a black skirt. He'd been ruined by all these literal-minded idiots.

But if he said any of that, he'd be patronised by clever arguments or swamped by gooey ones and generally made to feel inferior, and so by the time he got into the hallway he was virtually inarticulate with anger and frustration.

The elegant exterior of the terrace wasn't matched inside. Everything was wrong; the house had been stripped out, and the walls painted a matt, pale yellow, and the skirting-boards laden with thick white gloss, and in the long narrow lounge were orange easy chairs, of the kind where you lean slightly to one side and fall off.

Faces looked round at him and smiled. They didn't look weird at all, and Tom, caught out in a prejudice, felt even worse and couldn't find anything to say in the face of all this *bonhomie*. He was propelled to the hardboard counter at the end of the room. Behind the counter was a girl who was so pre-eminently normal and good looking and well-dressed and confident that he had to concentrate on not actually falling over on his way across the room.

"Tea or coffee?" She even had a nice voice. Tom wondered whether he'd ever give anyone the impression that he would decide for himself whether they were worth talking to. She handed him a mug before he could answer, which was just as well. "Hope you like both," she said, not too light-and-brightly. "I'm not sure what it is."

Tom smiled idiotically, and turned round to look at the room where they all seemed to be waiting for him. Tom turned back to the girl.

"Do they smile like that all the time?" he said. She almost laughed, which was encouraging.

"Been to this sort of thing before?" she said.

Tom nodded. "I went at school a couple of times, but it was either people going on about Galatians 7 or the twenty-fourth Sunday after Pentecost, or the rebel-types going on about Why I am Not a Christian or why I'm a Bhuddist or something." He paused for breath.

"The milk of human kindness does swash about," she said.

Tom looked across the room. There was a poster, advertising a talk by the Professor of Theology: 'Why God Must Exist'. Tom caught himself framing the sentence: 'Because if he didn't you'd be out of a job', and, not for the first time that day, decided to be honest and not to stand there making noises which would satisfy people or upset them. He put the mug down on the bar, and mimed a request for the GENTS, which was obviously out of the back door.

"Excuse me a minute, I'll just, is it, er, the –" and the girl nodded. Tom, smiling wildly, half-backed and half-sidled out of the door.

Outside, the garden had been gutted as well. There was a car parked, and bicycles chained, and two green doors, marked ♂ and ♀. Tom pushed open the ♂ door, and let it close with a bang. No-one was looking out of the barred back-window. He took a few steps towards the car (just interested in cars, you know); still nobody was looking; and he took three long steps around the corner and into the back lane.

*   *   *   *

Tom lay in the bath, the vapour condensing on the window and the new wallpaper lifting at the joins, and tried to ignore the ends of pink soap in the pink plastic bath-tidy.

It had been, he decided, a mixed day.

He'd made an excuse to Mrs Evans, and eaten pizza in the refectory and watched a video in the Union Lounge, and then, holding himself very carefully together, checked the car and then let himself into the house. There was only the sound of the Evans's TV from the back room. Outside the bed-hutch window, in the yard, was a small Japanese motorbike, with L plates, presumably belonging to the new resident. Well, he could hardly be worse.

If only, Tom thought, I had some sense of *direction*. He reached over the side of the bath and grabbed the STUDENTS' UNION HANDBOOK before the drips could run down his wrist. There were pages of programmes for the Music Society Concerts and a list of visiting theatre groups. Towards the end was a column headed

DEPRESSED? LONELY? GOT PROBLEMS?

You're not alone. Ring NIGHTWATCH *any time. There's always someone there to talk to. Absolutely confidential.*

Well, he thought, that was a comfort at least, but I'm a long way from feeling desperate. Still, maybe I could just close my eyes and fast forward and I'll be back home again. He closed his eyes.

Chapter Seven
SIGNING UP

Tom had half his breakfast with the new occupant, who was called Robbie. Robbie was about three metres tall, dressed in as much of the latest thing as he could afford, and was a totally psychedelic change from the neolithic Vince and the pestilential A. B. The first of these was still in bed; the second left when Robbie's conversation, which was on the strident side, got around to Vince's personal habits.

"He stinks," Robbie said. "It's absolutely disgusting. I don't think he's washed for a month, the room's full of fag ends and I won't tell you what he did in the sink last night."

A. B.'s chair shifted slightly. "Come on," he said. "Not over breakfast."

Robbie looked at his plate, and seemed to dismiss what he saw as some sort of optical illusion. "I don't know what you're getting offended about," he said. "I had to put up with it. Orchestrated farts all night long. You'd think he was practising –"

A. B. stood up. "I'll see you around, possibly."

"What's wrong?" Robbie said. "Perfectly good word. In Shakespeare." A.B., unimpressed by this excuse for vulgarity, went upstairs.

"He probably doesn't do them," Tom said.

Robbie was staring at the space A.B. had vacated. "Is he for real?" he said. "He's like some character out of *Lucky Jim*. Have you read *Lucky Jim*?" He didn't stop for an answer. "That's probably why he doesn't fart. People in books never do."

"Perhaps it's not germane to the story," Tom said,

feeling very impressed with himself for keeping up one end of this conversation.

"But they all did it, though," Robbie said. "Gandalf, I bet. Mary Poppins. Long John Silver, for sure." He looked down at his plate. "I can't eat this. I'll see you later." He got up and shouldered through an invisible crowd to the door, leaving Tom smiling both outside and inside, because he'd just seen what he should have been seeing right from the beginning: the wonder and delight of all this infinite variety. Not that it made the egg any more edible, but he went upstairs, surrounded by the peculiar smell of carpets and varnish and jam and eggs, hardly able to wait to get out and see more of this strange new universe.

However, when he got to the Students' Union and was wedged into his corner of the entrance hall, he discovered something about himself that he'd only suspected before.

He'd definitely inherited his mother's talent for *not* knowing what everyone else seemed to know. *She* never knew, for example, which day the dustbin sacks were collected; only after everyone else's were displayed around the village green did she haul hers out. And when the day changed, she tended to put them out two days early, so that they were ripped open by the local wildlife.

Tom was reading the STUDENTS' UNION HANDBOOK and feeling cheered by this thought when he realised that most of the Freshers were moving into the big hall which looked as if it had been taken over by a jumble sale. He leafed through the book and found an insert with a list of activities for the week which, presumably, everyone else had been fully aware of for months. From this, he discovered that he'd totally missed a general meeting of the Union the evening before, and that the present gathering was the Freshers' Fayre, where all the clubs and societies competed for custom among the newcomers.

Tom went cautiously into the hall, wondering whether he cared enough about anything actually to join.

He walked down the rows of stalls, and everywhere there were people BEING: being involved, and doing, and laughing and knowing each other. But, even if you didn't care, he had to admit it was interesting.

People were tempting him to be an archaeologist with computer terminals and lumps of rock and large photo displays and a few skulls; then there were piles of scuba-diving kit, and oars from the rowing club; the University radio station was doing a live show on the stage at the far end of the hall. Then there was the Philosophy Society which didn't seem to do much; then the Country Dancing Society, with bells, and the Green Earth Society, and from the balcony there was a cascade of silk contributed by the Parachute Club. Tom took a breath.

One of the two people sitting at the Philosophy Society stall, said, "Go on, join something. A free choice."

"It isn't," the other one said, before Tom could say anything. "All this freedom isn't freedom at all. The more things there are to do, the more you can't do. If he choses one, then what about the others?"

"It's a case of finding your identity," the first said.

"I'll keep looking," Tom said, escaping backwards. He tried to say "I'm just unclubbable," but it came out as a mumble.

Next was the English Society. Tom stopped. There were posters of Stratford Plays and Shakespeare in London. There were three students on the stall, two girls and a cheerful-looking man who said, "Thing to remember is that 95% of English Students are female." He paused as if that were an adequate statement about the subject. Tom paid and signed and smiled and felt a bit more human.

Then there was an argument going on between the Video Society ('Our movies are Ruder') and several people who had spilled over from the Feminist Society – which, thanks to some wit, had the next stall. Tom stopped a moment too long to listen. Having heard his mother on the subject of the legal and social inequalities attached to being female, he thought he might actually join the Feminists; lead the campaign against male exclusiveness in the churches, perhaps. But he was getting a rather unfriendly stare.

"What?"

"I'd like to join," Tom said.

"Another wit."

"I can't help being male," Tom said.

"That's what they all say."

The volume of the altercation with the rude video people seemed to be rising and Tom, who didn't like any form of shouting, moved away.

In one corner of the hall, the Contemporary Dance Society was limbering up. Tom caught the thought that all he could see was sweat and muscles, and decided that this wasn't his day to be human. Perhaps he could start an Outcasts' Society.

The last group of stalls began with the Heavy Drinkers Society. The man behind the table was reading the STUDENTS' UNION HANDBOOK. He was holding a glass, and looked up as Tom drifted by.

"Are you serious?" Tom said.

"It says here," said the student, "that if you want to start a society and have a genuine specialist interest and a group of at least ten people, there are union funds available."

Tom looked at him, thinking that all his aunt's worst suspicions about students would be confirmed.

"It's a branch of sociology and food science," the student said cheerfully, and grinned. "Well, we're a bunch of layabouts who visit breweries," he said. Tom grinned back. "Nothing if not honest."

The same humorist who had juxtaposed videos and feminists had grouped all the political parties at the same end of the room where they seemed to be taking turns at amiably insulting each other. Tom stopped at a safe distance, and the Heavy Drinker came and stood beside him.

"At this class of university, the Left does better than the Right," he said. Tom looked at the monochrome posters, with marching and fists. "But none of them actually do very well, because most people are here to work, whatever it looks like, and all that stuff takes time."

Tom walked slowly on and was struck by a simple thing. There were no masters or parents hanging about; a few porters in uniforms, but they were *employees*. This is our own show. Tom shook his head, and a voice said:

"Well, we're not proud. We're desperate. Join us."

Tom looked up. The last stall had covered all the nearby walls with old film posters and there was a neatly lettered nameplate: THE HOT CELLULOID SOCIETY.

There was a short, fair-haired man, apparently asleep with his feet on the table and Trish from the walking tour, brightly holding out a pen and a membership card. Tom wondered whether she'd noticed his defection.

"I like the name," Tom said.

The male said, "I think it's a bit cutesie-pie, myself. It was Trish's idea."

"It's for people who're fed up with TV screens and videos and the sexual degradation of women," said Trish.

"So we're not very popular."

"Shut up, Orris. No sex against women, no violence against men."

"Pretentious, in other words," the blonde-haired male said.

"Ignore him," Trish said. "That's Orris. He's our projectionist."

"I used to be a projectionist at school," Tom said and immediately wished that he hadn't because Trish said:

"Really? Sunday night, then. Basement of the Old Union. Get there by six. Projectionists are rare birds these days. All people know is how to shove cassettes into videos."

Tom took his membership card and turned back to the rest of the hall, rather wondering whether he should have mentioned that he'd actually been sacked from being school projectionist for incompetence after jamming the film in the projector twice in one evening.

However, he considered, this metamorphosis into a social being at last is clearly a good thing, and by the time he got back into the refectory, he had, in his poacher's pockets, membership cards for not only the English Society and the Hot Celluloid Society, but also the Architecture Society, the Squash Club, and the Local History Circle. He had passed the Christian Union by on the other side of the hall.

Exhilarated, he went back to the bookshop and bought the first two books on his booklist, and then changed his mind about working and got in the car and drove around the town for an hour, getting the geography into his mind.

Buying petrol made him rather nervous that his grant hadn't arrived and so he risked a meal at Mrs Evans's. There was no sign of Robbie or Vince, and Mrs Evans seemed to have grown wary of cooking for empty places. There was tomato soup, followed by a hot pork pie and chips.

A. B. found the pork pie interesting. "My brother," he said, opening up an awful prospect of a dynasty of A. Bs, "worked in a pork pie factory once. His job was to put lumps of fat on top of the trays of pies, so it would melt into them in the oven."

He continued to eat, apparently finding this reminiscence edifying rather than revolting, and Tom, falling back on childhood skills, spread his meal over the plate and hid as much as he could under his fork. Then he went to bed and read architecture and went to sleep on the peculiar pillow, really rather looking forward to Monday when you stopped messing about and began. So far, all there was was a handful of beginnings.

Chapter Eight
SUE AND THE WEEKEND

———————————●———————————

Zoe said:

> "...*in a world*
> *Of welcome faces up and down I roved;*
> *Questions, directions, counsel and advice*
> *Flowed upon me from all sides...*

That's Wordsworth. Haven't seen much of that, yet. How was the Biology Department?"

Sue was sitting on Mary's bed with a pad propped on her knees.

"Magic. I'm now an ecologist. This is the last pad of paper I use that hasn't been regurgitated."

Zoe looked at the pad. "Another letter to little sister?"

Sue nodded. "I won't be able to keep up this being funny much longer."

"Can't they do anything?"

"They don't know yet," Sue said. "They think it's fractured upper vertebrae, and that she could be paralysed for life." She shook her head. "The poor love can't move at all and they can't even say if it'll get better, let alone when." She paused for a moment. "D'you want to see?"

Zoe read:

St Trinian's Dorm
Friday Evening

Dear Jojo,

I hope they've been pasting these mistressworks on the
ceiling for you; actually, they're doing my reputation a bit of
good. Liz the cell-mate thinks I'm pining for my man at home
and writing ROMANTIC-ALLY. I told her it was my horse, as a jest,
which might have been a mistake. There's no point in going
to bed early because she comes in like a team of clog-
dancing rhinos and dismantles the wardrobes.

So, here is the news. I've noticed that none of the
second- or third-years actually talk to you unless they want
something; the girls tend to want you to join something, and
the men – well, my dear, I can't imagine. But it's just like
being back in the first year at school, a junior tick.

I've done signing in, which means going to the
Department. This is rather splendid. All the labs are new and
polished, and there's some big lecture theatres, and they're
all v. friendly – the people, that is. I haven't seen any
lecturers I fancy yet, but they all exude brains, and the
Professor of Ecology is all cuddly and looks like a koala
bear. Best thing is that they treat you as if you're grown-up.

Zoe said: "That's good, isn't it. My tutor said, did I
mind him calling me Zoe, and would I mind calling him
Toby? So I said OK, and he went into a long discussion of how
artificial it was, because it was all spurious and how he was
the authority figure so I was bound to say OK, anyway."

Sue looked at her. "Are they all like that?"

"Don't know," Zoe said. "He looks like Lord Byron,
though." She stirred her coffee. "I always thought that all
English Lecturers would be bound to be terrifically poetic,
what with reading all that good stuff, but Toby said that a lot

of concentration camp commandants read good stuff, too."
She paused, thoughtfully. "He said that one year, he was
doing all this introductory bit, like, what would you like to be
called, and they were saying, 'Jill' and 'Sue' and 'Fred' and so
on and one of them said 'Mr Smith'."
She looked back at the letter.

Then we were shunted off to have coffee in a sort of
sub-refectory. The ceiling is covered with small circles.
(Haven't found why, yet; don't go away.) Nobody had any
idea of what to say to each other to start with because it's not
done to talk about school or what Daddy does or where you
come from, because that's all behind us, so we sat around
like Trappists, and the lecturers went round enthusing a lot,
but it's difficult to know what to say to them.
    Then there was this thing called the Freshers' Fayre (this
doesn't say much, I know, the fact that they can't spell). I
signed up in a fit of insanity for the student newspaper (this
was Zoe's fault, because she told them I'd got a Word
Processor, and apparently the newspaper is stiff with English
types who can't drive the one they've got). Then I signed up
for the Badminton Club and the Foreign Travel Society and
the choir. The choir doesn't bode very well. The girl said
they had auditions *of a kind* but we know what THAT means. I
didn't feel like joining the Riding Club just at the minute. Get
back on your hooves and I'll see about it. (I enclose the
Student Handbook. It's all a bit clique-y, but I suppose I'll get
in soon and be just as bad.)
    My soul is safe, though (le mama will be pleased to
hear); I've been to the SCU (that means Student Christian
Union as distinct from the Students' Union which is distinctly
Un-Christian). Zoe's room-mate Mary is very keen, as you
might expect: she's the one who sits looking as though
someone has sat on her tuffet, so we went down with her just
in case anyone shouted at her. The chaplain is like a stork
and you have to talk to his belt-buckle and I'm afraid that at

the drop of a prayer-book he'd be taking us for jolly hikes.
But apart from that he shows distinct sounds of intelligence.

I ended up on the tea-urn (I'll rephrase that...), mostly
to get away from the conversation, which was a bit light-and-
bright. We were supposed to stand there looking wholesome
and friendly while the Stork went out and collected innocent
passers-by. The best bit was when one victim came in and I
dished up the tea (or tea'd up the dishwater) and he left it on
the counter and went out to the loo and didn't come back.
They sent a search party into the depths of the GENTS to see if
he'd got stuck, but he'd made a break for it over the back
wall. Had to admire his spirit, as Grandfather would say. Still,
they're not really that bad, and it's nice to have somewhere
you can go where you know they'll be civilised.

Lots of mind-boggling goodies ahead this weekend: the
social whirl, what. There's a dance of some kind, and you
can look at local antiquities or homes of famous authors, or
do a tour of the University, or go for a ride on the sea. I can
scarce contain myself.

"Can you think of a big finish? You're doing English."

They went along to the utility room for coffee. There
was a long cupboard on the wall, with jars of coffee and tea,
variously labelled, and Annie was ironing.

"Friday night. End of an exciting week." She looked
around. "Where are your roomies?"

Sue got her coffee jar out. "Mary's gone to a Christian
meeting, and Liz has gone off with her boyfriend."

"That was quick. What manner of man?" Annie said.

"No idea. But she's not reticent. Bulletins will be issued
shortly," said Zoe.

They shared coffee and biscuits and cakes. Mothers, it
seems, think daughters will starve.

"I'm surprised you haven't heard," Sue said. "The
whole of the Normandy coast probably knows. He's called
Robbie. I haven't seen him yet, but they came home last

night and shouted goodnight for about three hours."

Jojo's problem produced half a page of suggestions.

"How about a helium balloon? You could hang the letters from them."

"They'd float away."

"Attached to her nose with a small clothes peg."

"Good, next." Sue wrote it down.

Annie said, "How about a team of highly-trained bats. They could swoop over with one word at a time, so you'd need a team of highly-trained mice to chew up the letters."

"It's all the doctors, you know," Zoe said. "They should be forced to massage her with exotic oils day and night until she's better."

"Isn't it terrible," Annie said. "Poor thing."

They washed up their coffee mugs and went back to the rooms. Sue lay on the bed and took up the letter again. She wrote:

Well, I must away and begin my brilliant career as a student, Much love

and then she put the light out and lay in the dark for a bit, watching the swinging lights from the promenade moving across the ceiling.

She was just dozing off, when Liz came in. She did a very creditable pirouette across to the window, and looked out.

"You look cheerful," Sue said.

"I'll tell you about him tomorrow," Liz said, "I'll have to test him first."

Sue came back from badminton practice on Saturday afternoon to find Zoe taking Mary in hand. Mary objected, a touch sullenly, that she had no desire to be taken in hand and less to be taken to a dance. Indeed, as the conversation progressed and more of the corridor became involved, it became less clear whether she had ever been to a dance.

"We'll look after you," Liz said. "I'll bite anyone who even looks at you for less than a minute."

"Clothes," Zoe said, severely. Mary, with the air of one of the earlier martyrs, opened her wardrobe. There was a short silence in which it was clear that everyone was wondering how to shrink themselves into the clothes. They were new, expensive. Liz reached in and read a few labels. "You've got good taste, little one," she said.

"My father bought them," Mary said, rather dully.

Back in their room, Liz and Sue dressed themselves a little less ostentatiously as their means allowed.

"Poor thing," Sue said. "But you can't just put her out, can you?"

"What a fuss about us dressing her," Liz said, as if it were unreasonable to object to being forcibly fed into your clothes.

"Maybe she thinks we're what my little sister calls a bunch of Leslies," Sue said.

"It does look rather as though her body doesn't understand what clothes are about. Isn't it amazing how all her straps always *show*."

"We'd better keep an eye on her."

But, as it happened, there wasn't too great a need. When they got to the Union, all the bars were solid with people, and Liz lead her platoon purposefully into the hall, where something rather resembling Rourke's Drift was growing; a thin line of females on one side, and a savage horde of males on the other.

"Smithfield," Zoe said. "I might have known."

"Well, I'll go and pick me a side of beef," Liz said and disappeared into the mob as the lights went out and the lasers came on and a band with a six-armed drummer opened up. Mary looked, at best, dismal, and Sue and Zoe parked her at one of the tables ringing the room and took turns to sit with her.

At one point, Zoe came staggering back to them, weak

with laughing. "I just had this spotty," she said, "and he kind of steered me round to his mates and shouted, 'I've got one!' "

"Idiot."

Mary went to the LADIES.

"That should while away the evening," Zoe said.

"Poor thing," Sue said. "She's been sitting here as though she expected somebody to bite her."

"I wish somebody would," Zoe said.

The lights came up for the break and the band was about to wrap its gear, when faces began to look up. In front of the balcony that ran above the end of the hall (where, as Zoe said, all the real yobbos and zoogs festered), there was a lighting gantry, and out onto it stepped a rather muscular male, in jeans and a dark sweater. He swung along, rocking the lights, to the side wall, where there was a ledge about ten centimetres deep. There were no hand-holds.

There was a certain amount of leaning and grabbing from porters, and, among the faces looking over the balustrade, Sue recognised the elusive tea-drinker from the Student Christian Union. The climber, flattening himself against the wall and balancing on his toes, worked his way along the wall, clear of the gantry, leaving a dark smear on the pale paint.

There was a very definite silence. Dropping off a wall for nine or ten metres can damage your health. Mary came back and stood with them, watching.

The figure reached the proscenium arch, and climbed across another gantry, and then worked its way towards the University Crest in the middle.

"I hope it was a big bet," Liz said, from behind them.

The drummer, wishing to get into the spirit of the thing, started a long rolling crescendo, as the climber worked his way back along the opposite wall, until he climbed over into assorted uniformed arms. There was some spontaneous clapping.

"Did you enjoy that?" Zoe said, as they walked back

along the promenade. The lights were strung out along the seafront, dipping and rising, and the sea sloshed quietly. Around them there were groups and couples. All very· romantic. "I'm zonked." Mary looked out to sea. Zoe looked over her head at Sue and shrugged. "Don't worry, kid. There's more to it than bopping. At least, I hope so."

They came to the front of the Hall of Residence; couples were saying goodnight in huddles.

"Well, so far, so jolly good," Sue said. "I like Saturday nights."

Chapter Nine
IN WHICH TOM DISCOVERS ROOM-SPIN

Saturday night, late, and Tom was in bed, or rather on bed, with the Dreaded Room-Spin, talking to himself.

"Try to analyse the situation," he muttered, as if talking to a simple-minded child. "You lie down, and it's OK. You close your eyes and the bed gets up and makes a dive for the left hand corner of the room. You sit up and it makes for the ceiling, leaving the stomach behind. Open the eyes and it settles back on the floor."

Talking to himself didn't seem to help much. He tried sitting on the bed and putting the light off, hoping that the darkness would be soothing. It had the same effect as closing his eyes. The bed immediately rose up and tried to get out of the window. There was an unpleasant moment when Tom couldn't find the light switch again and he ran his hands desperately over the wall and there it was. The bed settled again in the pink light. His stomach felt awful.

With the light on, he decided to lie on the bed and die as peacefully as possible. He wondered how many pints he'd had. Vince had bought him one, and then Alf, and then he'd gone to the Union bar which was squashed full of people, and had had another one. Or two. The beer seemed to get thinner, the more he drank.

Someone seemed to be tying something very tight around his forehead, causing his scalp to revolve. He closed his eyes and then opened them very quickly, wondering whether it was actually possible to fall out of bed without moving.

He looked at the ceiling. After the Union bar they'd gone

into the dance. The man on the door hadn't seemed too keen on letting them in, but they went upstairs to the balcony, where there were some of Vince's mates, most of them smoking under the NO SMOKING signs, and a couple of couples locked together on the back seats. Tom had waited to be ignominiously thrown out.

Down on the dance-floor, under the lights, there was a mass of people doing dancing, the air pulsing with sound. Tom, who had never been initiated into the rites of dancing at all, except for one horrendous school dance, the thought of which still made him feel sick, had looked over the edge very cautiously and rather enviously.

Then Vince's mate, who was called Cal, and who kept calling everyone 'bonny lad', had decided to demonstrate what a great mountaineer he was, and had swung himself out onto the ledge that ran around the hall. That was a pity, really, because Tom had decided that the balcony was a good place for observers of life, but it had suddenly filled up with uniforms and they'd all been shooed away. Going back to the pub after that had probably been a mistake.

Tom was just wondering whether it was possible to sleep with his eyes open when the front door opened and closed, and feet danced up the stairs. Tom deduced that it was out of character for A. B., and Vince's snores were already shaking the windows. The cupboard door slid back and Robbie peered in, looking disgustingly cheerful.

"Hi, can I come in?"

Tom said, "If you can," meaning, if you must, and Robbie juddered the door open and closed it behind him, taking up what space there was.

"Hey, are you OK?"

"Great," Tom said, trying not to blink. Robbie, still bouncing slightly, sat down on the bed. Tom silently wished that he wouldn't. Robbie rocked back, and looked at the pink shade as if it were the most beautiful thing in the world.

"Isn't life good?" he said.

Tom was bereft of speech for a moment, then he said, with a great effort of articulation: "Look at me. A month ago I was a respectable schoolboy. Now I'm a drunken student. In three days. And I've got three *years* to go. I'll never stand the pace."

Robbie patted his leg, abstractedly. He seemed to have stopped listening.

"Do you want to know something?"

Apart from wanting to know how to stop feeling like this, Tom had no desires.

"I've got to tell somebody," Robbie said, bouncing again.

"Why me?" Tom said, before he could close his mouth. Robbie's goodwill was, however, unpuncturable.

"Good question. Answer is, you're the the only one half-way normal in this house. I mean, did you know that A. B.'s got a row of bottles on his washstand and one of them's labelled 'Tummy Mixture'?" Tom tried to ask how Robbie had acquired this piece of information, but Robbie rolled on over him. "And there's that idiot Vince. Do you know what he did last night?" No answer seemed to be required, although Tom thought that whatever it was was probably not calculated to make his stomach feel any better. "He's got this chessboard set up in the corner," Robbie went on, with a certain relish. "I mean, Vince. The neanderthal man compleat. Just before he falls into bed, he reads the chess problem out of *The Times*, and makes a few moves. Then he puts the light out and I'm just trying to get to sleep, which isn't easy with all the noises from both ends, and I just doze off when the rat gets up and puts the light on and lurches over to the board and moves one blasted piece and says 'I thought so' and then he falls back into bed and passes out, leaving the light on. I don't know how much longer I can stand it."

"Takes all sorts," Tom said, for something to say.

"That's right, that's right," Robbie said, with a disconcerting change of mood. "There's a lot of good in Vince, if only you could see it. Probably had an unhappy childhood. Poor background, you know." He laughed. Tom closed his eyes desperately and opened them again very quickly. "You know what, Tom. I'm in Love."

Tom focussed on him carefully. *Did I really hear that?* This was the sort of language that one simply did not hear, and here was an acquaintance of one-day-old apparently unembarrassed by such a revelation. A response, however, was clearly required.

"Oh, good," Tom said.

"Good isn't the word. Marvellous. Absolutely marvellous. I mean," Robbie said, as if feeling a slight need to return to reality, "I mean, that's so corny." He stood up and sat down again. "But she's absolutely wonderful."

"Good," Tom said, wishing fervently that he'd stop moving.

"Hair, eyes, everything."

"Fantastic," Tom said, with the awful feeling that he would soon have to hold both sides of the bed with his hands.

"People think you're weird if you talk about Love," Robbie said, talking mostly to the wall in front of him. "I don't see why. I feel like climbing onto the roof and shouting about it." He stood up again, shaking the bed. "Well, perhaps I'll go to bed and dream about her. See you in the morning, then." He stood up, patted Tom on the head, and slid out of sight and slammed the door.

It's great when it stops, Tom thought. Well, at least I wasn't sick on him.

He sat up a little and looked at his watch. It was nearly 1:00 am. He stared at the door, feeling worse, if anything. Well, he thought, it really begins tomorrow, *and I don't know anything*. Still, no point in panicking; they can't shoot you. Until tomorrow.

3

AUTUMN TERM

...easily I passed
From the remembrances of better things,
And slipped into the weekday works of youth...
...Companionships,
Friendships, acquaintances, were welcome all.
We sauntered, played, we rioted, we talked
Unprofitable talk at morning hours:
Drifted about along the streets and walks,
Read lazily in lazy books...and let the stars
Come out, perhaps without one quiet thought.
— Wordsworth (The Prelude)

"It says here," Tom said, "in the University Regulations, that 'students are required to pursue the course.'"

"That's OK, then," Alf said. "Nothing about catching it."

Chapter Ten
MOVING ON

———————————————————————●———————————————————————

By the end of the first week, rebellion was brewing at 54 West Park Street.

Tom, with what he thought was immense brilliance, had found out what the timetable meant and had sat through some lectures which made him wonder why he hadn't just settled for a nice life of moving cartons of cornflakes about, and rather more which had made him want to leap out and redesign the world at once.

He'd taken to taking a long time to walk home, admiring porticos and doorways and steps and sketching here and there, rather self-consciously. He'd been allocated a share in a drawing-board, and been given a keyword for the computer, and nobody in the class stared at him or thought he had three heads, and, unlike school, there was no feeling that you were stuck in the same room when you didn't want to be. Everyone wanted to be.

The School of Architecture had its own small library, with windows which looked out onto a square paved courtyard where the Biology Department was experimenting with something as yet unidentified. (Rather disconcertingly, they would come out wearing masks and gloves and take cuttings from an innocent-looking tree.) The room seemed to Tom to be a small piece of heaven, with more light than was usual, and he spent a lot of time there, simply looking at books most of which didn't appear on the booklist.

In short, all manner of things were well, and apart from occasional lapses into thinking that he didn't know anything about anything and that they would find out and have him hung up by his toes, he couldn't really remember being happier.

He measured this by the fact that he'd only taken the car for two more exploratory tours around the town – and one of those had been with Robbie to get a piece for his motor bike. Otherwise, he checked that it was still there, started it up every day or so, and pumped the rear offside tyre up now and again, and patted its bonnet when no-one was looking.

University life was having the same effect on Robbie. He was reading English and Economics, which was rather unusual (and geographically inconvenient), and he spent a lot of his time sprinting between distant lecture rooms. He also seemed to have discovered poetry, and if you put this together with his passion for Liz, which caused him to walk around just a fraction off the ground, and caused Vince to eye him threateningly, it made him something of a danger to shipping. Tom would not have been surprised had he been found composing an ode to Liz's eyebrow.

The snag was 54 West Park Street, and all that therein was.

All the students Tom had talked to among the architects were ensconced in comfortable, cheap Halls of Residence, or in freshly-painted Student Houses, or in homely lodgings with pleasant landladies who cooked a lot better than their mothers. This seemed downright unfair.

It would have been easy to say that it was he and Robbie vs. A. B. and Vince, but it wasn't that simple.

Nobody liked the food (except A. B.) and nobody liked A. B. Tom thought that the 'We Hate A. B.' Day, when Robbie and Vince set his breakfast place on the floor in the corner was going a good deal too far, but he hadn't the nerve to do anything about it. (A. B. merely shook his head at this childishness, but Tom could not help carrying the thought about with him that A. B. might well, that evening, have shut himself in his room and cried.)

10. Moving On

Everything about Robbie was experimental, except possibly the skin and the height. The 250cc Suzuki parked in the Evans's backyard had been bought with the proceeds of a summer spent working as night porter in a morgue. It had, Robbie said, left him with a disinclination to have anything to do with the medical profession, or dying. He'd had a supervisor with the sort of sense of humour that ran to turning the lights off suddenly on windy nights, with the result that Robbie still had a tendency to start at slight movements.

A week with Vince, however, did not treat him to many slight movements. Vince not only smoked the kinds of cigarettes which had double-strength Government warnings on the packets, but he stubbed them out and relit them to make them stronger, which, as Robbie said, seemed a good way to get cancer of just about everything, including the finger-nails. Anyone sleeping in the same room would have a short life-expectancy.

"He claims to have gone to a school where the kids used to sew razor blades into their lapels, so if a teacher grabbed them..." Robbie shook his head.

Tom, drinking coffee out of the machine in the Students' Union, listened as if to tales of some far-off planet.

Robbie said, "He's amazing. Do you know what he did to the chess club? They're all – according to him – weeds with glasses and they meet in dismal halls to play chess for hours. Old Vince called in on his way back from the pub the other night and beat the living daylights out of their champion in half an hour."

"It's an endearing trait," Robbie said, "but it doesn't make up for him being sick on the stairs last night."

"No, I can see that," Tom said.

"And when you think they've got a computer to help them assign rooms."

"Maybe it's a deliberate attempt to broaden your horizons."

"Still a few bugs in the system," Robbie said. "We've got to get out."

The question was, how could you move in a town which was bulging with students, with a waiting list for almost everywhere?

Deliverance came by curious means, and the first part of it involved, of all people, Alf.

Alf had arrived at the University somewhat after the last minute, his exam results proving him to be a lot brighter than anyone had thought, and so he had had to take whatever was left on the housing list. There was a rumour that he was running tours to show people just how revolting things could be. There was, he said, a madwoman in the attic, and the high-spots included a black, fossilised chip-pan and a strip of wasteland, called a garden, where it rained all the time. Tom, who, after two weeks was beginning to get a little sceptical about some of the things he heard, taxed him with this as they were running across the campus in a rainstorm. They sheltered in the entrance to the Modern Languages Block.

Alf said: "It's all true. I went and complained to the landlady."

"What did she say?"

Alf snorted. "She lives in a very neat and prim and tidy little terrace house with lots of cats, and she said I'd get used to it and there were lots of worse places."

"Where?" Tom said.

"I went to the Lodgings Officer," Alf said. "She didn't seem too impressed." She looked, Alf said, as though she thought for once she'd matched applicant and flat together quite neatly. He'd stood his ground, though, and she'd put his name on the file until a vacancy came up.

Then, while he was still standing in the office, the secretary, who was narrow and grey-haired and gave Alf a kind smile like a cup of tea, came in with some cards and placed them on the table.

"People do leave," the Lodgings Officer said am-
biguously, looking as though she was waiting for Alf to do so,
so that she could get the air freshener out. Alf nodded
politely, and got as far as the door (which the secretary was
holding open), when the Lodgings Officer said, possibly with
some reluctance: "Is it only you?"

Alf turned round. "That depends," he said, carefully.

"There's a flat for four," the Lodgings Officer said,
looking at one of the cards in front of her. "The students
failed their exams and didn't tell the landlady." She looked
at Alf over her spectacles. "If you can find three other people
by tomorrow morning, you can have it." She seemed to think
that this largesse required some explanation. "I haven't got a
foursome on my books," she said. "But I can find one."

"So," Alf said, standing, looking at the rain. "I need
three more."

"You've got me and Robbie," Tom said. "You need one
more."

All of which accounted for why, that evening, Tom was
sitting with his back against the plastic-veneered wall of a
small pub, waiting, while Alf bought a round of drinks, for
Robbie to arrive with his friend from the Economics and
Business course. The foursome.

The pub had been selected by Alf, who seemed to know
about these things. It had a front bar filled entirely by third-
year and research students, and, very often, an impromptu
jazz band. It was very different from the pub next door,
which catered for the local populace and had a fruit machine,
a juke box which looked like a huge flashing pile of boiled
sweets, and which served top-pressure lager from large tanks.

Alf's pub, in contrast, served real ale, and a particularly
venomous form of cider and had a back room where University clubs had parties.

"There are three kinds of students," Alf had said,

ushering a rather worried Tom into the pub. "Them as sits in cafés; them as sits in the Union Bars; and them as sits in real pubs. The aficionados."

"What about them as sits in libraries," Tom said, meekly, but Alf had gone to the bar hatch. The only free tables were in a kind of corridor which ran from the front bar to the back room where guitars were being plugged in and the door flapped and smoke was pulled out through the extractor fan.

Tom sat down, and contemplated the sexist calendar on the wall over Alf's head. There was a worried-looking barman who Alf addressed in a friendly tone as 'Des'. Tom thought that he would never have dared to do that because undoubtedly, after an hour or so, there would be a foul mortifying moment when the barman would stop and say: "The name's George, squire," and Tom would feel about ten millimetres high, and sink into the remains of the carpet.

So far, though, so good, Tom thought. He'd been at University for nearly two weeks, and he'd discovered where all the lecture rooms were, what his tutor looked like, and where to buy the best chips. He'd been to the Bursary, and they'd given him a cheque for a huge sum of money, and he'd found a bank and transferred his meagre account from home. They'd given him various plastic things which he'd immediately left in the Refectory.

He'd even gone down to the basement of the old Union and shown a film for the Hot Celluloid Society, an experience which he looked back on with mixed feelings. Mostly it had been funny. Trish had directed him and Orris in putting out too many chairs in a room with no windows and a polished floor. The chairs were stacked in a side-room, and fell out in tall piles when Orris opened the doors.

The projection box seemed determined to do the pair of them in, and the projectors were so old that Tom was faintly surprised that they didn't have small grates, and shovels, and piles of coal. The film cans, when opened, revealed films that had been re-wound upside down and backwards. Orris maintained that nobody would notice, but Trish made them rewind them correctly. This involved a fun machine called a re-winder, with two arms and a massively geared-up handle, which meant that the film got going very fast with no way of stopping it. You had to keep your nerve or the film went faster than the winder and started to climb up the wall.

By the time the small group of viewers had arrived, Tom and Orris were sweating and exhausted. The film (whatever it was – Tom couldn't remember) only broke twice, only one bulb blew, and only one speaker stopped working, which seemed to be par for the course. The audience gave a small round of ironic applause at the end and when Trish stood up and thanked the projectionists – she got Tom's name wrong which, as Orris said, was probably just as well.

Alf came back from the bar with four pints, accompanied by Robbie and his friend, Liam, who was about as opposite as it was possible to be to Alf, while still being human and male. Tom immediately suspected him of being at least a Union bar man, if not a library-type. He was neat, and if he didn't actually look as though he were practising to be a banker, he certainly looked as though he could buy all his clothes off the peg and they would all fit. One thing was certain: like Alf and Robbie he had put his previous incarnation thoroughly behind him. Tom, still wearing his invisible school uniform, took his pint cautiously.

"You're thinking," Alf said.

"Just," Tom said. "I was thinking of a woman I met in a queue. She expected gowns and bicycles."

"That's Oxbridge," Liam said. "We're your middle-classes, not yer upper-middles. We go to your provincial universities. Actually, the Oxbridgers don't recognise us as real universities at all. We don't count."

"Especially Alf," Robbie said.

"Don't you call *me* middle-class," Alf said. "I'm from the workers."

"Never mind," Robbie said. "We'll talk slowly for you."

"Look at us," Liam said, as if he hadn't been interrupted. "We're middle everything. We don't take drugs – apart from socially acceptable ones" – he lifted his beerglass – "because it's damn stupid and anyway we wouldn't know where to get any. We don't do wild orgies because we take sex seriously –"

"– and anyway it's too dangerous," Robbie said.

"– so we get a little drunk and have a little harmless lower-middle-class fun."

"What you mean," Alf said, moving his copy of *The Idiot* to the side of the table, away from the beer drips, "is that the middle classes can be slightly *sportif*, and society turns a blind eye, but the working-classes get duffed up."

"Not quite," Liam said. "Don't mix us up with people with REAL money, who can afford to buy education. It's all self-regulating. We can't afford to get too drunk, and we can't afford cars much, so we don't drive them when we're drunk much. We don't go to hunt balls or public schools, mostly, but we don't expect to end up out on the streets or get beaten up or bombed or starved. We don't get anyone pregnant –"

"– or get pregnant," Tom said.

"– or get busted for drugs or –"

"In fact, you're a bunch of boring –" Alf began.

"Just middle," Liam said. "Stop being so superior because you're inferior. Have a drink. My round."

Tom, who was nearly a pint behind everyone else, started to drink rapidly. Liam stood up, waited a moment for Tom's glass, stopped waiting and went to the bar.

Alf looked at his back. "I'll bet you," he said, "he's got a girlfriend at home, and they've got a deposit down on an engagement ring, a house, and a grave-plot."

"Are your digs rotten?" Tom said when Liam came back.

"Liam's in Hall," Robbie said.

Alf looked across at Tom, saying, without moving his lips, well, what do you expect?

"What's wrong with that?" Tom said. Tom had driven past the Halls on his tour; huge white-stone buildings, set in lawns, and looking down over the town. Although architecturally somewhat suspect, they looked like havens of civilisation beside the madhouse of number 54.

Liam spread his hands. "One thing and another."

"Try one thing to start with," Alf suggested.

"Well, to start with. I got there, in the minibus, with all these students."

"Snobby, eh?" Alf said.

"And it's like being back in school. Nothing but rules. And rows of showers and loos." Liam seemed disappointed by the unreasonableness of it all.

"It's got a roof," Alf said, apparently having forgotten that he needed Liam to make up the four.

"And I get to my room, and the bed's broken, so I complain, and I get accused of bed-wrecking." He sipped his half-pint and Tom wondered why he hadn't thought of asking for one and knew quite well. Not sufficiently macho. "I didn't come to university to be regimented around the place," Liam said. Tom thought that there must be more to Liam than met the eye. Liam went on, judiciously: "But it seems to suit a lot of people. They have a lot of fun," he went on bitterly. "They sing at three in the morning, and there's always the hosepipe fights and letting off the fire-alarm." He paused again.

"Jolly student japes," Alf said. He seemed to be suddenly approving of Liam.

"Nobody seems to take any notice of the fire alarms, except me and the fire-brigade," Liam said. "*They* don't think it's very funny, and you feel a bit of an idiot being the only one standing on the lawn at one o'clock in the morning." He looked at Alf. "But I don't intend to get fried on account of pride." Alf grinned. Liam said, "I didn't come to university to be mucked about by a lot of puerile idiots who nick the Hall Committee Notices."

"So there," said Alf. "Fancy joining us in a flat?"

Tom was intrigued by this new view of Hall life. "Don't they have wardens?"

"Keepers," Liam said. "The head one lives at one end of the site, and his office is at the other, and he always drives there in his car. It must be, oh, nearly half a k. Rumour has it that he locks the doors in case the students get him. Just one more," he said to Tom, who was edging his way around the table, his fingers locked through the glass-handles.

Tom spent a long time getting to the bar and a longer time getting served. Buying drinks was obviously a fine art. First you had to attract the attention of the barman. If you push there's trouble; if you wave too little the barman doesn't see you and if you wave too much he ignores you. At the moment, he was dunking glasses into a washer full of soap and four revolving rubber columns, and leaving a lot of soap in the glasses.

Liam came and stood beside him. "Just a half," he said. "I don't drink that much." Tom nodded.

Liam said, "Tell you the truth, I really can't stand being surrounded by all those students. I might get mistaken for one." He grinned, and nodded towards Alf and Robbie, who were apparently contemplating each other thoughtfully. "I think Robbie might be OK; what's Alf like?"

Tom started to say something and then was distracted by the fact that this was the first time that he'd been seriously asked a question like that, and by the implication that Liam saw him as some yardstick of normality.

"I only meant," Liam said, apologetically, "I mean, we might end up knowing each other all our lives, so it doesn't hurt to have a reference."

"I've seen worse," Tom said. "And basically, I need to move, soon." The barman was serving somebody else now. Robbie came by.

"Don't worry about another drink," he said. "I've got a date." He went to the door and went out. Outside, it was dark and raining, with a very lonely-looking lamplight. Tom had a momentary panic that they'd all drift away and leave him.

Liam was nodding. "Then we'd better work out how you can break your agreement with your landlady."

The gods, moving in particularly mysterious ways, chose Vince as their instrument of deliverance.

The following Tuesday evening (after a fairly unpleasant morning when somebody had written 'Tummy Mixture' on the milkjug, and A. B. had gone a very nasty shade), Tom was sitting resignedly waiting for the latest culinary horror. A. B. was reading *The Financial Times*, and Robbie was in the overstuffed front room, reading poetry. Vince passed down the hall and looked in.

"Waiting for your swill, then?" he said. "I wonder what she's messed up tonight?" He turned away and bumped into Mr Evans, who had come silently into the corridor behind him. Tom stopped breathing, thinking, it's times like this when being an innocent bystander is just the thing.

There was a certain amount of dancing in the hallway and sounds as though the hatstand was being crushed. Mrs Evans came out of the kitchen with a bowl of tinned spaghetti and dumped it on the table (where A. B., ignoring the whole thing, immediately served himself), and typhooned out into the hall. Tom got up and slipped behind her into the living room and stood next to Robbie, who was standing with a book of poems dangling in his hand.

They looked out of the window. On the pavement a slugging match was in progress. Tom and Robbie, neither of whom had ever seen anything like it, glanced at each other in silence. The two men were punching each other, hardly ducking or weaving: just standing as though they were punching at punchbags, and having about as much effect.

"It's terrifying," Tom said, but he meant that people were walking along the far side of the road without even looking across.

"What do you expect them to do?" Robbie said, reasonably.

The punching was developing into grappling, and the two fighters hit the lamp-post and rolled onto the pavement. Mrs Evans stood on the doorstep, arms folded, shouting abuse and encouragement.

"I'm too delicate for this world," Tom said.

At this point, just when Tom thought that ambulances might have been called, Vince and Mr Evans, as if by some mystic call, suddenly ceased to hit each other, got up, put their arms around each other's shoulders and walked across the road and into the small pub.

Mrs Evans, momentarily silenced, looked round for a target and saw Robbie who was grinning. She turned on him.

"What are you laughing at? It's disgusting. That creature is out of my house this evening. I won't stand for it." And Robbie, showing an admirable quickness of wit, said, "If he goes, I go," and Tom said, "Me too," from behind his shoulder.

"All right. Good riddance. You can all go. Students." She swept through the dining room and exchanged a glance of mutual understanding with A. B. and slammed into the back room.

"Mission accomplished," Tom said, wondering what his mother would say. "What do we do now?"

"Let's go and have a kebab to celebrate," Robbie said.

When you look at a demolition site, Tom thought, and you can see the shapes of two house-ends hanging on the two remaining house-ends, then this is the bit that's missing in between.

The new flat was on the top floor of a house built about a hundred years ago by somebody who disliked architecture. It was squat, had three floors, and the windows at the top being lower than the rest gave it a slightly worried if not homicidal look.

Tom's neglected car, coaxed back to life by some extended cleaning of its plug-leads, and at the end of its battery, had been loaded with luggage on a drizzly day and now was parked on the pavement outside the new flat. Tom had found a road around the corner which was on a steepish slope. If the handbrake held, that would be the ideal place to keep the Ford.

Liam and Tom and Robbie stood on the pavement, considering.

"Somebody's got to go first," Robbie said, looking at Liam.

The rest of the houses in the street were large Victorian affairs, many of them, mysteriously, having green shades at their upper windows and seemed peculiarly dead.

"Perhaps they're night-shift workers," Liam said.

"Morgue attendants."

"Drunken students who ought to be working."

"Strange satanic rites."

"Perhaps they just don't want to look out."

"Maybe the curtains are just nailed up."

"We're dithering," Tom said.

They looked down the street. Two of the houses were conspicuously tidy with red front doors. The forecourts around had overgrown hedges and black, dog-disturbed sacks of rubbish and chained bicycles, and ancient attempts at flower-borders, and flat black tiles with circular holes, and moss. The two neat houses had only paving stones.

"They're student houses," Robbie said.

Liam, as front man, knocked at the door and they shuffled in. Under the stairs was a door where the landlord and landlady lurked and suspiciously handed out front door keys with an extra one for Alf. Tom and Liam and Robbie went back for the luggage.

"Did you tell them we're saving Alf up for a nice surprise?"

"Lucky we signed the lease in the Lodgings Office,"

Tom said.

Robbie stopped on the doorstep. "Could this be the well-spring of inspiration of three future giants of business and letters and architecture?"

"No," Liam said. "Get in."

The stairs wound up with thin bannisters, and they came out, crab-wise, on a landing.

There were three closed doors, and one opened onto the communal bathroom, which was tall and green and hard, with a cat sitting on the windowsill. They bumped on upwards, and the ceilings got lower.

"Servants were obviously short in those days," Robbie said.

The top floor emerged over the bannisters, a dirge of faded carpet and magnolia walls; four doors leaning open. Ahead, there was a large room, with gun-slits of sash-windows under the eaves. This first room had three very odd beds, a wardrobe and a dressing table. The second had two easy chairs of great age, a dining table and four wooden chairs, a tiled hearth and a gas fire and a sink.

Robbie put his suitcase down.

"Is this a good idea?"

"It's ours," Liam said. He didn't sound entirely certain of himself.

"And there's no Mrs Evans," Tom said.

Tom went back into the bedroom. There was one (very saggy) bed behind the door, a bed against the left wall and another against the right wall with its foot against the windowsill. This last was a divan and Tom reserved it decisively by dropping his case onto it.

He edged around the foot of the bed and pulled the sash down. Checking that the frame wasn't about to detach itself and send him onto the pavement, he leaned out. There was a corner pub, and about three degrees of the promenade. Sea View.

At the back of the flat above the bathroom was a single

bedroom with sink, and a window looking out onto the usual rear roofscape, and with a wooden dividing wall between it and the kitchen. The kitchen was fairly rudimentary, with Adam's fridge, an ancient glass-fronted cupboard, a knobbly gas cooker and a large enamel sink.

They sat at the table in the living room with their first coffee and planned great things: they were going to cook every evening on a rota system, and pay money into a kitty for things like milk and washing-up liquid and posh newspapers. They fixed a rota for the single bedroom. Robbie wanted it straight away to have a bit of privacy with his new girlfriend, and Liam wanted it first to have a bit of privacy, full stop; and so they tossed for it and Robbie lost and insisted on making it best out of three. He lost twice more, and insisted, a touch sulkily, on having the single room for the second term. Alf wasn't there so he didn't get a choice. Tom, who kept quiet, ended up with the single room for the third term – which he thought was pretty intelligent because the exams would be coming up and he would be away from everyone.

Alf was allocated the worst bed behind the door.

"After all," Robbie said, "after what he's been used to it'll be luxury."

Tom unpacked his clothes into his third of the wardrobe and kicked his suitcase under the bed. By normal standards, the room was tatty and dowdy and disreputable, and his father would have laughed and his mother would have been very dubious about it. Tom, stopping for a second in the general attack on it, decided that it was really a rather good place to be.

Robbie was placing an impressive range of aftershaves and deodorants on the dressing table next to the window, and Liam came in from putting his bedroom tidy.

"OK?"

"OK," Tom said.

"Right," Liam said, "let's start again."

Chapter Eleven
SUE'S PROGRESS

Sue, with her collar up against the wind although it was a bright day, stood by the bridge and looked down into the harbour.

At the farthest end of the town from the girls' Hall, the river ran into the sea, and the University had a boathouse. Liz, of all people (a phrase that seemed to get used rather a lot about Liz), had not only taken up rowing but was in some sort of team, and Sue had come down to watch. She was supposed, herself, to be in a badminton tournament, but she had pulled a muscle in her shoulder. And there were other things to do.

She sat on the railings, hooking her toes under the second rail, and watched the boats swaying on the wide water. The houses edged down to the harbourside, neat and renovated, while behind them there were older terraces with gaps where they were being pulled down, and beyond them the sky was pale blues and greys. Fireworks tonight.

She slid a folded paper from her pocket, and read the print out from her Word Processor.

Dear Jojo,

I've had an insulting letter from the mama telling me to write to cheer you up, which seems to imply that my wonder-letters haven't up-cheered you so far. I know it's no good saying, look on the bright side; all those months of traction isn't going to be funny, but at least – well, you know. Sorry to hear about the latest batch of doctors: however, you may have a hairy nose one day. Still, the more specialists, the better. Perhaps you'll get a trip to London. They tell me they have wonderful ceilings there.

Sue looked across the harbour. Is this funny? It was odd how Jojo seemed to be slipping away from her, but the thought of her lying on her back, week on week, was a good one when things seemed less than bright. Not that they often did.

The course, as Zoe might have said, was brill, and there was a very small proportion of unspeakables; the laboratories were new, and the plant-breeding station was a dream, and she was starting a study of coastal ecology with the short and enthusiastic koala bear professor, who you simply had to rub against and knowledge stuck to you.

Apart from that, it was getting difficult to fit everything in, and Jojo got pushed to the odd edges of the day.

Well, I suppose being flat on your back for a month limits your sense of humour. Still, you could be Mary. Her *father* comes down *every weekend* to see if she's OK. Last Sunday I went into the utility room to get some coffee and found her crying in among her 26 pairs of knickers. I don't know whether it's because he came or because he went away. It's like talking to a wombat, sometimes.

Sue shook her head. Some letter-writer. She was about to crumple the sheet up into a ball and drop it into the harbour, when it struck her that if she just went on about how good her life was, and how great Uni. was, that would make Jojo even more depressed. What I need, she thought, is a psychologist. The letter didn't get much further.

Things are much the same. I'm still at the badminton and the swimming; Liz is still going out with the fragrant Robbie, and they're driving us all berserk because every night they're either shouting sweet goodbyes or having a row and, as we're three foors up, all the Hall and most of the south coast gets to know about it.

But the hot news is: I'm now Ace Reporter on the greatest student newspaper in – well, in the University – **APATHY**. I know you think as like us scientists don't know how to wright, but with this newspaper, it's probably an advantage.

APATHY came out once a week, or once a month, or every now and then, rather depending on whether there was anything to print. The Freshers' edition (which was full of re-writes of the previous year's articles on how disgraceful it was that nobody ever joined in anything) had been left by the previous year's staff, most of whom had either left, or who had resigned because it was their third year and they needed to catch up with work.

Sue began by producing columns of print from various scraps of manuscript, and then taught Phil, the editor, to use the Word Processor. Then she spent three evenings helping to paste the strips of copy onto sheets to go to the printer, and, finally, to fill in a gap, she wrote her first piece. The cutting was clipped to the letter:

JOIN THE COMMUNITY PROJECT

Is your life as worthless as everyone else's? Does that next pint seem jaded?
Yes?
Then get out and help somebody.
How?
Every weekend this term, a dedicated band of eejits is out helping the old and infirm (and I don't mean the Maths Professors). Out they go with their choppers and plungers to chop wood for the old people and unblock their loos and paint their kitchens – or just to chat.
Believe it or not, there are people out there worse off than you.

So, if you're tough, talented, or just wasting your life, get out of bed and get down to the **APATHY** office and see Phil or Zoe, and they'll sort you out.

Liz reported that this was causing qualms all over the town or at least in Robbie's flat, and they were still arguing about whether they were going to do anything. Sue had signed up, and here she was. She put the clipping and the letter back inside her reporter's notebook.

Coming along the prom was an ill-sorted couple. On the left, nearest the sea, was a tall slightly awkward figure who was called Fred. He played badminton and was wearing a tracksuit. With him was a short blonde figure named Orris, wearing the sort of donkey-jacket frequently found on building sites.

They went round the harbour, Orris explaining at some length that he didn't actually want to come, and that he wasn't feeling in the least bit charitable, and that he'd only signed up because his girlfriend was doing sociology and he wanted to impress her; and then the next day they'd raced each other across the bay, swimming, and she'd beaten him, so now they weren't speaking, but he couldn't see how he could get out of it now. Fred listened to all this in restrained silence.

They came up to the appointed house, which was one terrace-road up the hill from the demolition, and they looked down through the rafters of the houses below them to the harbour. The boats were moving slowly out, oars spread.

Everything was covered in stone- and brick-dust, and most of the houses in the street had windows boarded with thick planks. They stood for a few minutes. Fred consulted a piece of paper.

" 'Mrs Prothero. Widow. Age 79.' " He looked round. "I feel like a terrible do-gooder."

"Well, we can't stand here all day," Orris said. "Let's go and do some terrible good."

The next hour and a half made a mark on all three of them.

Orris knocked on the door and, eventually, an old woman opened it. She was over-inflated, as if she were full of water, and she smelled of stale clothes and pickled onions and had colourless saggy stockings and slippers which slopped. Fred and Orris and Sue looked at each other, feeling very young and firm and clean and worried about it.

Orris followed her into a house which seemed to be mostly full of wardrobes. The old lady, shuffling and flopping ahead of them, took them into the middle room where the light, in an elaborate brown fitting, was on because the side-window was virtually blocked up by furniture.

"Anything at all," Orris was saying. "Do you want any wood chopping?"

"I use the gas," Mrs Prothero said, fitting herself into an armchair. "But the outside lavatory's blocked."

"Fine," Fred said. "Fine, just the thing."

Sue went into the kitchen to make tea and found that she wasn't breathing through her nose. She washed the cups, then looked round for something to dry them on. There were no tea-towels and Sue began to suspect the quality of the water in the taps and then started, rather reluctantly, to wash around the sink.

Mrs Prothero came, lumpily, into the doorway, and watched her. "It's my eyes," she said. "I can't see to wash up very well. Isn't it terrible?" The kettle lead was frayed almost through and all the cups had a patina of grease.

Sue said, "It must be," because it was, and worse because Mrs Prothero knew it.

So, while Orris and Fred worked on the drains, Sue listened to a story of ungrateful daughters and dead sons, and wondered what she could have been like as a little girl, when she was thin and bright and quick. Sue tried to drink the tea, and listened carefully, and nodded, and thought how could she get her to wash before they came again.

After about three years, Orris and Fred came back in, looking yellow, and spent some time at the sink. There was a hard piece of soap with grit in it. Mrs Prothero watched them for a while and then pulled herself out of her seat.

"Horrid job, I should think. I think I've got some whisky somewhere."

Orris looked across at Sue and shook his head. Mrs Prothero shuffled into the scullery. Orris sat on the arm of the chair. Sue moved away slightly. "The bin's full of bottles," Orris said. "Poor old bag."

The poor old bag came back with four glasses in her hands, each one well full, and watched them carefully while they drank.

"I put some ginger ale in yours," she said to Sue. "Men don't have anything in whisky." Sue glanced round. She was out of range of any plant pots in which to deposit the drink and so she drank it. "That's it," she said. "I think there's enough for another." She shuffled out. Sue clutched her throat.

"Another one like that and you'll have to carry me out," she said.

"Who's going to carry *us* out?" Fred said.

Afterwards, when they were helping each other down the street (for the second glass, Mrs Prothero had obviously run out of whisky, and had topped up the glasses with gin), and Orris was describing the rat-holes in the garden, and what the drains were blocked with, Fred asked Sue to come to watch the fireworks with him, and Sue said yes.

And they went, and it was fine, mostly with the town people and children and a smell of raw gunpowder and hot dogs.

Afterwards, they walked back to the Hall and Fred said goodnight, and Sue came in and met Zoe on the stairs carrying books and files.

"Thinking of going to your room?" Zoe said.

Sue nodded.

"You'll be lucky," Zoe said. "I saw Robbie and Liz going upstairs."

"That's the third night," Sue said. She and Zoe were rapidly forming a persecuted-room-mates' club. "Mary asleep?"

"Mary's asleep," Zoe said. Sue turned resignedly around and they went downstairs to the basement lounge.

This was an odd room, without windows, but with drawn curtains hanging in imitation window-frames. It was used for meetings of the more intellectual societies, but, mostly, as somewhere to go for singles who had been denied access to their rooms by couples having got there first, or vice versa. Most of the chairs had high wing-backs and were turned towards the wall. When it was Sunday night and raining, you couldn't get a seat after about eight o'clock, and the lights tended to be turned down.

"I've been talking to Joy, the sub-warden," Zoe said. "She said that in the old days men had to be out of the rooms by ten, and on Sundays they were only allowed in two to four and seven to nine."

"Sounds like a good idea," Sue said, taking off her coat. They pulled two chairs into a corner, and put their feet on a radiator. There was a smell of dust and carpets, and burned air coming off the radiators.

"Apparently, in the real old days, you had to push your bed out into the corridor when you had male visitors."

"Shows a lack of imagination by somebody."

Zoe said: "Tell me about the fireworks. And Fred."

"Fireworks, well OK. Stood in the park. Whizz, pop. And Fred's a sweetie. I mean, he's not a great entertainer, but he doesn't grope."

"Much more exciting here," Zoe said. "We've got a mystery trumpeter."

"What?"

"Some idiot started playing the trumpet in the courtyard out at the back tonight. Really sweet. And when somebody went out there, he'd gone."

"He?"

"You could just see this figure. A tall he."

"He ought to meet up with Robbie. They could do a duet."

Zoe arranged books and files on the floor.

"What're you reading?" Sue said.

"It's called *Tristram Shandy*," Zoe said. She ran her hand over her tight hair. "Mad but good. He leaves blank pages for you to write your own description of the heroine, and there's a black page when somebody dies."

Sue said: "I don't understand you English lot. Give me a good ecosystem any day. Can I borrow some paper? I'd better get the letters column started."

The editor of **APATHY** had decided that they should have a letters column, as a good way of filling up space cheaply, but as nobody had written to them, Sue was given the job of starting things off. The first one was easy.

Dear Ms Editor,

I'm starting a campaign to rid the Union of sexist garbage, beginning with certain so-called newspapers which exploit the female body. Why should our Union dues (extorted from us undemocratically) be wasted on this degrading filth? How would the macho males like it if they were thought of as sex objects? These papers may be appropriate to building-site workers but they're a disgrace to the University.

Yours very sincerely,

Chairman, Women's Equity League.

"That should get a reaction," Zoe said, approvingly. "Full of prejudice. What's the Woman's Equity League?"

"I made it up," Sue said. "But here's a real one. Mary told me about it."

Sir,

I am very disturbed to discover that the 'Quiet Room', which was reserved as somewhere where people could go for contemplation and peace, has been taken over as a bottle store for the Union Bar. This is a sad reflection on the ways of the modern world and I ask the Union Executive to do something about it.

Yours, disgusted.

She sat, thinking for a while
"Have you written to Jo lately?" Zoe said.
"I'd better try," Sue said, looking at the wall. "What can I write about? I've done Robbie. And Liz is relatively calm these days. I think she's actually working."
"Tell her about Alf," Zoe said.
"She'll think I'm making it up."
Sue took a pen from her bag, rested Zoe's A4 notepad on her knee, and wrote:

Dear Jo,

Thanks for your scrawl. I'm getting up a collection to buy you a Word Processor. We can glue it to the ceiling and give you a long stick. I'm glad the cranking isn't too unpleasant, and the hospital sounds as well as it might be. We'll subscribe to your fund for sexier physiotherapists.

Zoe says I'm allowed to tell you about Alf, who she's started to go out with: she can't stay in with him because the sainted Mary usually goes to bed at half-past nine, when she isn't out being holy somewhere. I can't really describe him, except that he's nearly been thrown out because the porter thought he was a passing tramp. He seems to own one sweater and one jacket (no shirt), but he's doing Russian and Chinese or something and every time I've seen him he's always had some heavy classic stuck in his back pocket.

"How's that?"
"You forgot to say, he's absolutely smashing," Zoe said.

Zoe says he's gorgeous. He works in a pub on Saturday nights, which means that Zoe can get on with her work and look virtuous. He's the favourite son of the Italian chap called Carlo, who runs the pub. I've been in there and the spaghetti is wonderful. Carlo's a lovely man and he looks like he likes spaghetti a lot. The best bit is that his wife, who does the cooking down in the basement, is English.

Sue sucked the end of her pen.
"Go on," Zoe said, without looking up. "Light, bright, and sparkling. Tell her about the food."
"Ah yes. The cheese."

Let me give you the story of a typical day in this humble palace we call Home. Come the dawn, I'm awoken from my girlish slumber by the gentle cries of the gulls and the soft swish of the gravel caressed by the waves. The local troubadour plays under the window, and the uniformed eunuch pushes in the silver trolley with the scrambled quails' eggs (the eggs, not the quails) and the maid opens the curtains and the under-butler brings in the caviare-stuffed asparagus tips and the iced champagne. Then it's the ironed copies of *The Times*, and it's off for the massage.

Actually it starts with Liz snoring or the bin-men having bin-rolling competitions down the steps, or the sea chucking the gravel up five floors. I dreamed the other night that the whole place was being swamped by the sea, and Annie, who's doing psychology, told me that I was deeply sexually frustrated. She couldn't account for the suggestion that I'd be

less frustrated if my room was on the back. Then it's down to
the queues, but there's great bins of muesli, and the
Lambkins do a lot of toast.

But the best bit about the food is supper. That's about
nine o'clock and it's really rather exciting. One of ye
domesticks shuffles out into the hall with huge trays of bread
and cheese, and sometimes fruit left after dinner, and vats of
milk. She goes away, and then there's a pause and you can
hear the drumming of feet as men secreted in all the rooms
burst out and fall upon the food. Rumour has it that the
warden stands at the front door frisking them as they leave.
Alf and Robbie are deeply implicated in all this. Alf was
caught the other night shovelling mandarin oranges into a
polythene bag, and Zoe was about to rescue him, but he
convinced the warden that he was courier for the whole
corridor. Z. says he had the W. eating out of his hand, which
couldn't have been pleasant for her. Anyway, time for bed,
so I can surge on tomorrow towards my BSc. I got two Bs for
my first two assignments, so all I need now is a few Ss and
Cs.

"That's terrible," Zoe said.

"It's not even true," Sue said. "I got As." She put her
feet to the floor. "Come and help me throw them out." But
when they reached the rooms, the lights were out, and it was
quiet. Sue undressed in the dark and then went along the
corridor in her dressing gown for a shower.

Annie was drying her hair.

"It's just like school, isn't it," she said. "Only more men
around."

"Did you go to boarding school?" Sue said.

Annie brushed at her hair. "There's a few public school
drop-outs here, you know. We don't all go to Cambridge."

Sue glanced at her and turned on one of the showers to
see what the evening's temperature was like. Annie's voice
came over the curtain.

"Of course, Daddy was furious. Said he'd wasted all that money. He threatened to sue them, only Mummy said they'd only say I was thick. I mean," she said, hurriedly, "I don't mean that you only come here if you're thick."

Sue felt that some sort of comment was required. "It never occurred to me to go to Cambridge," she said. "My father says people just buy their way in there." As she said it, she had an uncomfortable feeling of doubt about this dictum; a loss of faith.

She was still troubled by this when she got back to her room. She switched on the bedside light and saw Zoe's pad and pen on her bed. She picked it up, tore the letter sheets off, and took the rest across the corridor, tapping lightly on the door. Zoe beckoned her in, and pointed to Mary's bed. In the low light from Zoe's bedside lamp, Mary was lying asleep, with her thumb in her mouth, and her arm around a large brown teddy-bear. Zoe looked at her rather affectionately, but Sue went sadly to bed and had bad dreams.

Monday morning, and Sue was in the Post Office, having run out of stamps.

It was another hard clear morning, with a rim of frost everywhere, and the air in the bright open hall of the Post Office was warm. Sue's nose began to defrost. She stood with her stack of library books in her arms, shuffling forward, when the woman in front of her, who was carrying two shopping bags, suddenly leaned back and kept leaning. Sue tried to catch the woman under the arms, scattering books and papers into the air, but she was a dead weight and Sue fell backwards onto the man behind her and the three of them splayed onto the floor among legs and shopping baskets and books.

A certain amount of crowding round and flapping went on, but Sue gathered the woman up and put her head forward and, when she had recovered enough to walk, helped her out into the street, carrying one of the bags, and, by doing so, moved into a new spectrum of university life.

"Better?" Sue said. The woman was just a little older than her, and too thin; a girl, really.

"My own fault," the girl said. "I forgot breakfast."

Sue steered her across the road and down the two blocks to the seafront and in to The Seafront Café, which was plastic and cheerful, and which had gravel lying on both sides, inside and outside, of its windows.

Every café (and pub) in the town had its own group of student clientele. The Seafront Café, unusually, hovered uneasily between the locals and the University. But it sold coffee and biscuits and when the girl, who was called Penny, felt better, Sue carried her shopping bags along the promenade to one of the Victorian wedding cake terraced houses.

Inside, there was an air of space and cleanliness with wide landings and Penny led the way to the top of the house. The walls of the highest landing were white and decorated with a long, very pale mural, a kind of seascape with cliffs and downs and a winter sky. Sue stopped on the stairs and looked along it..

Penny looked back at her. "Good, isn't it. That's Toby's. He's married to me." That sounded like a good way of putting it. Penny gestured her into the front room of the flat, and Sue put the bags down, feeling that she had walked into a different life, and trying to make a connection in her head.

The room was all light. There were two wide bay-windows with high sashes which, like her own window at the Hall, looked clear out over the sea. The walls were pale with paintings and a rug hanging; the carpet was off-white; and there were cushions and two long, deep sofas. There were low bookshelves with books on art and Zen Buddhism, and in front of one of the windows, an empty easel, with a stool and a tray of paints and brushes beside it. Such a splendid place of peace.

Sue went back along the landing and stopped in the kitchen doorway.

The kitchen had a cooker on an island in the middle of the floor and a staggering array of pans and utensils. It crossed Sue's mind to wonder why Penny was so thin. "What course are you doing?" Penny said. She was filling a copper kettle from a water-filter.

"Biology and ecology," Sue said.

Penny nodded. "That's brave."

"Why?"

"Well, men do science, don't they? Toby, you know, he's in the arts – English and painting – but women mostly do those." Sue was about to say that there was a majority of girls taking Biology, but the connection overrode the thought.

"Oh, *that* Toby," she said. "He's a friend of mine's tutor."

Penny's eye rested on her for a fraction of a second longer than was absolutely necessary. "Who's that?"

"She's called Zoe," Sue said. There was a pause. Penny slid the kettle onto the hob. Sue said, "What do *you* do?"

Penny smiled. "Nothing. I'm just a local. I used to work at Nick's caff – do you know Nick's? – you will – and Toby spent days in there drinking gallons of coffee, and he refused to go away until I said I'd go out with him. It was very romantic." She made coffee. "Now I administrate this madhouse. Toby thinks that you ought to have tutorials at home and not in college, so the place is always full of people, and once they come in, we can never get them out. You'll see."

Sue tilted her head.

Penny said: "You can be *my* guest, for saving me from breaking my neck. Come up any time." She smiled.

Sue looked around her. "I will," she said. "Thanks, I will."

Chapter Twelve
TALES OF FLATS AND LIBRARIES

———————————●———————————

Now that the system for sharing breakfast had broken down (it had lasted slightly longer than the cooking-in-the-evening rota, which had lasted as long as Alf's turn) and November was seriously upon them, there wasn't a burning incentive to get out of bed in the mornings. In the bigger bedroom, Tom and Alf had taken to lying in bed, waiting for Robbie's cabaret.

Robbie, oblivious of Tom and Alf watching him with increasingly wild surmise, sat, each morning, on his bed and shaved with an elaborate electric razor. He would then, as Alf put it, anoint himself with rich unguents, that is, aftershave and underarm deodorant, and, most intriguingly, talcum powder.

This last was applied by pulling forward the waistband of his jeans and directing the talcum powder into the gap. The entertainment value was considerably increased one morning, when Robbie, in a moment of oscitation (Alf had a collection of words like that) shook aftershave into his jeans instead of talcum powder and made an undignified exit to the bathroom amid muted hysteria.

However, one grey November morning, Tom woke up to find only empty beds and an empty flat and the air of everyone doing the right thing except him. He went into the kitchen, which seemed to be silting up with polythene bags of mouldy cheese and slices of bread.

He made himself some coffee and stood feeling guilty. After all, missing a day at school was something you only did with a great deal of fuss, parental notes, accounting to teachers, and things like that. On the other hand, here, nobody was watching. It was his responsibility not anyone else's, and if he chose to make it a free day, then, lo, it was a free day.

That line of thinking made him feel considerably better, but it still felt rather against the grain of things. Nevertheless, he went out into the frosty morning, feeling slightly roguish, pulled the grey scarf that his mother had knitted him around his neck, and decided to go and explore the library.

Tom crossed the town, passing those bits of the University that had floated off and taken the form of Victorian and Jacobean terraces and past the campus, which had already been used by one of his lecturers as the most convenient potted architectural history of the last thirty years, to the library, which contrived to be a bit of everything. There was a new concrete entrance, grafted onto some Victorian Gothic in one direction and some Edwardian brick in the other.

He stood for a moment, wondering about Orris's suggestion that the whole lot could be replaced by a couple of dozen hard disks, and Alf's that books were power and the greatest allies of the ruling class ever invented. The opposing view, launched forcefully by Robbie, that books were the great disseminator of democracy, had nearly sunk the flat-partnership on the second day.

Tom walked up the steps and the doors slid apart.

Inside there was an expanse of carpet under a concrete egg-box ceiling which was just a fraction too low and gave the impression that it was falling on him. There were, conspicuously, no books.

There were desks for librarians, display cases for manuscripts, microfiche readers, rows of terminals, and newspapers on poles, but no books. Tom walked into the hushed atmosphere, feeling as though he was walking on blotting paper. Perhaps Orris had already made his move.

There was an air of calm and learning, as well as mere warmth. Ignored by everyone, Tom took a random direction, through an archway that had clearly been cut through the wall of the original building and in five steps entered a most amazing world.

Here, there *were* books. Galleries of them; dungeons and attics, and spiral staircases with spiral bookshelves, and stacks and shelves and galleries bearing mystic symbols: PN, PR, PO. Tom felt, suddenly, as though he'd been swimming underwater for a week and that this was the air. He drifted between the endless spines of books, wondering – how do I ever absorb all this?

There were brown square boxes of old periodicals, and down the next corridor, law books, all bound uniformly in blue or black, and all looking too thick to open. There were doors covered with bookshelves and discreet arrows. On the twist of a staircase, there was a sudden slit view of the sea.

Every now and then he passed readers, sometimes with head resting on the shelves; once, lying down. Not for the first time, he tried to realise that this had been here all the time, all his life and before, and it wasn't being just invented for him, this minute, but he failed.

He went downwards into the basements where there were metal ladders to the stacks, books that were, presumably, only read once every hundred years, and the metal shelves were tight against each other and had to be pulled out on runners. For some reason, there were bars everywhere, so that it looked like a set for a nineteen-thirties thriller, where the hero is 'trapped with the heroine, while the poison-gas rises around their ankles, or the water pours in, or the snakes work their way down the ventilation shafts. Tom looked over his shoulder in the clinical fluorescent light; Robbie would feel at home down here.

He went back up the spiral staircases. Now it was like something from a medieval tale, and he wouldn't have been altogether surprised to find a turret room with a wimpled princess and a spinning wheel. The books seemed to be getting older, too. Now he was in the eighteenth century. He took down a copy of *The Gentleman's Magazine*, a softly dusted copy with a smooth leather binding and a cracked spine which shed little pieces of embossing. Inside, it had narrow columns of tiny print, with paper so soft that the type had dented it. He put it back, beginning to suffer from book-indigestion.

Through the next door there were books on, and in, different languages, Twee, Urdu; then on to philosophy and politics and history and economics. It was like Wonderland without Alice, and then, as he came between yet another set of shelves, he looked up too late and collided with Alice herself.

The books in her arms scattered and splattered open onto the floor and she fell backwards over the round pushable step, with Tom trying not to land on top of her, and bringing down some extra books.

Tom was jammed between her and the shelves. "I'm terribly sorry," he said. He tried to get back onto his feet without touching her anywhere, which was difficult. He put out a hand, which she ignored, so he used it to pick up some books, but all he could see was the swirl of copper-coloured hair, and brown eyes and a wide mouth. She was wearing a white coat. She picked up the books and held them in front of her. Tom slipped a book onto the pile, thinking that he really had to grab the moment, somehow. Grab a chance and you won't be sorry for a might-have-been, as somebody said.

"Are you OK?"

The girl nodded at him.

"I'm Tom," Tom said. To judge from her response, either he'd suddenly started to speak Twee and Urdu, or else 'Tom' was clearly a particularly unpleasant word in the local dialect. She half-nodded, and said, "Excuse me," and Tom flattened himself against the shelves and she swished by him, smelling of something unbelievably marvellous. Tom watched her down the row of shelves and then, just in case she turned round and saw him watching her, backed away and walked down the corridor at the end of the shelves.

He stopped at the Theology section. Perhaps I should be a monk, he thought. Anyway, it's all so stupid, convention. Why on earth shouldn't I just walk after her and. He came to a mental full stop. What do I do then? Perhaps there's a book about it somewhere.

He turned the corner at the end of the shelves and nearly walked into her again. He went into a pantomime of 'Sorry, excuse me, long time no see', all of which she merely registered with blank eyes. Tom walked straight over to the door and down the stairs, feeling bright scarlet. She was only about the same age as he was, but she clearly knew more about what to do when people bumped into you in the library than he'd ever know. All in all, it was a very strange feeling.

Tom came out into the pale sunshine, and, before he could take evasive action, was standing on the steps in front of A. B., who, far from seeming to bear a grudge, greeted him fulsomely. He even put an arm round Tom's shoulders. Tom tried to duck away in case anyone identified him.

"Well, how goes it?" A. B. said. "Still living with that funny lot? And when I say funny, I mean fun-ny."

Tom had a sudden surge of affection for Alf and Robbie and Liam. "Fine," he said. It didn't seem to fit into the conversation, but it was a noise. A. B. seemed to find it acceptable.

"Very educational, I don't doubt," A. B. said, his eyes bulging slightly.

"Takes all sorts," Tom said.

"To make a world," A. B. said, with the air of one uncovering a great and subtle witticism. Tom's regrets about 'We hate A. B. day' evaporated. It should have been a week. A month. The only thing that stopped him from uncharacteristically taking to violence was the feeling that the response served him right for producing a cliché in the first place. He stepped down a step, and A. B. did the same.

"How are things at Mrs Evans's?" Tom said. He ventured into irony. "Still dishing up the *nouvelle cuisine*?"

"No, the same old stuff," A. B. said, imperviously. Tom stepped down again, and A. B. followed. He looked around and dropped his voice:

"Actually, don't tell a soul, but I'm thinking of moving myself." He leaned forward, and Tom, before he could stop himself, leaned back. People will be staring. A. B. said, "Mrs Evans tried to get into your room the other day: I mean, it's Andy's room now; I mean, the other night, when Andy was in bed. She said she just wanted to make sure he was comfortable."

Tom searched in vain for a suitable response. "Andy had to jam his chair against the door." A. B. shook his head. "It might be me next."

Tom considered a galaxy of replies and settled on "True." Then, quickly, he said, "Well, see you," and stepped down the last two steps, then ran the next three in case A. B. should decide to follow. A. B. half started to and then stopped, and raised his hand. Tom, with the warmth of meeting his librarian around him, felt rather sorry for A. B.

He walked across the campus, and along a street with small, rather undernourished trees, and round the corner into 'The Lion and the Unicorn'. There was a row of high stools, and the heavy, laconic face of Carlo behind the bar. Rosie, his small round wife, was collecting orders. Tom asked for lasagne and chips and lemonade and lime, and looked beatifically around.

His euphoric mood wasn't even broken by Orris coming in and sitting next to him. He had a copy of APATHY in his donkey-jacket pocket.

"OK, who is she?"

"Who's who?"

"It's no good denying it," Orris said. "I've been following you, and you were distinctly skipping."

Tom shrugged. "Well, you know. I just met a girl."

"Good start," Orris said. "Identified the gender." He ordered lasagne and lemonade. "Well, come on. More."

"She's a librarian," Tom said. "Well, assistant."

Orris looked at him. "Not a Local."

Tom paid for his drink. It was very green. "I suppose so."

"Ah," Orris said. "You be careful, my boy. She'll be 'aving you."

Tom was surprised to feel rather hurt, as though Orris was saying something dirty.

"It's a hangover from the good old days," Orris continued, with the air of a man who has been at university for more than two years, and survived, against the odds. He did, though, sound slightly placatory. "Local girls think that anyone at the Uni. must be a good meal ticket. Bank Managers are the same. That's what they say."

Typical, Tom thought, of 'they'. He tried to think of a riposte, although he would actually have liked to push Orris off his stool, down the street, and into the sea. "What about the rapport between town and gown?" he said. "That's what it said in the prospectus."

"Seen a gown yet?" Orris said. "Load of old trot. Look, you've got to consider the infrastructure."

"Absolutely," said Tom.

"Put it this way. There you are, local fella, slogging away at some crummy job, and the best-looking birds go off with these student layabouts who get money for nothing, never do any real work, and know what the menus mean in frog, and who go away every ten weeks. What would you feel like?"

Tom looked at his lasagne, which had just arrived, without appetite. One minefield after another.

"More a question of what you'd do," Orris said. "This is really excellent lasagne." He smiled a rather dazzling smile at Rosie, who smiled back. Orris moved the crust of cheese with his fork. "What you'd do is congregate in mobs in dark alleyways and beat the living daylights out of anybody who stepped over the line."

"That's ridiculous," Tom said. "I'm not exactly from the aristocracy."

"Being working-class won't help you," Orris said.

"You're like me. You've read a book, so that's cancelled your credentials." He took the copy of APATHY, and placed it beside his lasagne, apparently having exhausted the topic. "You listen to Uncle Orris. He knows." He started to read and eat. Tom rather miserably unwrapped his knife and fork from the paper napkin, and speared a chip, and then resolved to be a new and better person, up with the lark, healthy eating, sports. He didn't dare look at Orris in case those pale eyes saw his thoughts.

Orris said: "Listen to this: it's a campaign to get rid of sexist newspapers in the Union."

"Jolly good," Tom said, relieved that the subject had changed. "Quite right."

"Ah," said Orris. "But it says: 'How would the macho males like it if they were just thought of as sex objects?' That must have been written by a woman. All the macho males have been *dying* to be looked on as sex objects for *years*." He ate a little more. "This is really very good. How are you eating these days. Is that kitchen still disgusting?"

Tom considered. "Well, I suppose so."

"I'll have to show you the proper way to eat," Orris said. "How about breakfast to start with."

"Now?"

"Say, Monday. I'll call round for you. Say, seven o'clock."

"On Monday? In the morning? Do they still do it?"

"Say quarter to," Orris said. "I'll show you the best breakfast in the universe. Start the week well."

"Well, OK," Tom said. "But don't ring the bell."

Tom's getting-up-with-the-lark campaign didn't begin very well. The first morning of it, he managed to get into the kitchen by 10:30 to find Liam ostentatiously counting the milk bottles, one or two of which had been washed out, and one or two of which were not quite green. Tom picked up the kettle, weighed it in his hand, and put it on the gas cooker.

"How long have we been here?" Liam said. "How many days?"

"Five, six weeks," Tom said. "Something like that." He dragged the bar stool from under the counter and sat on it. *The Times* of two weeks ago was still next to the sink, another small monument to failed co-operative living.

"Thirty-five days, say," Liam said. "So how is it that we've got fifty-three stinking milk bottles here?"

"Same reason we had to burn the tea towels," Tom said. "The other two are slobs."

Liam glanced at him for signs of irony. "Anyway, we'd better clean them up. The landlady says we might be inspected by the Lodgings Office."

"Why?"

"The blokes downstairs have moved out, so they're inspecting that one, and they might come up here. I think it's just a threat."

"What do you mean, moved out?" Tom tried to picture the blokes downstairs. "What are they called? Mike and something? Doing economics."

"Not any more," Liam said. "Mike's gone home. Packed it in. The other chap couldn't afford it on his own. He's got a place in Hall." He moved some of the bottles forward, disturbing two ancient Chinese take-away boxes.

"What do you mean, packed it in?" Tom said. "You can't. We only just got here."

"Well, he could," Liam said. He picked up a milk bottle experimentally and tilted it over the sink. A glob of grey matter with green mould on it flopped out.

"But what's he going to do?" Tom said. Even in his greyest moments, the idea of actually going home had never seriously occurred to him.

"Apparently he got a late place," Liam said, "and he didn't really want to come to university anyway."

Tom looked at him, thinking that out there was a world of adults and lack of sympathy and going to an office every day whether you needed to or not. He picked up a bottle. There was a patchy grey fog inside it.

"His father was getting him a job in the local Town Hall," Liam said, pouring out another bottle. "Give me a hand with these, will you." They worked their way downstairs with armfuls of bottles, and noses averted, Tom thinking of Town Halls, with their polish smell and frosted doors, and wondering how anyone could do it.

The milk bottles stretched from the front door, along the pavement, and round the corner, in a putrid double row.

"Should we have washed them out?" Tom said.

Liam looked at them rather doubtfully. "Probably," he said at last. "But it'll be a challenge to the bottle-washer." They came back up the stairs.

"Probably had a girlfriend," Liam said. "People do that; leave to make money quickly; get a house, get married, all that."

"I still don't get it," Tom said.

"University's not the only thing in the world," Liam said. "Most people don't go, and they seem to get along."

He went off to lectures, and Tom sat and drank black coffee and read *The Times*. I wonder, he thought, will I be any happier being B. Arch, FRIBA? Or will the day come when I'll have to go off to some Town Hall? At least it'll be later rather than sooner. He assembled his folders and let himself out of the flat, ignoring the milk bottles. Perhaps going to university is a subtle act of cowardice.

After five weeks, there was only one thing that the four of them did together. Catering, newspapers, and milk having failed (the milkman left them a quite unnecessarily abusive note and refused to deliver again), they discovered that they all felt the same about Sunday mornings.

Tom had a residual feeling, when he heard the town bells, that he should be in church, but he resisted it reasonably easily. Church seemed to go with a certain village ambience, and Flat 2, Number 21 Norfolk Road was about as bereft of that sort of ambience as it was possible to be.

What they did instead was to sit in the plastic café on the seafront, reading the papers and drinking coffee and watching the thin sun on the sea, or the grey waves coming over and spattering gravel on the steamed-up glass.

On Sunday mornings, therefore, Liam got up and bathed, Robbie anointed himself, and Alf rolled out of bed, already in his sweater, and put on his jeans and trainers. Tom, who sometimes felt that they'd cornered all available personalities, wrapped himself against the November wind, and they all went down to the corner shop for an argument about newspapers.

Robbie tended to buy the sort of newspapers banned in the Union, on the grounds that they were of sociological interest, and Liam bought the posh ones. Alf read the racing pages, but took *Middlemarch* with him for real reading. Tom suffered from slight home-sickness, corner shops being rather like village shops, and he usually bought whatever kind of newspaper hadn't been bought by the others. Then they went out down to the sea and walked beside it and skimmed stones and dodged the licks of waves, or sprinted between bits of shelter, if it was throwing itself across the promenade.

In The Seafront Café, they had desultory conversation over the newspapers. Tom was alternately amazed by the diversity of life, and the fact that he could never remember anything that had been in the newspaper the week before. Robbie read out the rude court reports. There was an amicable fug, and the water condensed on the window and ran down among the decorative gravel trays and the green plants.

And, that Sunday, the door opened and a group of girls came in. The first was Alf's girlfriend, Zoe, who looked like two or three cheerful puddings balanced on top of each other, and the next was Robbie's girlfriend, Liz, who had a lot of very blonde hair. The other two were mixed; one looked as though she disapproved of the whole business, and the other was the girl from the tea-urn in the Christian Union, all that time ago.

Zoe waved cheerfully, and the four girls lined up at the bar.

"Four coffees, please," Liz said, and then, "What is *that*?"

"What?" said the café-man.

Alf, who had left *Middlemarch* beside his cup and was on his way to greet Zoe (Robbie, clearly of the opinion that Liz would get to him sooner or later, was still reading), slid backwards into his seat.

"We're not with them," he said. "Can't you do something, Robbie?"

"Me?" said Robbie.

"That filthy degrading object," Liz said, pointing.

The café-man turned, rather elaborately. Tom folded his paper over.

"I can't see any filthy degrading object," the café-man said.

"The nut-card," Liz said. "It's rude."

The hanging card was half-covered with packets of peanuts, which also half covered one of Robbie's objects of sociological interest. The man looked at it and turned back.

"Well, it isn't yet," he said, "but I have hopes."

"How would you like to have a picture of a naked man up there?" Liz said.

"I'm not that way inclined," said the café-man. "That's why it's a woman."

"It makes me sick to look at it," Liz said.

The man had obviously decided that enough was enough. "Then don't," he said. He put the coffees on the chromium and glass counter. "Sit with your back to it."

"You know what you are," Liz said.

The man looked at her carefully. "Yes, I do," he said.

"I'm an extremely patient café-owner, who has to put up with snotty over-privileged students to make a living, but don't push your luck." He smiled and, rather to Tom's surprise, Liz smiled back. Tom was feeling like hiding under the table.

Liz took the coffee and they came over to the table. Tom shifted along the red-plastic bench, and the limp girl with the secret sorrow sat beside him. Zoe sat on Alf's knee, and Liz and Robbie started a rather strident argument about Robbie's reading matter. Tom looked over at the girl with the shrewd grey eyes, and she smiled at him. Now that the aggro had passed off, Tom relaxed again and began to think that, after all, there were few places he'd rather be.

"Cleaned up the kitchen yet?" Zoe said. She looked over at the intelligent eyes. "Oh, this is Sue. Sue, Mary, Tom." Sue nodded at Tom, and picked up a colour supplement. "They've got this disgusting male slum," Zoe went on. Mary looked into her cup.

"We got rid of the milk-bottles," Liam said.

"I heard," Zoe said. "You should see their cooker. And there's a frying pan that's beyond belief."

"It's only a bit black," Alf said. "Anyway, Tom's the one who uses it." Zoe looked over, as if surprised at this.

"It's my patent quick breakfast system," Tom said, talking rather quickly, rather than having to sit saying nothing. "At night, you put the bacon in and melt the fat, and the bacon sinks into it, and then you turn the gas off and in the morning, you just turn the gas on, and it's partly –" He stopped. Sue was looking at him rather guardedly.

"You mean you have fat, and you leave it in."

"Only a couple of centimetres," Zoe said. "Anyone for more coffee?"

Tom felt a trifle mystified. It was a good system and you could use all the bread that kept appearing for soaking up the fat. Frozen hamburgers were even better; you could use the chunks of cheese, too, folding them into delicious squidges.

The response he was getting, however, didn't suggest that Sue thought that these were examples of the finer things in life.

He said: "Some people have no feeling for the finer things in life." There was a general rustling of newspapers.

Mary said to him, "Where do you go to church?"

Sue said: "Have you joined the community service yet?"

Tom said, "My friend Orris dug somebody's drains up the other week. He was still looking ill the next day," and wondered why Sue looked at him as if he was an interesting specimen.

"Why didn't you go?"

"Is that an awkward moral question?" said Liam.

"Sure sounds like one," Alf said. "OK. Who's going to get us out of it?"

"Can't do everything," Robbie said. "Got our own lives to lead. Alf's got all that sleeping to do."

"And by the time Robbie's ponced himself up," Alf said, not without a touch of malice, "another poor old biddy'll have frozen to death."

"It's a serious point," Liam said. "I mean, the world is full of misery. Starvation. We're OK. Why don't we just give it all up and devote ourselves to all the other poor sods?"

"Well, why don't you?" asked Mary. There was a second of silence, while they realised that she had spoken.

Robbie, who seemed to have taken something of a dislike to her, said: "Because you end up like them, that's why. Powerless. At the bottom of the heap, and that doesn't do anybody any good. I mean, look at all those marchers and protesters, and all that crew. I know they mean well, solidarity with the poor and the vegetables and whales and all that, but they never get anywhere, and they never will. You've got to have real power, get to the top, then you can change things."

"Hurrah!" said Zoe, coming back with the coffee.

"When you get to the top," Alf said, "you won't *want* to

change things. You'll be another greedhead fatcat."

There was another, longer pause. Then Robbie looked round, and leaned a little towards Mary, and said: "OK, you win. Where do we start?"

Tom was up until half-past one in the morning working on an essay; that is, he was writing an essay, but even sitting in the pinkish light at the dining-room table in what he had to admit was a tatty room, he felt positively inspired. It was the next best thing to poetry. Unlike school, when everything seemed to be pretty much a sausage machine, and all the teachers knew the answers anyway, now he felt that his bit of thinking in his bit of the library, with his selection of books, was different.

At half-past one, Liam came out of his room to make a coffee. He'd been working on his economics and, to Tom's utter amazement, they had a conversation about the economics of building on green-field sites as opposed to rebuilding the inner cities, and Tom went to bed at three, and set his alarm clock, and put it on the chair by the bed so that he could grab it as soon as it went off.

He opened the door to the dark, freezing November morning, feeling catatonic.

Orris was standing cheerfully under a street lamp with his donkey-jacket collar turned up as a vague gesture against the cold. Tom, who had his scarf up around his ears, and his gloves on, decided that he was clearly insane.

"Are we mad?" Tom said.

"You won't regret it."

The town was most odd at this time of the morning. The street lamps gave off orange light under the freezing mist, and on some street corners, where the streets ran towards the sea, the mist swirled and curled and turned in the light, looking like orange candyfloss. They walked away from the sea, towards the back of the town where the train station and the bus station sat next to the cattle market. The road passed the derelict goods station which was being razed. Diggers stood frozen on the black gravel.

"How did you find this place?"

"Natural talent for the disreputable," Orris said. His breath clouded in front of him.

The bus station was in an orange glow. Tom thought, perhaps all bus stations were built simultaneously in 1952; huge green iron sheds between grey-stone straight blank walls. There were rows of silent double-deckers, and the streets looked as though the bodies had just been swept up.

"Amazing how safe you feel at this time of the morning."

Orris nodded. "Only mad eskimo muggers survive."

He walked on, head down, with the back of his neck open to the frost. Orris appeared to have a theory about everything, but Tom couldn't bring himself to listen to one about freezing necks.

They walked past flat plastered facades with frozen rotten window frames, political posters fading on the windows. Everything was in suspended-animation decay.

"Politicians," Orris said as if reading Tom's mind. "No sense of humour. At the last election, I collected all their stickers and posters and stuck them in the window together. All very democratic; and one of the candidates had the nerve to come back to complain."

"I hope you voted for him," Tom said.

Over the buildings it was still dark, and there was frost on the beaten-down edges of the pavement. They came out into a square with frames of market stalls around the edges, and there were the lights of a café.

"It's the British equivalent of the taverna," Orris said, and he pushed open a door covered with advertisements for milk and cigarettes, with a swinging sign, and they went into a fug of smoke and condensation and the smells of coffee and sausages.

There was a large man with an apron mostly over his stomach, behind a dark-swabbed counter, with a line of deep-friers and gas rings behind him. Ghosts of ancient fires marked the wall.

"You can have tea in half-pints or pints," Orris said. "None of your metric rubbish, and the best food."

The man behind the counter smiled hugely at them, as if to say that seeing them had made the world all right, after all.

"Morning, Orris. Brought me a new victim?"

"Tom," said Orris, edging the word in.

"Welcome to our little shrine, Tom," the man said. "I don't recommend the hamburgers, but the sausages were obviously from happy pigs. Seen my new toy?"

He pointed at the end of the counter where there was a toast-maker consisting of a small conveyor-belt or treadmill. The bread slices went on short metamorphosing journeys through a small oven, and fell out of the far end. Tom looked round curiously. There weren't all the deadbeats that he'd expected, although there were a few, thawing out after the night, watching.

The large man was juggling with frying-baskets. "The trick is the temperature of the oil," he said, clearly delighted with the whole thing. "Above 470° the flavours don't transfer, so you can cook anything with anything."

There was bacon curling on a wide grill, and he took a handful of mushrooms out of a cardboard basket and dropped them into the oil. "Portion control," he said. "Can't get field mushrooms this time of year, but this is the way to cook these objects." He took sausages from a flat-sided cardboard box. "Made by a little mate of mine round the corner. Must be good 'cause he hasn't got many fingers left. He eats it raw to show you how good it is."

They took their plates and large patriotic mugs of tea, and jammed themselves behind a small plastic-topped table.

"All good stuff," said Orris.

"If you can afford it," Tom said.

"What's this, a social conscience?"

Tom looked round and looked at his plate. "I feel very lucky," he said. "Privileged."

"Only if you think you're privileged to be breathing," Orris said. "It's just a matter of degree. You're privileged because you've got more on your plate than those poor sods over there. And you're incredibly privileged because you can sit on your backside in a university contemplating abstract beauty instead of getting up at six and going to work in a Town Hall. And you're incredibly privileged because what you're actually doing is being trained for free to get even more privileged." He took a breath.

The food was amazing. Tom said, because it seemed a useful thing to say, "That's right, make me feel terrible."

Orris sliced bread into his egg. "No chance," he said, "because the minute you get back to the *better* part of town, you'll just be thinking how underprivileged you are compared with all those people at private schools, and the 5% who own 90% of the land, or whatever it is." He stopped, and grinned a grin. "Sorry. Politics."

Tom leaned back on the bench. It seems, he thought, as if university is just a series of exclusive clubs, and this is one of the better ones. After all, I can sort out the moral problems over the next three years.

Tom closed his book and looked at his reflection in the black window. The light was fluorescent and hard and outside there was night and rain and the sea. The pubs would be shut soon, and, anyway, the most interesting people only used them as staging posts to go somewhere else. He leaned over slightly so that the warmth from the central-heating pipes came up his sleeves.

He slid the book into the tidy row against the board that

divided the desk from its twin, and opened two folders and spread out the paper in artistic disarray. There was a notice on the wall: *Please remove all books from desks when you leave.* This was not, despite what it said, a way to start major fights all over the library, but a device to stop the unscrupulous from hogging the best desks. This one, in the Modern Languages section, looked out over the roofs to the sea and the beach, and got a lot of sun, and had superior chairs.

One evening, when the throwing-out bell had roused Tom from a pleasant dream about being locked in the periodicals annexe with the librarian with the copper hair, he'd gone back to the flat without putting his books away. When he'd got back the next morning, rather worried in case his notes had disappeared, or that there would be a short note barring him from the library, he found things exactly as they were. Whether this was because the librarians had better things to do, or because they were suitably impressed by the piles of books was hard to say, so Tom kept his place by selecting the most intellectual books at random each evening and leaving them on the desk.

But she didn't work in the evening, it seemed, and so Tom took his coat and went out of the library into the cold and spattering rain, and the patches of light. He reminded himself, with a considerable effort, that he was quite tall and might look uninviting to potential muggers, even if they had been insane enough to be out.

He went across the campus and into the streets.

Around every corner, hard rain flicked unpleasantly into his face. He put his head down and trudged. A good word, that, he thought, trudge, trudge. A hand fell on his shoulder and he stifled a scream.

"Well, if it isn't the two-pint wonder." It was Vince, with his shirt open at the neck.

Tom said, "You scared me to death."

"Not difficult," Vince said.

They walked on. "Going my way?"

Vince nodded.

"But the pubs aren't shut," Tom said, before he could stop himself, and then thought that he must have come some way to be able to venture suicidal remarks like that.

Vince grinned, showing his yellow teeth. "Boring evening," he said. "Some bloke's birthday party. We went on a pub crawl, and he passed out at the fifth pub." Vince seemed philosophical about this. "So we had to carry him round and prop him up in the corner of the next five."

"What happened to him?" Tom said, thinking that this took him into a new and horrible world. Every time he raised his chin to speak, iced water sliced into the gap between chin and collar.

"Dunno," Vince said. "We left him at the eleventh."

Tom put his head down, trying to imagine how anyone could possibly think that sort of behaviour was sensible. All this might count as seeing the world, but he rather preferred the warm library-side of university life.

They came down to the sea, and turned up towards number 21. There was a mizzle of rain here, blowing under the streetlights. Tom fingered his key out of his pocket and Vince stopped at his elbow with no sign of moving on.

"Like to come in?" Tom said.

"Yes," Vince said. "Specially as I live here."

Tom groped around for the light switch, trying to get the right expression onto his face.

"You what?"

"First floor flat," Vince said. "Me and the Geordie boy, Cal McKechnie. You remember. Climbed round the hall that time. I've been sleeping on his floor. Then the flat came free."

They went up the stairs, under the forty-watt bulb.

"Have you met the landlady?" Tom said.

Vince considered for three steps. "Well," he said, "when you're born my shape, you soon get used to sending the pretty boys in first."

They circled up to the first landing. The top flat was dark, but this evening there was obviously life in the kitchen on the first floor. The light was bright and the place clean and respectable, except for a loaded ashtray of Vince's cigarette butts. Cal was sitting on the breakfast stool, looking at Robbie, who had his head on his arms on the kitchen table and seemed to be in tears.

"Eyup, bonny lad," Cal said. "Is this yours?"

They stopped in the doorway.

"What is it now?"

"I tried to end it all," Robbie said into the table top.

"He tried to end it all," Cal said.

"Not very good at it, were you?" Vince said.

"What happened, for Pete's sake?" Tom said.

"I threw myself off the prom into the sea."

"He threw himself —"

Robbie's head came up. "Will you stop talking about me as if I'm not here."

"He's not very wet," Tom said.

"He missed," Cal said. "The tide was out. I thought I'd better bring him home before he got arrested."

"I could have broken my neck," Robbie said.

"But it's only two metres," Tom said, trying to be reasonable. Robbie seemed to be taking himself entirely seriously.

"Why don't you try the gas oven?" Vince said. "Here's some money for the meter."

"Do you want to hear about it or not?" Robbie said. He went on before anyone could answer. "Liz has finished with me. So I threw myself off. I landed on a stone. This one," and he ducked down and brought up a two-handful-sized stone. Then he dropped it on the floor. The reverberation shook the walls.

"Get him out of here," Cal said, "before we're thrown out. We've only been here one day." Cal and Vince heaved Robbie up, dragged him upstairs, and left him sitting on the top step.

"You'd better sign for him," Cal said.

Robbie was ignoring them.

"Have you ever been in love, Tom?" he said. Vince laughed and went downstairs. "Isn't it terrible. How's your librarian?"

"What librarian?" Cal said, leaning on the doorpost.

Robbie seemed to revive out of his misery. "We're not allowed to know her name," he said unkindly. "She's got the most amazing hair, though. Copper."

"Oh, Karen," Cal said. "Very nice if you like that sort of thing."

"What sort of thing?" said Tom, rather more quickly than he intended.

"You know. Vestal virgin. Can't be doing with it, myself. Had to get rid of her. Bonny lass, though." He looked at Tom. "You OK?"

"Fine," Tom said. "Just wonderful."

Chapter Thirteen
MORE EXCLUSIVE CLUBS

―――――――――●―――――――――

There was a break between lectures at eleven o'clock, and Sue went down to the small common room beside the library in the basement of the Natural Sciences Building. It was a long, narrow room, with a coffee machine in one corner, and a coin-operated photocopier in the other, which always had a queue of people in front of it, and a table covered with the debris of sandwiches and plastic cups, and, today, piles of the new edition of **APATHY**.

Sue, smiling at lecture-friends, coaxed a hot chocolate from the machine (because it was the only drink that really resembled what it said it was), and took the plastic cup and a copy of **APATHY** out to where the wide stairs came down. Under the last flight was a large wedge-shaped carpeted space, which was ideal for small conferences and stretching the legs out, and, for a minute, avoiding discussing projects and people. There was a girl sitting there already. She was slim, with a mass of copper-coloured hair. They made 'may-I-I-don't-mind-please-do' faces and smiled at each other.

Sue sat down, placed her cup carefully on the carpet, and took a pair of small scissors from her bag. She opened the paper and began to cut. The girl watched her and Sue said, smiling, "It's for my little sister. I do bits for it." She indicated the paper. The girl nodded. Sue said, "It's rubbish really." She handed over the clippings.

THE GOOD . . .

This week the Union opened its voluntary Day Care Centre

in the cleaned-out cellars of the Old University Building. For the whole term, dedicated teams of noble students have been digging out the junk and doing in the rats, and painting and refurbishing. Toby from the Art Department took a crew of brush-wielders in to paint murals and line out the walls. The Electrical Engineers (led by the noble Kev) put in new plumbing or whatever they do, and in response to the St Mary's Hall Feminist Group Challenge, a mob of Rugby players and other disreputables went on their hands and knees with buckets and brushes and scrubbed the place out. From Monday it will be open to provide a warm place for Down-and-Outs (this does not include Vince and his mates) and the catering Students are going to do soup and things at lunchtime.

We need help and donations.

Call in and ask for Trish (who might be in the Sociology Department (4401)) or go to see the Rev. at the Anglican Chaplaincy, or Fr Harry at the RC Chaplaincy, or Terry at the United Chaplaincy.

Do someone **ELSE** a bit of good!

. . . AND THE NOT SO GOOD

The Principal (bow, scrape, grovel), Dr M. Usrey, announced today from the Oval Office that he was gravely concerned about reports from the police about rowdy behaviour in local pubs by students (rah, rah). He said that if any formal charges were brought, he would not hesitate to rusticate the offenders. (The Med. School is being consulted to see if this is painful.)

— Super Soo, Ace Reporter.

Going Up

THE GOOD EATERY GUIDE
This guide is being compiled with no
thought to the digestive tracts
of the selfless investigators, who don't
get free nosh, despite foul rumours.

We're using the main refec. as the base-
line of 100% – which means, for example
that Di the Chip on South Parade rates
3% and the Grill Room at the Esplanade
(so we're told) about 900%.

Here are the first three entries: all
information received will be checked
out and treated with maximum bias, and
ignored if we don't like you.

(250%) **THE LION AND THE UNICORN** New Ferry Street (better
known as Carlo's)

You can't miss Carlo; he looks like one of those Italian tenors
who obviously go in for all-in wrestling as a sideline. He
smiles all the time, which is not surprising considering the
food. Our drinks correspondent tells us that the beer is
pretty average but you can get superb bar snacks, like egg
and chips that don't smell of eggs or chips, and real lasagne
and stunning spaghetti, and anyone with money should try
the spumoni for afters. All this is dished up by Mrs Carlo,
called Rosie, who is wonderful and is chained in the
basement. Try it! – Z.S.

(56%) **THE SEAFRONT CAFÉ** West Promenade

Notable for plastic seats and sexist calendars and peanut
cards. Has the big advantage of being open most of the time
and early on Sunday. Coffee ok, but avoid the cheese

sandwiches (made with grated cheese and they scatter-everywhere). Beans on toast good value for the poor and high fibrous.

(250%) **NICK'S CAFÉ** (or **TOADS** or **FLATLAND** or **GANDALF'S**)
Lewes Street

This is an institution, and does the best cheese sandwiches in the universe, although them as knows sez that Nick is still using the same sack of dried onion soup powder that he bought the year the Principal graduated. Nick changes the name and the décor every six months, which shows there's gold in them there toasted sandwiches (good). Best combo is the leek soup (v thick) and garlic bread (if you're not going out tonight or s/he has some too). – S.M.

The girl's reaction was slightly muted, but she smiled politely. Sue said, "Which course are you doing?"

The girl spoke very quietly. "I'm not, actually. I work in the library." Sue was about to say that she hadn't seen her before, and thought that that sounded rather rude, when the girl said, "I've just been transferred over from the main library. My name's Karen."

"Sue," Sue said. "Like it here?"

"I think so," the girl said. "It's quieter." She got up, ducking her copper hair below the angle of the underside of the stairs and smiled, dropped her cup into the tall black bin by the door and went back into the library.

Sue looked at her watch and took the letter to Jojo out of her bag and opened it. A quick check.

Heaven

Dear Jojo,

I'm sorry about the bedjacket. The old dear would insist on doing it, and I had to drink more gin, just to be polite. Fred

says if he ever wants to have his wicked way with me, he'll
send me round to la Prothero's to get me tanked up first.
Anyway, Liz goes to visit her every week now and they
seem to get on like a house on fire.

Then I've found this most amazing place: it's the old
Union Snack Bar – there's this Old Union building they use
for art exhibitions, and I think they have a film club in the
basement – and it's all *grey* (not black rubber like the new
one), and there's two squash courts we play on sometimes.
They don't get so packed out as the Sports Centre. So,
anyway, there's this nice snack bar with a cuddly lady who's
been there since they built the place. She only does
sandwiches and pies, and NO FISH. (I'm on a campaign to stop
the cooks in the refec. cooking the fish for Friday on
Wednesday. They must do. Liz says it's the first thing you're
taught at catering school.)

But she has her little ways – the lady in the snack bar,
that is. I went in the other day and said, "What's the soup?"
and she said, "Oxtail, Mushroom, and Tomato," so I said, "I'll
have the mushroom," and she said, "No, all together." Well,
Zoe laughed.

Actually, I said 'Heaven' because I'm lying on the
biggest sofa I've ever seen – I don't touch either end – in
Penny and Toby's flat, and the sun is kind of flooding in
everywhere, and it's warm even when it's freezing outside.
There's scatter-cushions and a very posh carpet, and Toby's
paintings are everywhere. Did I tell you that he works half-
time in the Art Department *and* the English Department, so
he's pretty good.

I come round a couple of times a week, when it gets too
mad at Hall, what with Alf and Zoe hiding cheese and milk
everywhere, and, of course, the Mad Musician. I forgot to tell
you. He's incredibly talented, whoever he is. He's now
playing the oboe and then he went on to the violin, and then
the heavy mob lay in wait for him and caught him dragging a
kettle-drum or something into the yard. Rumour has it that he

said he was serenading somebody, but he wouldn't say who, despite the rubber hoses and being locked in room 101 with the warden. And there's always Mary mooding around the place, so here I am.

Toby, when he isn't painting, cooks like a dream. He's very much into killing sex-stereotypes. He calls the cooking 'inspirational', but Penny says that's because there's vast quantities of cream and brandy in everything. *He* says it's because he's trying to break out of the usual expectations, so they have eggs and bacon at three o'clock on Sundays and crêpes for breakfast. I can't understand why he doesn't get fat.

You meet all kinds here. Yesterday, I had to step over somebody doing Yoga in the middle of the hall. He said that he'd been slung out of his flat for doing it. His landlady said they were all Christians there and she wasn't having anyone with shaved heads and wearing pink sheets wandering around.

And Nick, the man who runs the café which keeps being something different, is here a lot, too. He's very nice, although Penny thinks his middle name is Faustus because he doesn't seem to get any older.

Toby knows all these people in the art world and in the local music, and Penny runs meditation classes and dances. It's like the University in one little room. And it's the only place I've been for a long time (apart from the Revd. Aunt Gill's) where they say grace at every meal.

Sometimes they all link hands, but mostly somebody brings a book and they read out a bit from the *Upanishads* or from Lao Tzu, or even *The Bible*. Toby says it concentrates the mind on the food. There's a lot of brown rice around, and we had the most amazing bottle of wine last night. (We get invited to dinner every other week and Toby has this wine collection. You have to drink it by sips.)

Mind you, there are rumours. Annie, the girl who keeps on having shower-conversations with me, said she'd heard that Toby was on drugs and, anyway, there must be something wrong with somebody who keeps on hanging around the same University all these years. Actually, I asked Toby about the drugs next time I came round here. (He was painting a still-life of vegetables and he said he had to be quick because it was going to be ratatouille within the hour!) He said that he'd been around the University for fifteen years and he'd never come across drugs himself, but there was some of it about, and he helped to distribute the Anti-Drug pamphlets. So you can tell the mama she can have no fear on that score.

Must close: Penny's come in followed by some character with a guitar.

Love and high fibre, and hope the sores are getting better and better.

She shook her head, put the clippings and the letter back in the envelope, and sealed it.

On the notice-board outside the lecture-theatre was a poster for a major film on whales and ecology in the last week of term. Sue went in and took her seat, where her notes had been left from the previous lecture, thinking how amazingly quickly term had gone; hardly a minute since they'd driven down.

The lecturer strolled in, arranged his notes on the bench, tried out the overhead projector, waited until the last people came in and shut the door, coughed, and began.

Chapter Fourteen
AN EVENING AT HOME

Tom thought: I hate Saturday Nights.

He sat in the living room with his virtuous books in front of him and a flagon of beer to cheer himself up, but it wasn't working.

The output of the overhead light seemed to have diminished, and the gas fire wasn't really competing with the draughts. All the place needed was a few bars at the windows and a few scraps of food and bones on the floor.

Tom gave up the book and went across to the window and put his forehead on the glass. Out there were wet lights on the wet road, and the dark wind. He could have gone out, but that just meant sitting in the corner of a bar somewhere or on his own in the cinema. At least he felt that he was earning his living, this way.

At five-thirty, Liam had come in neatly from playing squash. He had had a bath, dressed himself immaculately and had gone off to see his neat girlfriend. (Tom had only met her once, and Liam kept her well out of the way.) Alf hadn't been in. He generally went straight from playing Rugby to Carlo's and would now be on one side of the bar or the other. Tom looked at his watch. It was nearly eleven, which meant that Robbie would be in with Liz at any minute for their evening row in the bedroom.

Tom took a drink and wondered why he drank beer at all. When he'd asked his father that, his father had said that it was one of those things that men were supposed to do, and even now Tom couldn't work out whether he'd been joking or not.

But, having got thus far with being depressed, Tom started to think of other good things he could get depressed about.

First of all, there was the car. It had stopped starting because the battery was virtually flat, and the carburettor was almost certainly full of salt, and there was a slow puncture in the nearside rear tyre.

On top of that, he didn't actually need the thing. One day he'd gone out to get into it and it hadn't been there. He'd had a very bad moment of panic, involving incredibly complex and exhausting imaginary visits to the police, before he remembered that he'd driven to the University in it the day before and then had forgotten to bring it home.

And he was the only person not contributing milk and cheese to the household.

And he hadn't seen Karen for a week.

And at the last film society show, things had got so bad that Orris had persuaded him to go round to the pub next door while the film was running to cheer themselves up. They were showing an ancient French classic (which seemed to take place in much the same sort of run-down surroundings as Tom was sitting in), and when they came to make the fifth change between projectors, they found that they had reels three and seven left. They looked at each other. Presumably nobody had noticed so far, so they missed out reel three altogether, and slipped quietly out for a cider. The film hadn't broken, for a wonder, but it hadn't done Tom's nerves much good. Trish, who had noticed their absence, was remarkably uncivil about it. Tom was seriously thinking of resigning.

He'd done some house-painting for an old man who didn't seem to like him very much, and complained at every minute spot of paint that sprayed from the roller, so he was going to give *that* up, which made him a moral failure as well.

Even Orris had made friends with his girlfriend again

because it was too cold to go swimming across the bay, and so there were no breakfasts in good company.

And he hadn't seen Karen for a week.

There was a thumping on the stairs and Robbie and Liz went into the bedroom.

Tom sat down and looked at the unhelpful books. Maybe I should have gone into the Town Hall, he thought. Whatever happened to life? Romance? Excitement. We need a few orcs in here.

The sound of shouting from the bedroom increased, and there was a certain amount of thumping. Tom turned in his chair, and then the bedroom door was banged open, and then the living room door, which jammed against the carpet. Robbie came in, red, and breathing hard and he didn't look entirely pleased to see Tom.

"Hi," Tom said.

Robbie's eyes became rather small. He rocked back on one heel. He said: "Got a cigarette?" contriving to make it sound like a threat.

"I don't smoke," Tom said, wonderingly. Robbie took steps in several short directions. Tom said: "You don't smoke either." Robbie glared at him, as if he'd said something very rude and personal, and then spun round, went across the hall into the kitchen and took the pile of dinner plates out of the kitchen cupboard. He lifted them up, like a sacrifice, and dropped them on the floor. One fragment zinged and flicked its way into the living room.

There was a very deep silence. Tom, who was trying to think of an appropriate reaction to any of this lunacy, looked at the fragment of plate. Robbie turned again and slammed back into the bedroom.

Tom got up cautiously and went to the kitchen door. Pieces of plate lay neatly around an epicentre in the middle of the lino. Tom wondered whether or not to start to clear them up, and then the bedroom door banged open again and

Robbie shouted, "Tom. Come here. Liz wants you to take her home."

Tom turned round very slowly, as if he had been invited to walk home with a sabre-toothed tiger. Never, his father used to say, interfere between man and wife; this seemed near enough to come into the same category. He stepped across the landing.

In the bedroom, Liz was starting to get up from the bed, saying, "OK, come on, Tom," and Robbie, without looking round, put out a hand and pushed her backwards. Tom, who didn't think that any violence was entertaining, half-started forward, but Liz was apparently spring-loaded and she came back off the bed swinging a bag. Robbie doubled up under the impact, and the door slammed shut about one centimetre from the end of Tom's nose. It was a second or two before he could move, looking closely at the woodwork. I've obviously been reading the wrong books, he thought. I thought love was being nice and kind.

He took his nose away into the kitchen, and found the dustpan and the moulting brush and the black sack and began to sweep up. The bedroom door banged open again, and lightish feet went downstairs and then heavyish feet. The front door closed firmly, and then it opened again, and banged shut.

Tom carried on brushing, philosophically. Shards of plate were embedded in the grease under the cooker, and he was on his knees trying to dislodge them when Zoe's voice said, "The front door was open, so I came up," causing Tom to bang his head on the grill-pan handle. He slipped on the pieces of plate, trying to get up.

Zoe took his arm. "Having trouble?"

"No, no," Tom said. "Pretty average. I'm afraid Alf's not in yet."

Zoe looked into the living room. "The ratbag," she said. "I've been looking all over. Did he leave a note?"

"Don't think so," Tom said. It didn't seem like Alf's style.

"I'll try Carlo's," Zoe said. She went into the living room. "Don't mind if I look round? This place is quite famous, you know, what with you lot, and Vince and Cal downstairs."

"I can imagine," Tom said, caught between being pleased at being included in the notoriety, and thinking what his father's view of it would be.

She stopped at the table and looked at Tom's books. Tom thought it might be unseemly to push her out of the way and slam them shut. She said, "Do you spend every evening working?"

"Not if I can help it," Tom said.

"This is fun," Zoe said. She held up Tom's dictionary. "Good idea. I like it."

Tom came and stood by her. On the blank pages at the back of the dictionary, Tom had written out his favourite quotations, not in a very neat hand.

"It's not my idea," he said. "I read about two characters who pasted a huge sheet of card to the back of their bedroom door and covered it with quotations. Only I didn't have a whole door."

"Salinger," Zoe said. "I read that." She read down the page.

"Nothing so absurd can be said, that some philosopher has not said it. – Cicero.

"People must not do things for fun. We are not here for fun. There is no reference to fun in any act of Parliament.
– A. P. Herbert

Love does not vex he who begs his bread. – Euripides.

137

The bright day is done, and we are for the dark. – Antony and Cleopatra.

I'm not sure you should be allowed to stay in on Saturday nights.

He seldom errs/Who thinks the worst he can of womankind – John Holme.

Hmn. Who was John Holme, then?

Look not for mind in woman.

I know that one. John Donne. Another sexist pig." Zoe, who seemed to be amused by most things, seemed to be amused by this. "Never mind. We thought we had the girl for you, but she's fallen for some idiot musician. Nearly literally." Tom wondered what she was talking about. "I'd better go." Zoe went to the door. "Try not to get too excited. All this riotous living." She smiled and went away down the stairs.

Tom went back into the kitchen and filled the kettle. Liam came up the stairs and into the kitchen and looked at the floor.

"Don't tell me. Let me guess."

Tom lowered the kettle onto the flame.

Liam said: "There I am, walking back on the prom, minding my own business, when Liz comes sprinting past me into the Hall and then Robbie comes sprinting past me and he goes into the Hall, and then the porters throw him out and he stands on the prom shouting and crying." Liam shook his head. "And then I find Alf hiding in a doorway across the road. He says he's waiting until Zoe's left, and then I meet Zoe on the doorstep, and she says, 'Look not for mind in woman,' and off *she* goes. They're all mad."

He got his mug out of the cupboard, with a resigned look. The front doorbell rang.

"That'll be Alf," Liam said. "I suppose he's forgotten his key. Well, I'm not going down."

Tom went onto the landing and the bell stopped, and the first-floor bell began to ring.

"Better let him in, I suppose," Tom said. "He'll ring the landlord's next."

He started down the stairs, and Alf, apparently tired of the lack of response, shifted his finger to the lowest, the landlord's bell. Tom sprinted down the stairs, swinging on the flimsy bannisters, but the landlord was already at the door when he came down the last bend. He retreated cautiously. The landlord wrenched the door open.

"What the hell do you think you're doing?"

Alf straightened up and slid past him into the hall. He was eating from a bag of chips.

"Thanks, very civil. Appreciate it."

The landlord said, "Do you know what time it is? It's nearly midnight."

"Oh, right," Alf said, moving sideways along the hall.

"They're not allowed visitors after midnight," the landlord said. "It's a rule. In the lease."

"Jolly good," Alf said. "Right on."

Tom backed away up the stairs, and Alf followed him, still eating.

When Robbie came in ten minutes later, Alf and Liam had gone to bed and Tom was brushing his teeth. Robbie undressed in silence. Tom closed the door and was about to get into bed, when the landlord came rather noisily up the stairs. Tom opened the bedroom door again. The landlord was standing on the first step down as if reluctant to venture onto enemy territory.

"It's after midnight," he said.

Tom wasn't quite sure what to do with this information.

"Oh, right," he said.

Robbie loomed over his shoulder.

"What?"

"He says it's after midnight," Tom said. Liam emerged from his bedroom in a neat dressing gown and the landlord turned to him as a representative of respectability.

"You're not allowed visitors after midnight," he said.

Robbie snorted. "We know. It's in the lease. Are you going to read it to us or can we go back to bed?"

Liam raised a placatory hand.

"We'll bear it in mind, thanks."

The landlord said, with a slight air of desperation: "But what about the person who just came in?"

Tom said, before Robbie could actually start a fight, "That was Alf. He lives here." There was a slight thump as Alf rolled out of bed and put his head round the door.

"Me. Alf. I live here."

"Why haven't I seen him before?" said the landlord, sticking to his case.

"Just lucky, I guess," Robbie said.

"He does live here," said Liam, reasonably. "He signed the lease with the rest of us."

The landlord looked at them suspiciously, and went away downstairs.

"Another fine mess you've got us into," said Robbie to Alf. They went back to bed.

Tom said, "Goodnight," to Liam.

"Can't blame him," Liam said. "I sometimes forget he lives here myself."

Tom closed the door and navigated by the shape of the window back to his cold bed. He had just got his feet down to the bottom where the sheets were carved from solid ice when there was a bang on the door. Tom was out of the bed as fast as he could, beating Robbie to the doorway. The landlord was on the landing, holding up the lease.

"He doesn't live here."

Tom tried to be reasonable. "But he does actually."

"His name isn't on the lease," the landlord said doggedly. "Robin, Liam, Thomas, and Claude. No Alf." He waved the paper. "No visitors after midnight."

There was a silence. Robbie looked slowly round at Alf's bed. "Claude?"

Alf appeared in the doorway. "Well, my mother's French. And you can't expect me to go around calling myself Claude."

"Why not?" Tom said. "Very suave."

Liam said, from his doorway. "So, you see, he does live here. Sorry about that."

The landlord was about to say something else when the unmistakable sounds of Vince and Cal coming home sounded from below. "You'll hear more about this," the landlord said, and went hurriedly downstairs. Robbie and Alf went back to bed again. Tom and Liam shook their heads at each other.

"Let's have another coffee."

"Look on the bright side," Tom said. "At least there aren't any fire hoses."

Chapter Fifteen
IN WHICH A PARTY IS THROWN

Sue came into Nick's Café, out of the rain which was blowing horizontally in from the sea, carrying a large streaked cardboard box in front of her.

Nick came round from behind the bar, which was in the middle of a metamorphosis from all black to butterfly colours, and held the door wide for her. Zoe paused in collecting cheese sandwiches and cups of chocolate and watched him admiringly.

"I ask you. Most café owners would sling you back in the sea."

"It's a survey," Sue said. "These are samples."

Nick took the box and stowed it away at the back of the counter behind the climbing plants. He was stocky and curly-haired and seemed to look cheerful and depressed on alternate days. This was a cheerful day.

"You're a wonder," Sue said.

"You're not so bad yourself."

Sue unwrapped the layers of scarves and anoraks and wriggled behind a table opposite Zoe and Alf, who was still reading *Middlemarch*.

"Times like this, I'm glad I'm doing English," Zoe said.

Sue shook her hair and ice-water drops fell onto the table. Nick came down and took her coat away and hung it up and went back behind his counter.

"Isn't he amazing," Zoe said. "One of my lecturers was saying he's been here for twenty years, and he never changes. He's starting to be an institution."

"What a terrible thing to be," Alf said.

"Guess who we just saw," Zoe said, "coming along the prom. Mary and her mad musician. It was disgraceful. They were actually *holding hands*."

"Have to get married now," Alf said.

"I thought you were doing Russian," Sue said, looking at *Middlemarch*.

"Russian's easier," Alf said.

"We're educating each other," Zoe said. "I'm reading *The Brothers Karamazov*. The first page is great," she said, before Alf could speak. He blew on his chocolate. "They're looking for volunteers to clean up the flat."

"For the party?" Sue said. "OK."

"You wouldn't have said that if you'd seen it," Zoe said.

Sue sipped her chocolate. "Who's going?"

Zoe nudged Alf. "Don't know," Alf said.

"What about the food?" Sue said.

Alf put his book down. "I can see there's a fundamental ideological gap here," he said. "Parties aren't for eating at. They're just somewhere to go after the pubs shut and people jump on each other."

Sue looked over at Zoe. "Well, that's different. Sounds very exciting," she said, ironically.

"It will be for Tom," Zoe said. "They've moved his bed into the living room to make a sofa."

"What happens if he wants to go to bed?"

"We're not stopping him," Alf said. "We'll just sit on him."

They finished their chocolate and Nick said he'd look after the samples for an hour, and they walked back from the sea and along the sidestreets. The spray drizzled down over the buildings.

As they got to number 21, Cal and Vince came out, carrying sports bags. Sue, who had not met Vince in the flesh before, stepped back.

"Comes as a shock, doesn't it," Zoe said. "Coming to the party, Vince?"

"Yes and no. Me and Cal are down as bouncers. On the door."

"Are you expecting trouble?" Sue said.

"Always a few hard cases about after the pubs shut," Cal said.

"Like Vince, for instance," Zoe said.

Vince grinned. "Fr'instance. But if we sit down here in the hall, we can be as uncouth and brutal as we like, quite legit. Fights sort of come to us." He waved a hand, and Cal followed him out into the drizzly afternoon.

"They're going to play rugger," Zoe said. Sue was watching them go. "See what you would have missed if you'd gone to Cambridge."

Upstairs there was the sound of a vacuum cleaner and, as they came onto the top landing, there was a bang, and the vacuum cleaner stopped.

"Brilliant," Tom said. He glanced at Zoe and Sue and Alf and nodded. "Only Robbie could do that."

Robbie was kneeling in the doorway.

"Do what?" said Alf.

"Nothing."

"Nothing," Tom said. "We've wired up the stereo on the other side of the living room."

"And there's no socket there, so we've had to twist a few wires together. No problem."

"No problem," Sue said.

"He just managed to drop his cigarette lighter on the join," Tom said. "Kerpow."

"I didn't know you smoked, Robbie," Sue said.

"He doesn't," Tom said. "It's part of his suavity kit."

Alf went downstairs and mended the fuse and Zoe took over the vacuum cleaner. Then they pushed what furniture there was against the walls and Robbie tried to change the overhead bulb for a dark red one, to add atmosphere. When he touched the fitting, a sharp circle of sparks ran round it and the vacuum cleaner stopped again.

Robbie got down off the chair, rather shaken. "That's stupid," he said. "Isn't there a separate power circuit and a separate light circuit?"

"You're kidding," Alf said and went downstairs to mend the fuses again. Sue went into the kitchen, where Tom was stuffing paper and bottles into a bulging sack.

"Can I help?"

"Anything," Tom said. "It's pretty horrible in here."

Robbie helped Tom to move the sack onto the landing. Sue said: "Where's Liz. Rowing?"

"No," Robbie said. "There's some competition on, so she's gone to see the Prothero."

Zoe came out of the bedroom with a dustpan and brush. Tom said, "Prothero?"

"That Prothero woman," Robbie said. "The one who fed Sue the whisky. Liz goes round there and talks to her every week. She's got her onto the weak whisky. They make bedjackets together." Robbie sniffed. "It's incredibly un-romantic. She always smells when she gets back."

"She never told us about the bedjackets," Zoe said.

"Well, she wouldn't," Robbie said. He went downstairs with the sack.

Zoe looked at Sue. "Endless surprise," she said.

On their way out, Sue helped Tom to carry a box of empty bottles down. They paused on the first landing where all the doors were shut.

"Hang on," Tom said and walked to the bathroom door and banged on it. "Anybody in there?" He listened.

"What *are* you doing?" Sue said. She turned to Zoe. "I thought he was the normal one."

"Stand back," Tom said and opened the door. A large cat clawed its way rapidly along the landing and down the stairs. Tom left the door open and picked up his box. "That's the landlady's. The bathroom window is its private en-trance." They went on downstairs. "You have to leave the window open and it scares you to death if you're in the bath.

And if you don't leave the door open, it does unspeakable things in there."

They came down to the hall. "What's the landlady going to say?" Sue said.

"They've gone away for the night," Tom said. "We sent Liam down to tell them about the party and the landlord said they'd had that sort of thing before, so they've gone." He held the door open for them. "See you later?"

"Maybe," Zoe said.

"I suppose we could just call in," Zoe said. They came out of the shower room and went down the corridor. Zoe opened the door of her room, and half-started across it very quickly and then pulled up. Sue stood in the doorway. Mary was leaning a very long way out of the window.

"You OK?"

Mary looked round. Her hair was damp and she was quite different; Sue thought, I might not have recognised her.

Mary said: "Listen."

From down in the courtyard, there came the sound of a piano. They all squeezed themselves along the window ledge. Down in the bricked courtyard was an upright piano, with what looked like a tarpaulin over most of it, and a tall male playing rather well. The air was damp and gave a fine aura around the street-lamps and the window lights.

"He's mad," Zoe said. "Did he push it out there?"

"It's Michael," Mary said as if she were hugging herself. "He proposed to me last night."

Zoe and Sue looked at each other, both thinking of stupid remarks, like, you've only known him for a week.

"Isn't he wonderful?" Mary said.

"Pretty spectacular," Sue said.

Sue and Fred went to a concert in the town arts centre and sat in what used to be an old school hall, under high beams. Around ten, they bought a bottle of wine and went to meet

Zoe at Carlo's. Alf, who had been washing up, was released onto the world and they walked back to the flat. Alf and Zoe entwined their way ahead.

"Isn't it illegal to work when you're on a grant?" Fred said when Alf was out of earshot.

"Apparently Alf doesn't get much of a grant because his father's well off, and he doesn't approve of what Alf's doing, so he won't make it up." Sue had heard Zoe on the subject.

"Doing Russian's pretty clever," Fred said. He was an historian.

"I mean going to university at all," Sue said. "Alf's father thinks it's a waste of time and he should be making a decent living."

Fred shook his head.

The door was opened by Tom, rather to Sue's relief. Vince was an acquired taste that she had not yet acquired.

"Hi, come in. Foul night."

"Indoors or outdoors?" said Zoe. "Where's Vince?"

"Not back from the pub yet," Tom said. "Do I look frightening? I'm supposed to keep out the undesirables." He let them in and closed the door. "Are you sober, honest, and clean living? Well, I earnestly advise you to go home now. You can put your coats in our bedroom."

Sue went up the stairs, with Alf and Zoe and Fred behind her. In the first floor living room, there was one dim light, and a tape deck playing slow music. One couple was swaying in the middle of the room. In the top flat, there was more noise and more people. Liam was in the kitchen with a small, neat girl. He didn't introduce her. Alf said to Fred, "If I were you, I'd hide that wine in the oven and drink whatever's around. Then you could probably take it home with you." He poured drinks for them from an open bottle, and took Zoe to dance in the noise room.

Fred, who thought this was most unethical, opened his own bottle, poured wine into the two plastic cups, and he was about to go downstairs to dance, when Sue took the cork off the cork-screw and recorked the bottle. She carried it down-stairs and hid it behind a chair and left their cups on the rudimentary mantelpiece, and they danced.

Shortly after midnight, when the leg of his bed suddenly went through the floor under the weight of ten bodies, Tom decided that he'd had enough.

The top room was jammed with people and because he didn't have anyone to listen to, Tom could only hear the noise. He was sitting on the windowsill (hunched, because the window was shorter than his back), with a cup of wine. The music from the stereo in the top room and the cassette in the room beneath combined with the voices of sixty people and the smoke and the weight of bodies to hammer at him. The biggest effort was to keep moving, wine raised out of knocking way, and a cheerful smile so that he always seemed to be going somewhere or just looking for someone, just for a moment, so that no-one would suspect him of being on his own. Nobody else seemed to be alone, except Vince, who was sitting down in the hall with bottles of beer and Tom didn't feel inclined to join him. Cal, not surprisingly as he was tall and good-looking, was dancing, if you could call it that, and even Liam was downstairs in the more demure room with his more demure girlfriend. Robbie wasn't anywhere obvious.

Tom eased into the kitchen, where more earnest con-versation seemed to be going on, and reached round behind the cupboard where he'd hidden his bottle of wine. It hadn't been opened yet and it had a large black T scraped onto the label, just in case of arguments. Holding it down by his side, he worked his way across the hall, passing Cal, who was on his way downstairs, presumably to take over as bouncer. Tom went into the small bedroom and met, in the half-light, Sue and Fred, who were buttoning their coats. Even in there, the noise was overpowering, and Tom nodded at them in what he hoped was a sympathetic way and waited until they'd gone. Then he took his coat and scarf out of the wardrobe and put the bottle of wine into the poacher's pocket and ducked downstairs.

At the bottom, Cal and Vince were debating something. Vince said, "Ah, the two-pint wonder," but not as if he meant it, and Cal said, "A word in your ear, hinny. You live here."

Tom tried to look worldly. "Ah, I know of another small party," he said.

"Hope she's nice," Cal said.

Tom turned towards the door and stopped, looking at Vince. "What's wrong with him?"

"He's labouring under the injustice of this world," Cal said. "We've just been arrested."

"What?"

"Nicked. Apprehended by the peelers. They let us out, though. Didn't want to lower the tone of the cells."

"Are you serious?" Tom said. As the police to him were people who protected him from the rest of the world's nastiness rather than being, as they obviously were to a lot of people, the enemy, he had a little trouble taking such an enormous statement on board.

"Refusing To Leave Licensed Premises and Language Likely To Incite A Breach Of The Peace," Cal recited.

Vince roused himself from his state of dejection, or whatever it was. "Mistaken identity," he said. "We were having a private argument with the landlord of 'The Red Lion', when these rozzers came along and started causing trouble."

Tom had a sudden insight into what his mother would say if she could see him.

"You were lucky not to get assaulting a policeman," Cal said to Vince. "Lucky they were such a fun-loving lot."

Tom let himself out of the front door into a horrible night that blew at him freezing air and threw icy rain at him. He pulled his hood up and buttoned and tied until he could just see out and set out for Orris's flat. The temptation to take the car was quite strong, but the idea of being next in court to

Vince charged with drunk driving, or worse, wrecking his chance of escape, or worst, somebody else's, froze any parts that weren't already frozen. Not surprising that an idiot like Vince got arrested. A joke's a joke. How immature. The rain hit him again.

He'd been to Orris's flat once before in passing. It was on the edge of the town where the hills that formed the headland came inland and shouldered the houses. Orris's flat was in a house in a terrace that backed onto the woods, and Orris (so he said) could go out of the back door of his house, up through the woods, and along the hill to the cliffs, looking down on the roofs of the girls' Hall.

Tom moved from street-light to street-light, expecting, against all logic, to get jumped on at any minute. The wind hacked at him at all the junctions. Even the chip shops were closed, with blank windows.

Tom came up to Orris's house, and had to go up the steps and along the short path before he could read the house number. He put his face against the glass panels of the door. Nothing but dark.

He considered; he could always go back and sit in the car for a bit, or just go back and slip into the party. In the light from the street-lamp, which was behind blowing trees, he could see the names; three flats. The second scrap of card read, ORRIS: TWO RINGS. That meant that there was only one bell, and so he was quite likely to wake the whole house, but it was that or defeat. The idea of facing the derision of Vince and Cal made him lift his finger and push the bell, twice. It rang immediately on the other side of the door. Tom got ready to run, but, almost at once, there was a glow as a door opened high up behind the glass, and the hall light came on, and Orris, wearing a silk dressing gown, opened the door.

"In," he said as Tom opened his mouth. Orris shut the door behind him and gestured up the stairs. On the half-landing were two doors, apparently made of cardboard. One was open to a dark bathroom, the other, at the back, to a small oblong pink room, but there was warmth and light.

They went in. Orris's room looked very much as though it had been painted in pink undercoat, but no-one had ever got round to putting a top coat on. There was a small oven with two electric rings on a white stand with a rack of plates under it, a gate-leg table under the window, an ancient arm-chair, a bookcase piled up with paper, and, across the far wall, a tired bed. On the table was a Word Processor, its screen glowing greenly, and, beside it, a chess-board.

But the most distinctive thing, for Tom, was the curious smell of burned paraffin from Orris's large, square, chrome-plated heater. It permeated the air with an oddly soporific heat.

"I heard you were having a party," Orris said. "I take it it was awful."

"My bed fell through the floor," Tom said, hardly able to move his lips.

"Sounds pretty typical," Orris said. "I hope you've got a bottle in there. We'll have some bacon sandwiches and I'll beat you at chess."

Playing chess with Orris was an interesting experience, because Tom, who could never bring himself to concentrate more than one and a half moves ahead on the grounds that it was only a game, tended to play hopefully rather than tactically. His only technique was to look intelligent and hope that his moves were sufficiently illogical to look daring. Orris, in contrast, played with a sort of suppressed frenzy and, when things were clearly coming to a head, had a tendency to say, "Damn, mate in two," and while Tom was looking, mysti-fied, at the board, he would move Tom's rook, his own king, and then Tom's bishop, and say, "There you are, well played."

That happened twice, and they ate bacon sandwiches which didn't taste anything like any bacon sandwiches Tom had ever eaten, and drank the wine and Orris gave Tom both his extra blankets and Tom went to sleep in the arm chair, with his feet across the bottom of Orris's bed.

The next morning was bright and clear and, despite the arm chair, Tom woke up late and washed in Orris's pink bathroom and drank coffee and played chess again and ate honey sandwiches.

Then he walked, feeling scruffy but very satisfied with life, back across the town, with the bells ringing, in a sharp, bright morning, with the pavements frosty and white. The nearest bells were ringing from a large church, set back in a crisp churchyard, with railings keeping out the encroaching houses. Tom stopped at the gate, standing aside for old ladies to walk by, feeling very ambivalent. And then, on a whim, and with a distinct feeling of doing something daring and different, went in.

He had the slight feeling of being looked at by everyone, but the smart woman and man handing out the service books seemed briskly friendly. He sat at the back. There was a choir and he thought he recognised some girls from the architecture course. He took communion, partly because he would have felt more conspicuous NOT taking it, and kept walking past the Priest when he left, and arrived outside his own flat towards lunchtime. The landlord was standing in the road, inspecting some broken glass.

"Morning," Tom said. "Had an accident?" It was clearly the wrong thing to say.

"You had a good party last night?" the landlord said.

"They did," Tom said, self-righteously. "I've been out all night. That is, I mean, I spent the night, that is, I just got back. I missed it. I wasn't here." He stopped for breath. The landlord didn't seem to be impressed.

"The wife'll be having a word," he said. It wasn't a threat; more a statement of flattening fact. Tom nodded helpfully and let himself in.

He went up into the flat, where the doors looked Sunday-morning shut. The living room with the sunken bed had some bottles in the corner, but no wreckage. Even the kitchen looked more or less unscathed, apart from the eight sticks and the wooden disk that had been the stool. Liam came out of his bedroom.

"Ah, the wanderer returns."

"How did it go? I see someone had an argument with a window."

"A mere accident. Touch of jollity with an empty plastic barrel."

Tom looked at him. "You seem very cheerful."

"Well, why not?" Liam said. "Last week of term. Nobody got arrested, the police weren't called, the floor didn't collapse. There was a bit of bother when Robbie went to sleep with his door locked and people couldn't get their coats, but it's been pretty quiet since then."

"All well, then."

"Fine. And your parents called in about half an hour ago."

"What?" Liam was making coffee, and Tom came round in front of him. "Say again."

"Parents," Liam said. "Apparently they turned up last night on their way from somewhere to somewhere else, and when they got here the party was starting, so they didn't like to interrupt. So they spent the night at 'The Esplanade' or somewhere and came back this morning."

Tom had a sinking feeling. "What did you say?"

"Wasn't me," Liam said. "Alf went down. He told them you'd gone out last night and you hadn't been back and your bed hadn't been slept in." Liam poured water into his mug. "Yes," he said. "Struck me as tactless as well. They're probably down the police station now."

153

Chapter Sixteen
LAST WEEK OF TERM

———————————●———————————

In the projection box at the back of the Biology Lecture Theatre, Tom was connecting up the projector. The box was purpose-built, except that the speaker had to be carried down and plugged in on the front desk. Tom did this while people were filing in, and then went back up the rake of the hall. The box was equipped with faders for the lights and the sound and there were two films.

Tom had come into the School of Architecture a little late, on account of phoning and placating his mother. In his pigeon-hole was a note from Trish which said that Orris claimed to be too busy to show films any more, so would he like to do a small job for her. Phrased like that, Tom thought, there wasn't much choice, and so he'd cleaned the carburettor and pumped up the nearside rear tyre, and (thanks to the slope) had driven up to the big Halls to see the President of the Natural Sciences Society (who reminded him somewhat of A. B.).

"What's your fee?" said the President and Tom, acting on Orris's advice, suggested two flagons of beer.

The two flagons were sitting in the projection box and Tom often asked himself afterwards why he had assumed that it was necessary to drink both of them during the course of the film. Seemed logical at the time. The fact that he did may have accounted for why the first film was shown with rare professionalism, the lights dimming and sound fading up at the beginning, and the same smooth operation in reverse at the end. It might also account for why the second film ended with the projector being switched off in the middle of the credits with a deafening groan from the speakers and, when the lights eventually came up, why the projectionist was seen to walk unsteadily down to the front and to unplug the speaker, and to bump it on most of the tiers of the hall on his way back. Tom sat in the box, rewinding the film very slowly, and thinking that he could write a homily on the embarrassments caused by alcoholic drinks.

Consequently, when the lecture finished, Tom mingled himself with the rest of the audience and didn't wait to be thanked. The only people he recognised in the crowd were Sue and Fred, and he stayed well back from them, and hid in the GENTS until he thought that everyone had gone.

When he came out, there was only a porter checking the rooms before he locked up.

"Goodnight, sir," he said.

Tom half-looked round to see who the porter was speaking to, but it seemed to be him, so he nodded and went out through the two sets of doors. The porter locked them behind him and Tom was on the first step down before he realised that somebody was standing on the top step, clearly waiting, and, just as clearly, it was Karen. She had her anorak hood up but the copper hair flowed out from around it. Tom felt his stomach melt, followed by his knees.

He stopped. "Hi." Karen inclined her head slightly. Tom made an immense effort of articulation. "Are you waiting for somebody?"

Karen turned towards the door. "I thought my friend was going to be in the lecture," she said.

"I'm the last," Tom said. The campus seemed to have drained itself of people. "He's just locked up." Karen looked back again. Tom, having got so far, said, "Can I, I mean," and stopped because, 'Can I walk you home' sounded like a song rather than something sensible. And corny, with it.

Karen said, "I can look after myself, thank you."

She walked down the steps and Tom, who could see that he'd probably never have a chance like this again, fell into step beside her. "Do you live far away?"

Karen named the next street to Orris's. Tom decided on the lie direct. "Amazing," he said. "I live in the next street." Karen didn't react. Tom said, "Should I walk on the other side of the road?"

Karen looked at him sharply, with her chin tilted, and then relaxed a little, but as they came clear of the shelter of the campus the wind and the rain came at them and they didn't speak. Tom, sneaking glances at her profile, wondered what it would be like to walk closer to her and to put his arm round her.

Tom blinked the rain out of his eyes. At every corner, it seemed to find a new way down his neck. They came to a rise in the terraces, and to the right there was a short street with a row of old terraced houses, and a telephone box opposite them. It looked, Tom thought, like a scene from one of the classic French films without reel three. They stopped under the street-lamp.

"I'll be OK now," Karen said, managing to suggest that she would have been OK anyway.

She walked quickly and precisely across the road and along the house fronts, past the phone box, and up the steps of the end house. Tom, with a terrible lonely feeling in his stomach, stood under the street-lamp and watched her. It was wet and cold.

Karen stopped with her key in the lock, and looked back down the street; then she came back down the house steps. Tom, not quite breathing, walked across the road and they met by the telephone box. It seemed sensible to go in where it wasn't raining. The door closed heavily, and suddenly he was very close to her and her hair and a smell of perfume and rain. Tom felt quite drunk and not with the beer.

There was rather a long silence, except for the rain hitting the telephone box and running down the panes.

Karen said, "Look. I know you like me, but it's not a good idea." Tom made a strangled noise. It would have been very easy to lean forward ten centimetres and put his nose into her hair. He put his hand on the handset for support. Karen said: "I've got a boyfriend. He wouldn't like you."

Tom nodded his head, thinking of Orris's dictum. There didn't seem much to say. He already saw himself slogging home through the rain and getting into the cold bed, and then glimpsing her once a term. He felt endlessly miserable.

Karen, however, didn't seem to be in a great hurry to leave. The phone box glass was steaming up. She put her hand up and stroked the back of Tom's hand and said: "You've got penis fingers."

It went very quiet inside the phone box and inside Tom's head. Tom thought: did I hear that? I couldn't have. Nice girls don't.

She was still stroking his hand. Tom swallowed and said, with great difficulty, "I beg your pardon?"

"You've got penis fingers," Karen repeated cheerfully. She lifted his forefinger.

Tom swallowed again, thinking, I knew it; I'm just not equipped for this world. One minute she has a boyfriend, and the next she's saying things like that. Is this what people usually say to each other in phone boxes?

Tom said, desperately: "How do you mean?"

"Well," Karen said. "You ought to play the piano."

There was an airless moment, and then Tom was caught between the urge to laugh hysterically and to start crying, and she lifted onto her toes and kissed him quickly on the lips and pushed out of the box. "See you around, and don't think about it any more." She went away down the street and into her house.

Tom looked at his hand, thinking this is the most embarrassing thing that has ever happened to me. Thank heaven people can't read your mind.

He pulled the hood of his jacket up and went down into

the town, hunched against the rain. He passed the sidestreet where the Ford was all ready to go, tyres pumped up, tank full with the last of the money. And then it'll be Christmas and working for the Post Office, and then too much to eat in the Village Shop, and the silver band playing on the village green on Christmas Morning. Tom, keeping his hands in his pockets, smiled into the rain.

Chapter Seventeen
GOING DOWN

———————————————●———————————————

The last **APATHY** of the year was a single sheet, with information about when the next term started, and train timetables and an application slip for Union minibuses, and the term's football league tables. The first item was a sociological note:

More Christmas Upsets are caused at home by people forgetting that they're not still in the front bar of 'The Lion and The Unicorn', so, as our sociolinguistic colleagues have it, take good care about your style shifting, or, in other words
MIND YOUR $&*#@#!!$ language!

On the back was an agony column.

AUNTIE SAM'S AGONY COLUMN
Any Problems? Remember, a trouble shared
is a trouble doubled.

Dear Sam,

Now that it's nearly the end of term and we're being threatened with no more lectures for a month, I don't know what I'm going to do. Several of us work junkies are planning to kidnap the lecturers and force them to lecture at us all over Christmas, but if this fails, where will I get my fix? I've been distraught at the thaught. What do you advise?

Yours in desperation,
Alfie.

AUNTIE SAM writes:

You are clearly unfitted to University life as perceived
by the media, but you would fit in well with the
dedicated and selfless team of journalists in the **APATHY**
offices where incessant working would not be a stigma.
You don't want people pointing at you, do you?

Dear Sam,

I'm having trouble with the persons of the opposite s**. I
suspect that this is because I happen to like certain
bits of their bodies, but they seem strangely reluctant
to share my enthusiasm. Is this because I'm just too
handsome, talented, and modest for all women, and they
can't live up to my standard, let alone my huge motor
bicycle?

Yours desperately,
Robbie

AUNTIE SAM writes:

You're clearly a revolting egotistical male chauvinist
candidate for the sausage factory and you have won the
free lobotomy prize for repulsive people. Hope this
helps, and have a good Christmas.

This didn't go too well at number 21. Alf, with his
rucksack, was getting a lift home with Zoe and her parents,
and, as he left, he'd passed a copy of **APATHY** over to Robbie,
who was sitting on the Suzuki. Alf waved cheerfully and went
off down the road. Robbie read it unsmilingly.

"I'll murder her."

Liam opened the boot of the Ford and, with an air of
great reluctance, slid his suitcase over the rim, in among what

looked like a decomposing mass of oil, rope, water-cans and tools. Tom was piling his carrier bags of washing onto the back seat.

"Don't take on," Liam said. "There must be hundreds of Robbies in college. Well, dozens. Well, a few." He slammed the boot lid, then slammed it again, then adjusted the rubber seal by tearing a piece off it and slammed it again.

"Alf thought it was funny," Tom said. It was a fine, clear day, but not oppressively hot, and he was trying to get the driver's window to stay up.

"Some people can't stand a little satire."

Robbie, obviously one of them, tore the paper into four and threw it into the air. The pieces drifted down among the milk-bottles delivered to the landlady.

Tom settled into his seat and untangled the seat-belt.

"Have a nice Christmas."

Robbie shut his helmet down, revved the engine, and kicked off down the road.

Tom checked round the car, and drove down to the promenade. They took a look at the sea and then drove back through the town towards the station. Liam waved to a couple of people.

"Good isn't it?" he said. "I feel really at home here now."

They passed Orris coming out of a chemist's shop with an armful of Winchester bottles. "Oh no," Tom said. "Not home-made wine."

"Something to look forward to."

There was a traffic jam near the station and they sat, Tom trying not to look at the temperature gauge.

"Well, what do you think of it so far?" Liam said.

Tom looked back over the most curious three months of his life and decided that it was good.

"I've been reading University Novels," Liam said. "Quite amazing. They're all about these loony lecturers, and sex, and University politics. Have you noticed any of that?"

"No," Tom said, thinking that he scarcely noticed the
lecturers at all, really. The jam cleared, and Liam got out on
the station forecourt.

"See you next term."

Tom drove out through the short suburbs and up the hill
onto the downs. At the top, he pulled into the lay-by to have
another attempt at the window. He put a hand on either side
of the glass and yanked it up. It stuck for a moment and then
slid out of sight into the door. Tom was so distracted by the
thought of four hours driving with the window open that he
quite forgot to look back at the town before he drove away.

SPRING TERM

There are as many fools at a university as elsewhere... But their folly, I admit, has a certain stamp – the stamp of university training, if you like.
– William Gerhardie

"Spring Term," Robbie said in disgust. "There was ice on my blanket when I woke up this morning."
"Cheer up," Sue said. "Soon it'll be warm and soft again."
Robbie looked at her.
"In the meantime," Zoe said, "you could always burn the furniture."
"That wouldn't last us very long."

Chapter Eighteen
COMING BACK

Tom, after a journey which had taken him several years, slithered the Ford down the long hill into the town, and turned onto the promenade. His right hand was numb with cold, his shoes were full of ice and the needle on the temperature gauge was just into the red band.

Although it was only four o'clock, it was falling dark, and the snow flurries out over the bay were pale against the black clouds and the dark sky. As he nursed the car along, the snow started to fall properly, and the wipers, which had been failing under the frozen slush for the last two hours, virtually gave up.

"Come on, come on, nearly there, you swine," Tom said. He'd been talking to the car for more than fifty kilometres and had stopped thinking how odd it was. "Another half kilometre. You can do it." All the way, it had stuttered and stopped, and forced him out into the icy wet to wipe its engine and burn his hands and get slush down his back and he comprehensively hated it.

He signalled to turn left up the street to the flat, changed down, and simultaneously a green light came on on the dashboard, and a burst of steam waved up from both sides of the bonnet. Tom looked at the temperature gauge, which was hard against the peg. He turned the wheel quickly, and the car slid round and stalled and stopped, angled awkwardly out from the kerb. There was a smell of hot metal and burning oil and rubber and a hissing noise.

The wind drummed on the window and the snow melted with hisses into the engine. Snow blew in through the gap in the window (which had never, for some inexplicable reason, been mended).

Tom said, aloud, "Well, nearly made it," and sat and composed a mental letter:

Dear Mother and Father,

This is a complete waste of everyone's time and money. I don't want to be an architect, even if I had the brains. I've forgotten everything I learned last term already. Please can I come back and work in the shop and be warm and useless.

Then there was the thought of going back to that grotty flat, with those uncivilised idiots downstairs (his mother had clearly disapproved even of the expurgated version of Vince's doings, and he'd had to search desperately for things to tell her which didn't make her purse her lips). That thought, however, brought the thought of the gas fire, and how, if he pulled his bed up in front of it . . .

Swallowing his rebellion and despair, he opened his door; and the wind smashed it out of his hand and it crashed wide with a nasty wrenching noise of metal and the side of the car buckled outwards. Tom slid out onto the snow and pushed the door. The hinges protested, but it did shut. The snow was already piling up under the wheels, except where steam was still hissing into the black pool of water under the front of the car. The water smelled burnt.

The car was farther from the kerb than he'd thought. He opened the boot lid, trying to hold on to it in case it blew off, and the snow started to fill it up. He dragged out his suitcase and the three carrier bags of food and other things that wouldn't fit, and slammed it shut.

Behind him, Cal said, "Weelah. Given up parking near the side, bonny lad?"

Tom turned. There, with what looked like coal sacks on

their backs were Alf and Vince and Cal, and Tom surprised himself by being amazingly glad to see them, disreputable as they were.

"It doesn't work," Tom said, into the snow. "Lost a radiator hose, I should think."

Alf's shrewd eyes looked at him from under a woollen cap. "Look on the bright side. If it'd been a horse you'd have had to shoot it. Still, you can't leave it there," and they put their sacks down in the snow, and ranged themselves against the back bumper, and bumped the car round until it was parallel with the kerb, leaning on the snow pile. Then they each took one of Tom's brown paper bags and marched up into the shelter of the town and the flat.

All the lights were on and the landlord, who apparently had a short memory, met them in the hallway and welcomed them back. Cal and Vince went in to warm up their flat and Tom and Alf went upstairs, where Robbie and Liam were sitting in a fug, toasting muffins against the gas fire and drinking hot chocolate.

Tom pulled his bed up and they sat and opened their post-Christmas loot, and listened to Robbie's tales of the morgue, and how Liz had gone to the Bahamas for Christmas, and how Cal and Vince's case was coming up in two weeks. Tom contributed the story of how, in a fit of profiteering, his father had sold the family turkey to a needy customer on Christmas Eve, and how one of the huge blow-heaters at the central Post Office sorting office had filled the place with smoke and there was a traffic jam of trolleys and skips trying to get out. Tom still savoured the smell of hot dust and string.

He sat back on his own bed in his own flat, and looked at the snow flowing past the window in the fluctuating street light, remembering that he really should have phoned home, and then thinking it was too late anyway, and feeling that he might just survive, after all.

Nearly a mile away, down in the Hall on the promenade, in
the utility room on the fifth floor, in a superior fug generated
by the large central heating pipes and the kettle and the
ironing-board, a party was going on. It was centred round a
bottle of sherry given to Zoe by an aunt, a bottle of ginger
wine which nobody at Annie's house would drink, and a
bottle of brandy which Liz had bought at the airport. Not a
lot seemed to have been drunk but there was a lot of giggling
going on.

Mary had been greeted by a brief trombone salute from
the back yard and was now sipping a glass of ginger wine with
a faraway look. Liz's tan was being given qualified praise, and
Annie told a sad story of how, when she was delivering a
parcel on Christmas Eve, an elderly lady had apologised for
being so long in answering the door but it was because she'd
just heard that her son had died.

Keeping up this cheerful vein, Sue described how she'd
met Toby, coming back on the train, and he'd said that the
second term was the worst because people get really miserable and fed up and some have been known to do themselves
in.

"A fun-lover, obviously," Zoe said.

"A lot of people break up with their boyfriends, Toby
says," Sue said, thinking that leaving Jojo had been her
problem. She'd been very brave, just lying there. They kept
saying it would be better, but with the foul machines and
being miles from home you couldn't make jokes.

"Come on," Zoe said. "Tell us."

So Sue described how Jojo's traction was proceeding,
and that maybe she'd be better in six months, and maybe not,
how generally incompetent the medical profession was, but
how brilliant Jojo was becoming at computing, and then she
burst into tears and had to be comforted with brandy and
Mary came and put her arm round her.

Then, to distract their attention, Zoe called for a fuller
and more lurid account of why Liz was exceedingly brown all

over, which was mostly because she'd been to the Bahamas with her family. This led on to why she wasn't at Oxbridge, with that kind of money, and Liz said that even her father's money wouldn't buy her into that bunch of snobs. She'd been thrown out of some posh private school because she didn't fit in and, anyway, her father had made his money out of tyres rather than cheating people at share dealings or inheriting it from the slave trade.

Annie said that was a load of old prejudiced rubbish, but before an argument could start, Liz hit her forehead and demanded that they go and wish Mrs Prothero Happy New Year, and Sue and Zoe and Mary and Liz set out into the snow with Mary's big bedside torch, and the bottle of brandy, and struggled across the town, singing, 'Good Queen Wenceslas'. They found, not as Sue had expected, an empty house, but rather a worse-for-whisky Mrs Prothero, with whom they had a drink (most of which was transferred to a strategically placed plant pot – Liz having learned from experience). They left her the bottle, and went back through the snow singing carols, to be cheerful with Mrs Lamb over supper.

And, much later, Sue sat on the window-seat and looked down at the snow driving past the window, sent out an ethereal encouraging thought to Jojo, and went warmly to bed.

Chapter Nineteen
ORDINARY LIFE

———————————————●———————————————

Even before the snow cleared, life settled down to a pattern, even if it was a rather intricate one.

Tom ate breakfasts of toast and, now and again, met Orris down at the cattle market for a dose of hyper-calories. Orris's girlfriend had beaten him at something else, although Orris wouldn't say what, and they both handed in their resignations to the Hot Celluloid Society after three nightmare evenings when films broke incessantly, bulbs blew, they missed out another reel, and Tom showed an entire half-film at the wrong speed and no-one noticed the difference.

The rhythm of lectures and workshops and essays became easier and no less entertaining, and as Tom never went across to the Natural Sciences library, Karen became a rather stomach-dropping memory.

The landlady didn't appear in the flat to wreak revenge for the party, and no-one appeared from the Lodgings Office. Liam, who was clearly intent on taking a first class degree (and, as Alf put it, being filthy rich), more or less took over the living room as a study, when he wasn't in the library. Robbie, with the luxury of a single room, fell out with the enigmatic Liz almost immediately over how much time she was prepared to devote to him as opposed to old ladies, rowing trips, and, of course, work. The ensuing desperation brought him to more and more spectacular depths of despair. Liz, despite a deputation from Liam and Tom when they met on the prom one evening, was unimpressed.

"Can't you do something?" Liam said, reasonably.

"I'm not doing what he wants me to do," Liz said, and

Tom and Liam had retreated, in rather bemused silence.

And Alf, who was collecting an interesting number of threatening letters, first from his lecturers, then from his Professor, and finally from the Dean, had riposted by writing directly to the Dean on various matters of University politics. Tom, who only just managed to grasp the rules of the game, couldn't quite fathom this behaviour. That Alf was permanently broke and spent more and more time working illicitly in Carlo's bar was rather more comprehensible, although he was never quite sure what to make of the ethics of the thing.

He saw rather more of Zoe than anyone. She took to waiting for Alf at number 21, rather than anywhere else, and not only cooked and cleaned things to pass the time, but lent Robbie her lecture notes of lectures that he'd missed on Byronic mornings. That was how Tom knew so much about the remarkable progress of Mary's love life.

Just as Liz still spent a certain amount of her time (despite intervention from Joy, the sub-warden) shouting insults at the wailing figure of Robbie on the prom, so, conversely, at the back of the hall, Mary spent part of every evening in silent communion with Michael (whose parade of instruments had been banned by the warden).

When Zoe, who was getting rather fed up with having to vacate her freezing bedroom and retire to Annie's or Sue's rooms, or, worse, the basement, or walk across to number 21 in the rain, suggested, tersely for her, that Michael and Mary might go out together, Mary looked faintly shocked. Zoe gave up and talked to Tom instead.

She reported, in passing, that the estimable Fred had been replaced in Sue's evenly-paced life, or at least, supplemented, by an equally estimable (and boring, Zoe said) second-year biologist. He, like Fred, was left amicably on the front doorstep of an evening.

"Nothing personal," Sue had said, when Zoe taxed her on the point. "Pleasant company. When I find the dream man, you'll notice."

"You've been reading the wrong books," Zoe said.

Sue became part of the University badminton B team, and was on the selectors' reserve list at swimming, and took Annie and Liz for runs up to the top of the cliffs. She had an ambivalent relationship with the choir; she and Zoe had been to several practices, and sang, some Sundays, in the largest local church, but they'd retired from the choral pieces. Now that the **APATHY** office was full of Word Processor literates, she was a little less in demand there. Which was just as well because her course stayed satisfying, her tutors liked her, and, apart from toothache in the second week, all was well in the world.

Tom, for his part, played squash with Orris.

This was not competition standard. The one thing that was obvious to Tom, when he took his racket and went up to the sports hall one afternoon, was that there was nobody in the Squash Club who would last more than five minutes on the court with him; before leaving derisively, that is. The games he watched seemed to transform the sport into a brutal exercise of slogging the ball backwards and forwards until somebody got bored, he assumed.

Orris, when the subject came up, had never actually played, and regarded the game as a rather more energetic variant on snooker. He seemed a likely lad. Their games turned out to be generally amiable, but not much to resemble squash.

In the third week of term, Tom came into the flat one Wednesday lunchtime. Alf, carrying Rugby boots, met him in the hallway. "Your mate with the peculiar name's in the kitchen," he said and went out into the damp day.

Tom went up. In the kitchen, which still had a high cheese-factor, Orris was leaning on the cooker reading Tom's book on cooking for students, which Tom had left, unopened, on the windowsill.

"Is this real?" Orris said.

"Why?"

"Well, for a start, you need more bits of equipment than

you'll find in the whole house," Orris said. "And it tells you how to boil eggs, for crying out loud."

"Some people don't know how to boil eggs," Tom said, reasonably. "Look at Robbie."

Orris wasn't distracted. "Who wants to boil an egg, anyway?"

They went downstairs. On Wednesday afternoons, there was a half-day as far as lectures were concerned. Ostensibly, a lot of people did sporting things.

"That book," Orris said, settling his donkey-jacket around him, "makes the basic error that what students ought to eat should be simple, cheap, and nutritious."

Tom couldn't really see an argument about that.

"Edibility has nothing to do with it," Orris said. It was a pleasant day, if you liked the damp, with some thin sunlight. "You can eat cheese and apples if you want it to be cheap and healthy. The real truth is that food's got to be impressive and it's got to be easy to clear up and it mustn't leave a smell."

They went up towards Orris's flat for a demonstration. "I'll show you the secrets of scrambled eggs."

Tom thought that you just cracked them into a pan, but having the feeling that this should be a holiday afternoon, he followed Orris into his flat.

Orris assembled ingredients on the small table. Tom sat on the bedhead.

"It's pretty easy to impress your average woman," Orris said. "They're all FCSS at heart, and they're secretly impressed if you do anything except fry." He took down a frying pan. "Note: it's black. This doesn't help the flavour, but it adds no end to the ambience."

Tom nodded, fascinated.

"Into the pan," Orris said, "place an extravagant lump of butter." He held up a lump of yellow fat, encased in transparent paper. "Note," he said, "the essence of the thing is the waxed paper. Very classy. It could be hair oil, and the fact that it came out of the supermarket wrapped in standard butter-paper is something you overlook." He looked at Tom to check the reaction. "Hide the supermarket wrapper in the deepest bin. Get UNSALTED if you can. Extra points."

"Right," Tom said.

"But only if you're going to use it quickly. It goes off. Then," Orris went on, "only use a WOODEN spatula."

"I give up," Tom said.

"(a) they cost next to nothing," Orris said, with the air of a true scientist, "and (b) they don't melt." He waved his spatula, which had a burned lip, in the air in the pink room. "Amazing how we always get given sets with blue handles which melt. And if they melt, that's it for the evening."

Tom looked at the room with its ambience of unpainted-ness. "You must get some amazingly gullible girls in here."

"You'd be amazed," Orris said, without much conviction.

He slid the ball of butter around the pan. "Note the wristwork. You've got to look like an artist." He picked up his milk carton. "Then you add the top of the milk – not if you're in your flat. And then you get to the eggs."

Tom passed them over in their brittle, supermarket egg-hugging plastic box. Orris produced another ancient fibre-cardboard egg-box from under his cooker, and transferred the eggs.

"You can always use a brown paper bag," he said, "but it's easy to break them. Only the absolute pseudos stick on mud and straw." He took an egg in one hand, and cracked it against the side of the pan and opened the shell with his fingers. "Classy," he said. "You have to be careful that you don't crush the egg completely. That can be a disaster. Then you dispose of the eggshell immediately, trying not to leave trails of albumin all over the cooker. Fork it round. Then, the piece de resistance. You crumble in some Stilton. White Stilton beats Blue Stilton, like single Gloucester beats double Gloucester."

"Expensive."

"Nope. Cheese-ends from the deli, reconstituted." He juggled the eggs lightly until they began to set.

"Now, suppose you were an attractive female," Orris said. He looked at Tom. "Stretch the imagination. I'd have dim lights, and I'd place the whole pan in the middle of the table; two forks, chunks of brown bread and, of course, the unsalted butter. Or you can use plates."

They sat down with two forks. Tom thought it was the best scrambled eggs he'd ever eaten.

"You can use plates," Orris said, "but you have to warm them. If you haven't got an oven, the safe way is to put them into the sink with hot water, then dry them with a tea towel. *Not* one of the foul rags lying around your kitchen. Preferably a clean one with an expensive logo."

"What's the dangerous way?"

"You can grill them," Orris said. They finished eating. "See. Quick, clean, not much to get out of the way afterwards."

After lunch, Orris absorbed himself in his video-screen, and Tom went out, much cheered, down onto the prom. In other universities, he thought, people walk by rivers or in parks. The sea is a good thing, on the whole. Soothing. Feeling soothed, he went into the library and worked for the afternoon.

Then he came out and walked down to the sea again.

It was dusk and the sea looked steel grey. Coming along the prom was Robbie, and Tom discovered the meaning of 'livid'. Robbie was actually a different colour.

"You won't believe it," Robbie said.

"Try me," Tom said. "I'm dead gullible." They walked by the railings. "Where have you been?"

"I've been to see Vince and Cal in court," Robbie said. "What a farce. Ruined my faith in British Justice." He was forced to stop and gesticulate.

"What happened?"

Robbie said, "We all got marshalled into the back of the

175

court, and we sat there while they did some other cases. I
mean, it was all OK. There was a local yobbo who attacked a
visitor with an iron bar and he got probation and community
service and it all looked reasonable." He took a breath. "But
then there was some girl from the German Department who'd
been run over on that Belisha crossing at the bottom of Park
Road. Broke her glasses, got a scar for life near her eye,
stitches in her leg." Tom had to walk faster to keep up. "Gets
dizzy spells. And this stupid defence counsel stands up and
says, 'She's only very small and so you couldn't blame my
client for running her down.'"

"Really?"

"Really. And she was wearing a light-coloured coat, so
he couldn't be expected to see her. It was like Alice in
Wonderland. So instead of chucking the defence counsel out
for insulting their intelligence, they let the guy off, because he
had to use his car to drive to work. And it turned out he'd
been done three times before."

"Can't be typical," Tom said. "Can it?"

Robbie shook his head. "I hope not. But then Vince and
Cal came on." They stopped at the end of the promenade and
sat on the rails, with their backs to the Hall. "Mind you, they
didn't actually look their best. I think Vince had done up one
button on his shirt."

"Justice is supposed to be blind."

"Not when it's got a gut like Vince's poking at it,"
Robbie said. "Anyway, three policemen turned up and read
out of their notebooks about how they'd been called to the
pub, and outside on the pavement, they'd found Vince and
Cal swearing a lot and inciting the people to riot. So they
nicked them, and Vince was supposed to have said, 'You can't
do this to me, it's a police state.'"

"Doesn't sound like Vince. No swearing."

"Plenty of that," Robbie said, "but it was so bad that the
policeman couldn't bring himself to read it out, so it was

passed up to the Bench on a piece of paper. And the old dragon who was chairperson, she's the Prof. of History's wife, I thought her face was going to freeze solid.''

"Sounds like the real thing," Tom said.

"Yeh, sure," Robbie said. "But it wasn't *fair*." Tom thought that Robbie must be the most unlikely defender of Vince imaginable. "I mean, the next thing, this useless defence man gets two students to stand up – I didn't know them, perfectly respectable types – and they said they'd been walking down the street opposite the pub, and they hadn't heard anything, and there wasn't anyone else around, anyway, and they hadn't been incited to anything. It just looked like a bit of high spirits."

"Oh, come on," Tom said. "You can't call Vince getting drunk, 'high spirits'."

"Anyway," Robbie went on, ignoring him, "one of these students couldn't remember how many police there were, or what was actually said, and the magistrate laid into him for not remembering properly. And the police had it all written down, word for word. And do you know what she *said*." His voice rose to new heights of indignation. "She said to this student: 'When you saw another student, one of your *kind*' – as if we were lepers or something – 'being bundled into a police car, why didn't you go to help him?' " Robbie was at a loss for words. "It was insane."

"What did Cal say to all this?"

"Ah well, Cal did his best. Turned on the charm and said he was just an innocent bystander."

"I bet. What about Vince?"

"Well, he'd had it, just by standing there. The magistrate asked him whether he'd said those things, and he said he might have done, when the police were kicking him, and she said he'd better not make any allegations against the police and he said why not, they were making allegations against him."

"How to win friends and influence people."

"So she just said it was disgraceful language, and Vince said, 'Well, everyone uses it.'"

Tom considered. "Well, they do, don't they. In his circle."

"So they got done. A big fine, and now they'll probably get sent down or rusticated or something as well. Remember what the Principal said, unless Sue was making it up. They got more than the yob who mugged the visitors."

They walked back along the prom, and came to 'The Lion and the Unicorn'.

"Well, I'm sure it's not typical," Tom said.

"I suppose it can't be," Robbie said. "But it's frightening, the prejudice against students."

"Vince isn't a very good example," Tom said. "Anyway, was justice done? Do you think they did it?"

Robbie stopped. "Of course they did it. No question. They certainly refused to leave licensed premises, and they were certainly swearing in the street, and I wouldn't like to try to put Vince into a car if he didn't want to go, so I should think there was a dust-up and they were lucky not to get done for assault."

"Well, then," Tom said. "They got what they deserved. I mean, what a rotten job if you're a policeman."

"You don't see, do you," Robbie said. "They might as well have strung them up on a lamp-post. There was no evidence or anything like."

Tom, wondering whether these were moral niceties that he should understand, pushed open the door, and at the bar were Vince and Cal, buying pints, and not looking conspicuously like victims of the police state.

"Ah the two-pint wonder and talcum man," Vince said cheerfully.

"You got back quickly," Robbie said.

"The police gave us a lift," Cal said.

"What?"

"No hard feelings," Vince said.

"I bet the one whose leg you nearly broke had a few," Cal said.

"Well, he was trying to break mine," Vince said.

Tom had a recurrence of the feeling that this was a world he didn't understand. In his world, nobody kicked anybody, the police were helpful and hardworking and pleasant and honest and a jolly good thing to have around.

"Oh well," Robbie said. "Here's to innocence."

They lifted their glasses.

"What I always said," Vince said. "Innocence is no defence."

"Right," Robbie said.

There was a pause.

"You know," Cal said, "it would've been all right, if you hadn't sworn at that copper."

Chapter Twenty
EXTRAORDINARY LIFE

———————————●———————————

Sue spent Friday evening working in the **APATHY** office, pasting together the new edition. Zoe was supposed to be helping her, but she hadn't arrived and the editor was on a field trip, the assistant editor was at a chamber concert and the assistant assistant had gone home for the weekend to see her boyfriend.

Sue could hear the faint sounds of the evening revels proceeding down in the great hall and the bars, but in the office, with its large table and computer and with its low desklamps and piles of paper, things merely seemed intelligent. There was one item which needed to be printed for the front page. Sue looked at the notes left on the desk, went over to the computer, and composed.

STUDENTS RUSTICATED BY DEAN

Two first-year students, Calvin McKechnie (Economics) and Vincent Andrews (European Languages) have been rusticated by the Dean for three months following their conviction at the Magistrates' Court last week. Cal and Vince were charged with refusing to leave 'The Red Lion' when asked by the landlord, one evening last term. They are then alleged to have shouted in the street and to have sworn at the police.

When interviewed, the Dean said that a warning had been issued by the Principal and that the University had no option but to act. "This sort of thing not only damages the image of the University, but of all students," he said.

"Students are paid to do a job, and have a responsibility to set standards. The vast majority of students are good citizens. A tiny minority like McKechnie and Andrews can do a lot of damage to our public image."

Interviewed at the Central Police Station, Inspector Dave Price said, "This was more than just the usual high jinks. We don't want to look like a bunch of fascists, but this sort of thing has to be kept in bounds. It is our job to protect the public."

Sue pursed her lips, and, while the story was printing, composed a tail-piece to run across the bottom of the back page:

RAG WEEK RAG WEEK RAG WEEK RAG WEEK RAG

Don't forget! Two weeks to Rag Week! We expect the best parade ever, and the best money-raising stunts ever! Remember, all the profits go to charities – and there's no rake off. See you there!

RAG RAIDS

We're organising coaches to go to other university towns to sell rag magazines. It's free – except we want a deposit refundable when you turn up for the coach. Prizes for the biggest collection of loot. Join up at the Rag Office in the Union.

It didn't seem very inspired and she was wondering about it when Zoe came in, looking most un-Zoe-like. She walked up and down rapidly, breathing conspicuously. Sue watched her.

"Tear up some of that scrap paper," she said.

Zoe seized the pile of computer print-out and strangled

it; then she tore it in half and dropped it into the metal wastebin and stepped in and jumped on it.

"Feel better?" Sue said.

"No," Zoe said. "Ygh. Ygh. I've just had the most foul
conversation with the most foul man." She sat down in the
editor's chair. "You know Mary's gone out tonight."

Sue couldn't quite follow the logic, but the report itself
was very pleasing. "With Michael?"

"Of course. To the chamber concert. Not very exciting,
but they hold hands." Zoe made an effort to hold herself
down. "They'd just gone – this was about a quarter to eight,
when Mary's father came up."

"Haven't met him," Sue said.

"Don't," Zoe said with great feeling. "Hitler without
the moustache. He marches in with hardly a knock, and
demands to know where Mary is. I mean, just demands."

"What did you say."

"I told him I didn't know and would he mind knocking
next time." She flared her nostrils. "He told me not to be
impertinent, and he supposed that I'd been the one leading
her astray."

"Astray where?"

"That's what I said. He said he'd heard that she'd been
going out with men and I'm afraid I laughed. I mean. Men.
Mary. And then he said – well never mind." She kicked over
the wastebasket. "Anyway, we had a big row, and he said he
was going to report me to the warden and I told him if he
didn't get out of the room I'd scream and have him charged
with assault and attempted rape and he left. The worm." She
looked across at Sue. "Well, I know. Abuse of power. But he
deserved it. You should have seen him."

Sue cut the last piece of paper to shape and stuck it into
the gap.

"Come on. I'll walk back with you and make you a
calming cup of chocolate. Stop gnashing your teeth."

But when they came up the stairs to the third floor, they

could hear a man's voice, shouting. Zoe nodded at Sue, and they walked quietly up to the door of Zoe and Mary's room.

Mary was being told off. She was being told that she was a slut, a disgrace and not fit to be in the world, let alone university. She was being told that universities were full of degenerates and that she was becoming one, and that she was cheapening herself and it was disgusting and she was disgusting. All of this was in such a loud voice that they couldn't tell what Mary was doing. Zoe put out her hand to the door handle, but Sue caught her by the arm and they went up to the sub-warden's flat, and brought Joy down.

She listened for a moment and then knocked decisively on the door. The voice, the ranting, stopped, and they could hear crying. The door opened. A short man was standing there.

"What the hell do you want?" he said, loudly. Mary was sitting on the bed behind him.

"I want to know what's going on," Joy said.

"Mind your own damned business," the man said and slammed the door. Joy caught the handle as it shut and threw the door open. The man spun round.

"It is my business," Joy said. "That girl is in my care."

"I'm her father," shouted the man, "and I'll —"

Joy shouted back. "Will you keep your voice down. There are thirty girls on this corridor trying to sleep or work and You Are Disturbing Them!"

The man looked at her and then at Sue and Zoe and then at Joy, flaming at him. Then he said, "I'll be back tomorrow, young woman," and walked out.

He came back the next day.

Sue and Liz were gathering their sports gear together when Joy knocked at their door.

"Do you have any idea where Mary is?"

"I haven't seen her since last night," Sue said. "Zoe said she was still in bed this morning, when we went out."

"You don't know where Zoe is?"

Sue shook her head.

"She could be anywhere," Liz said. "Why?"

Joy came in and shut the door and leaned on it. "It's that man," she said. "Her father. He came back to take Mary out to lunch, so he said, and he's been going on at the warden about letting Mary go out."

"That's insane," Liz said. "It's Saturday lunchtime."

Joy shook her head. "He's frightening. Do you have any idea where she might be?"

"She might have gone to see Michael, the mad musician," Liz said. "Trouble is, I don't know where he lives. I don't even know his name come to that. Apart from Michael. Do you?" Sue shook her head again, and Joy, with the air of Joan of Arc about to walk onto the bonfire, went off to report.

That afternoon, Sue came second in the two hundred metres butterfly, and nowhere in anything else, and gave up her pretensions as a swimmer, and turned down an invitation from the third-year zoologist who won the freestyle to go to the Union dance. The Hall Rag Float was about to be designed and Sue was going to the meeting.

On the way back along the prom, she met the tall figure of Michael, for once not carrying or pushing an instrument, and she was rather taken aback when he crossed the road to her and said, "You're Sue, aren't you? You don't know where Mary is?"

"No," Sue said. "Isn't she back yet?"

Michael shook his head. He had very quiet, fine features, and very fair hair and seemed always about to apologise for something.

"It's been terrible," he said. The wind was rising now as the evening closed down over the colourless sea and they stopped in the lee of the bandstand. "Her father's been here all day."

"I met him last night," Sue said.

"Isn't he vile?" Michael said, but making it into a real query, as if he needed confirmation of such an unlikely thing. "He's been terribly rude to me. He's accused me of the most terrible things. He even accused me of knowing where she is, but I haven't seen her since last night."

"Don't you have any idea where she is?" Sue said.

"I've looked everywhere," Michael said. "The music library's closed, and she wasn't anywhere in the department. Nobody's seen her. I'm really worried. I mean if that — that man's been upsetting her." He paused and looked out at the sea. The possibilities seemed to hang in the air. They started towards the Hall. "The only place I can think of is the bay where we went for a walk. Our first walk. We went up over the headland and walked for three or four kilometres; then there's a bay with a stream and a beach. She really liked it. She said she'd never been so happy. She might have gone there." It obviously seemed silly to him as he said it.

Sue didn't ask why she might have gone there, but, she thought, thinking of Mary's face last night, she might well have gone somewhere where she'd been happy.

"If only I had a car," Michael said.

Sue took a couple of paces while the thought struck her and then took Michael by the arm and turned him round. She said, "Come on," and she marched him back along the promenade and up the sidestreet to number 21 and rang the top bell.

Tom opened the door, with a pen behind his ear, and Sue explained and Tom went quickly upstairs and came down in his green coat and a long scarf and with Zoe following him, and they all went up the street and round the corner. The Ford was parked on the short slope.

"You're lucky," Tom said. "I only fitted a new radiator hose yesterday."

It was getting darker now and on the streets shops were closing up, and chip shops and kebab bars were starting to do good business. They drove out of the town, with Zoe and

Michael in the back seat leaning forward over between Tom and Sue. Tom seemed to be coaxing the car with his stomach muscles, and only listened to the story and Zoe's violent interventions. They drove past the back of the Hall and the road wound past Orris's and Karen's houses and up through woods and out onto the open downs. Now they could see the white light of a moon between black clouds.

"How did they find you, Michael?" Sue said, over her shoulder. "We don't know your surname."

"They didn't," Michael said. "Apparently Mary's father hounded the warden, and she pretty much lost her temper. She couldn't see why an eighteen-year-old shouldn't go out for lunch on Saturday, and Joy said that it was pretty obvious why she wouldn't want to have lunch with her father. Turn here, I think."

They had come to a junction with a lane and Tom turned left. Ahead they could see the dark sea, just distinguishable from the dark land. The air was cold and heavy, and the wind from the sea was picking up. Michael was looking through the windscreen as he talked and the headlights picked out high hedges and then the road turned back on itself and started down into a valley. The moon gave very black shadows on the black night.

Michael went on: "Then Mary's father made her ring up the Professor of Music to make him look through his files to find out who I was, and he refused point blank, and then her father went to the police, and they refused to do anything either."

"Good for them," Zoe said.

The lane turned with steep hairpin bends four times, and Tom straightened the car out and the lane came down, past hedges and a field with the spikes of frozen marsh grass standing stiffly up, and then the road ended in a small turning circle with banks of gravel around it, half a metre high. The headlights swept the circle, then Tom backed up and said, "Hang on," and drove the Ford up the gravel bank immediately ahead and then turned the wheel. The Ford settled unsteadily with its headlights still rather high, beaming along the beach. The moon, unhelpfully, was behind clouds.

"Will we get off?" Sue said, looking at Tom for the first time.

"The back wheels are still on solid," Tom said. "I'd better leave the engine running, so the battery doesn't go flat." He leaned over and pulled the choke out a fraction, and the engine note rose. "Excuse me." He leaned further across Sue's knees and pulled a big black rubber torch out of the glove box which refused to shut again. "Christmas present," he said.

They got out into the desolate cold and looked down the beach. "This is hopeless," Zoe said.

Unexpectedly, it was Tom who said, "Look, somebody stay here, in case she comes to the car, I mean, if she's here. Dab the accelerator now and again; it'll keep the lights brighter." Zoe hesitated, then sat in the driver's seat, with one foot on the gravel, and Tom and Sue and Michael walked down the gravel and over the sea-grass and onto the beach. Michael took a few strides to the left, and Tom and Sue to the right, and then, in the verge between the torchlight and the headlights, which brightened as Zoe dabbed the pedal and revved the engine, Tom saw a shape, and they ran to it.

Mary was standing quite still, with her shoes in the sea, and the end of the waves starting to lap over them. Tom and Sue both put their arms round her, and she put her head up and started to shake, and then she was sick down Sue's coat and over Tom's trainers, but she didn't say anything when they got her back into the car.

Zoe sat, illegally, on Sue's knee in the front seat, so that Michael could hold Mary in the back, but she was stiff and shaking and upright and wouldn't speak to him.

They drove down into the town in silence and the smell of vomit, and Michael talked softly and gently to Mary, and Tom parked outside the Hall on the double yellow lines while

Sue and Zoe went in to see Joy. They were quite a long time, and then the warden came out and looked into the car, and Joy came out and sat in the passenger seat, and Zoe came out with a bag of clothes, and Tom drove Michael and Mary and Joy and Zoe up to the hospital and its bright lights and Joy and Zoe took Mary in, and Tom and Michael sat not talking to each other.

After a while, Michael got out and thanked Tom and went away down the hill.

The second thing Tom saw when he went into the Dean's outer office on Monday morning, after a square short man with rather protuberant eyes, was Alf who was sitting in one of the three chairs along the wall rather in the attitude of somebody in a good seat at the theatre. Tom sat down beside him.

"What are you doing here?" Tom said, in an undertone (which seemed appropriate).

Alf shrugged. "I wrote to the Dean about what I thought of rusticating Vince and Cal. He wanted to see me."

Tom nodded. The short man was looking out over the secretary's head, out of the window towards the car park. The inner door was open and Tom could feel a vague presence. The Dean seemed to be waiting, just out of sight. Tom looked at the secretary, who was rather like an older version of Karen, with the same extravagant hair. Only her eyes were even more shrewd and quiet.

The corridor door opened and Sue came in, ahead of Mary, whose eyes seemed to be focussed about six million miles away. Zoe came in last and let the door close behind her. The short man, without a word, reached out and took Mary by the wrist, and, very sharply and roughly, pulled her into the Dean's office, her body seeming to follow, feet last. The door banged and rested two centimetres open.

There was a calm voice and then a loud voice almost at

once. Nobody in the outer office moved. After a few minutes the door opened again. The short man was holding it and talking loudly at the Dean. Mary was sitting with her back straight, her feet tucked demurely under her chair, hands resting on her lap.

The man said: "I'm taking her away. Now. Not fit. Not a fit place."

The Dean said, "Perhaps Mary has an opinion of her own."

The man said: "Mary has an opinion when she's told. Come along," and Mary shuffled her chair back, and followed, shoulders down, head down, eyes on the carpet. Tom thought, why doesn't she do something, but she looked as though she was on a lead. As she came past, Zoe put out her hand to touch her arm, and the short man's bulging eyes turned on her with intense disgust. Zoe's hand formed into a fist, just for a moment, and they went out. The door closed on silence.

Then Alf said, "The sod," and in slow motion they all got up and went to the large corner windows looking out over the car park. The Dean came and stood beside them. He was a compact man with fair hair and glasses. Below them, the car park was laid out with grass islands with young, bare trees.

They waited and then Mary's father came out and Mary followed, like a beaten spaniel. She was put into a car. She didn't look back.

"Poor little cow," Alf said.

The Dean put a hand onto the glass. "That must be the most unpleasant man I've ever met," he said.

Tom said: "Where's Michael?" After all, if this were a movie, he thought, Michael would leap out and club that swine into the ground.

Sue said, "He was going to come with us, but Mary wouldn't speak to him or look at him, so he went off."

They watched the car pull out of the car park. It was a

bright morning. The car turned among the houses and was hidden among them. All the people in the office looked at the houses for a few moments.

Then the Dean straightened up and rested his eyes on Alf. "What do you want, Alf?"

"You wanted to see me," Alf said. "Vince and Cal. Injustice and all that."

The Dean looked out of the window. "Well," he said, breathing in, "I don't want to see you now. I can't do anything about it, even if you're right, and just now I think I'd prefer to say a short prayer of thanks that none of us has fathers like that. Go away." He went into his office. Tom wasn't sure that he could remember what he looked like.

They went into the corridor.

"Surely we can do something," Zoe said.

"Let me know when you think of something," Alf said.

They went down the corridor and down the stairs.

Sue said, "Tom, I forgot. Can you help us with our Rag float? We're going to need somebody with a car."

"Your charm strikes again," Alf said.

"I didn't mean it like that," Sue said.

"Yes you did," Zoe said. "But *I* like you, Tom."

Sue and Zoe watched Tom and Alf walk away across the campus. Sue looked round at Zoe.

"What's wrong?"

"Nothing," Zoe said. "Nothing I'm not used to." They walked towards the library. "I'm just regretting a bit that I didn't get the chance to tell Alf what Mary's father called me." Sue waited, but Zoe said, "Just the type you'd expect to be a racist," and she didn't mention it again.

Chapter Twenty-one
RAG WEEK

On Sunday night, Tom left the garage at the back of the Hall, where the final stages of the great pneumatic typewriter were being assembled, and drove back along the prom.

His car was full of grey fragments of latex foam, which had rubbed off the twelve carloads of the stuff that he'd carried from the factory near the railway station. One of Zoe's English set was a local girl whose father managed the factory. The rubber pieces were off-cuts, waiting to be remelted, and Tom had the unrewarding prospect of taking them all back when the typewriter was disassembled.

He and Robbie, despite several protests of sexism (from themselves), had been elected to construct the wooden frame-work to be placed on the lorry (which would arrive on Saturday), on which all the white cushions and the long black roll would be placed. Neither Tom nor Robbie had the faintest idea of how to do this, and they were saved from total ignominy by Orris (of all people), who had fallen out with his girlfriend terminally and, as she was involved in building the float for one of the other Halls, had joined in as a gesture of revenge.

Unusually, his theories on how to build the structure actually seemed to work. He had borrowed an impressive set of tools from his landlord (with whom he was on excellent terms), and assembled enough wood by the simple expedient of making Tom drive round the town stopping at all the demolition sites and skips that were standing in the road, and scavenging.

They were then allocated the Hall garage and Orris drew

the shape of the lorry on the floor with chalk, and they assembled the borrowed workbench, and sawed and hammered and swore, and Orris and Robbie, the one eccentric and utterly reasonable, the other totally conventional and wildly emotional, soon established a deep and abiding dislike for each other. Tom kept in between them, feeling very much as though he'd been conned.

"Why's that then?" Orris said. He was eyeing the construction expertly, holding what had clearly been part of a window-frame. It was very cold in the garage, and the lighting, fluorescent tubes swinging very nakedly between the beams, could have been improved.

"My idea of getting into the girls' Hall wasn't quite like this," he said. "I mean, I get lumbered with driving around all day, unloading tons of foam, carrying it up thousands of stairs – and instead of being surrounded by grateful women, I'm stuck here in the freezing cold with you two."

"We're the best bit," Robbie said.

That being as it may, after they'd finished for the day, Tom drove back to the flat and parked the car and then, as it was not quite closing time, walked down to 'The Lion and the Unicorn', to reward himself with a manly drink. Robbie had gone into the Hall, and Orris about his inscrutable business (which was to work, as was his wont, until the early hours). Tom pushed open the door into the warm, and the only person there was Vince who raised his empty glass in greeting.

"The two-pint wonder. Just in time."

Carlo, who was reading *The Times*, got up and pulled two pints without being asked.

"That's on the house," he said. "A farewell present."

"The only money I've got is the bus fare home," Vince said, "and Carlo won't let me spend it."

"You bet," Carlo said, from behind the paper. "He might not leave."

Tom sat on the stool next to Vince. There was a sharp smell of stale clothes. He said: "What are you going to do? Three months, isn't it?"

"I've got a job on the council at home," Vince said. "Assistant shoveller on the local tip. I follow the bulldozers and swat rats."

Carlo looked over *The Times*. "Nepotism," he said.

Vince said: "He means I've got an uncle who's in charge of Environmental Services, which means the bins and the rubbish tip. You don't get classy jobs like that without a bit of pull."

Tom took a sip of beer, caught Vince watching him, and drank some more. "You'll be back for the exams, then."

"Unless I get promoted."

Carlo said: "Ask him where he got the bus fare from."

Tom said: "Where?"

"The chess club," Vince said. "They had a whip round."

"Must have needed a bloody big whip," Carlo said.

Tom looked up at the glasses inverted in the rack over the bar. He hadn't actually wanted a beer, but it was worth it for the sense of belonging.

Carlo said: "I hope I'll see you in here all next week." He pointed to the poster pinned at the end of the bar.

"Sure," said Tom.

Feeling rather guilty, Sue sent Jojo a postcard on the way up to 'The Lion and the Unicorn' on Monday lunchtime:

Remember I told you about those mysterious rings on the ceiling of the coffee room? Yogurt pot tops. You remove them carefully from the pot, spin them with skill, and they ascend and stick to the plaster. This BANNED by the management, and is a stupid game, especially as mine didn't stick. Hope you're tractioning jolly well.

She walked up past Nick's Café, and saw Michael sitting in a corner with a double bass on the seat next to him. He looked, even through the steamed-up windows, very dejected. Sue pushed open the door and went in.

Nick looked over at Michael. "I'd buy him a coffee if I were you. He doesn't look too bright."

"Do you blame him?"

"No," Nick said. "I heard about it. It's tragic, really. You get these nutters. One in ten thousand." The chromium machine choked and expectorated and Nick put a coffee and a hot chocolate on the bar. "I'll just take for the chocolate," he said. "He can have the coffee on me in return for the joke." He went out into the back of the café.

Sue took the drinks to the end table and sat down in front of Michael.

"This is from Nick for the joke. What joke?"

"Oh," Michael said. "I asked him if he minded me bringing the bass in here, and he said no, as long as I bought it a drink. I think that was the joke. He also said he was going to turn the whole place into a musical café and would I come and play. To play. That might have been a joke, too."

Sue put her hand on his hand, that could do so many things. Michael looked at her and tried to talk, but his mouth went very slack and he took out a handkerchief and pressed it to both eyes.

After a while, he said, "I can't forget the way she looked; just switched off. How can you do that to somebody?"

Sue shook her head.

"I've written, and the letters come back, and I've phoned, five times, and all I get is an answering machine, and I've only once got the nerve up to say something after the beep. But I've heard nothing." He sniffed loudly, then blew his nose, trying to turn his head away so that he wouldn't actually blow at Sue. Sue helpfully looked behind her at the empty café. "I'm going to go down there after the end of term."

"Good on you," Sue said.

There was a pause. Then Michael said: "I don't suppose
you know anyone who'd like these?" He held out a neat,
heavy envelope. Inside were two tickets for all the concerts in
the University and the town, for the rest of the term and next
term.

All of which was why, when Sue arrived at 'The Lion
and the Unicorn', the first heat of the Great Spaghetti Eating
Contest was over. Zoe and Annie were sitting at a small table,
finishing their soup and bread, and at the next, the contest-
ants, Robbie, Tom, and Alf, were contemplating their empty
bowls – all, that is, except Alf. Sue sat down.

"That was lucky," Zoe said. "You just missed the most
disgusting exhibition. They're supposed to see who can eat a
bowl of Rosie's spaghetti bolognese quickest."

"Who won?" Sue said, amazed.

"I did," Robbie said, leaning over. "That means I get a
free meal and another one on Saturday in the final."

Rosie came over with soup and bread without being
asked. "Last year," she said, conversationally, "one boy was
taken to hospital with throat burns because I'd made it too
hot."

Sue leaned over. "I don't think you're going to win,
Alf." Alf was still eating.

Tom said, "You don't appreciate the subtlety of all this.
Alf doesn't actually intend to win. He gets a free lunch every
day anyway." Sue and Zoe arranged their soup bowls. Tom
took an envelope from his inside pocket. "Haven't had time
to open the mail yet."

Rosie brought three cups of coffee over to the table. Zoe
was reading the EVENTS listing.

"There's been a ban on stunts that offend the natives,
after the fuss last year," Rosie said helpfully. "Some of the
Biology students put on white coats and picked on the small
village where the Principal lives and visited every house
telling them that the water was contaminated and that they

couldn't use it. They were going to take a van full of barrels out and sell the stuff when somebody rumbled them."

Zoe was reading. "Climbing the High Street on Tuesday. Mass marathon on Wednesday. Street fête on Thursday. World Dart-Throwing Record Attempt. Yard of ale drinking contest. Three-legged race around the pubs. Drink the Union dry. (There seems to be an emphasis on alcohol, wouldn't you say?) The chaplaincy's doing a sponsored pray-in. There's a concrete canoe race. Discos every night and plays or concerts every lunchtime in three different places. A charity sports day on Saturday morning, and then the big parade on Saturday, with a barbecue and a torchlight procession. Then there's the Superior Dinner Dance at the poshest restaurant as an alternative. Will that do you?"

"Boring," Robbie said.

Tom opened his letter. There was a crest on the envelope.

"Your knighthood come through, then?" Robbie said.

Tom unfolded the foolscap sheet. "It's the Old School Society," he said. "They want me to come to a reunion."

Robbie picked up the sauce bottle and held it under Tom's nose. "Now Mr Rowlands, tell the waiting world, and this sauce bottle, what your reaction is to this kind invitation."

Tom didn't have to think. "I wouldn't go back there if you paid me. Well, depends how much, but a lot."

"Why not?" said Liam. "I'm going to my reunion."

"You would," Robbie said. "It's pathetic. Who wants to remember school – except those idiots who were good at it and've been total bummers since."

"Come on," Liam said. "It's just nice to go back to see the place."

"Why?"

"Makes you feel lucky. It's like visiting somebody in hospital."

Robbie put the sauce bottle down, upside down, to drain

the last centimetre of sauce. Tom tried to steer his mind away from bicycle sheds and intimidation and chalk and uniforms and incomprehension and school dances and prefects who confiscated the only water-pistol he'd ever owned, and he hadn't even been using it.

"I wouldn't go back," Tom said.

"Not even to get even?" Alf said. "The day I get my PhD, I'm going to go back and –"

"I think you're rotten," Liam said. "Teachers are people. They try. And it's a lousy job. I liked my teachers."

Tom digested this with his spaghetti.

"Well, maybe."

"Use the newsletter to light the fire with tonight," Alf said. "That'll be some satisfaction."

That evening, in the ghostly light of the Hall garage, Robbie didn't turn up and Orris, who reckoned that they'd done all they could until Saturday, took pity on Tom's increasingly depressed state and invited him back for supper.

"It's only women," Tom said as they drove up to Orris's house. "Lack of them. I mean, Robbie's got Liz, and Alf's got Zoe and Liam's got his mystery woman and I end up as taxi driver and good chap."

"You know Liz is dressing up as a bottle of correcting fluid, don't you?" Orris said, ignoring him. "Come and have a cooking lesson and then if you ever *do* get a woman, you'll be prepared," and they went in to an evening which raised Tom's spirits almost by each second.

The room had its slightly oily fug and Orris switched on the three table lamps and took a brown bottle with a distinguished label from the narrow cupboard just inside the door. Then he took two tumblers and wiped them on a clean tea towel. Tom looked around. The most striking characteristic was that although almost every item of furniture was both cheap and old, it was clean. Orris was clean, the cooker was clean. You could, probably, have eaten off the carpet.

Orris poured two clean glasses of brown liquid. Tom looked at it dubiously.

"Don't look at it like that," Orris said. "Good British Sherry."

Tom looked at the label.

"Rule One," Orris said. "Always buy your cheap sherry from the jug-and-bottle and re-bottle it. If you buy it in a cheap bottle it just looks cheap and nasty."

Tom tasted it. "But it is cheap and nasty," he said. "Leave this stuff and it'd crystallize in the glass."

Orris shook his head. "Basic psychology. You *know* what it is. If you put it in this bottle, there's less chance of being confused with the old men gobbing down by the town hall."

Tom, vividly remembering his room-spin, let the glass touch his lips and held it away from him.

Orris bent and opened the oven door. There was a vague smell. He prodded and then closed the door and set up the chess-board. Tom played his usual game of attempting to keep up with Orris's mercurial moves until Orris said, "There. Mate in three. I'll get the supper out."

Tom stared, mystified, at the board for a few minutes and then gave up. Who was about to mate whom was not at all clear. Orris had taken a roasting tin containing three foil parcels from the small oven and placed it on the top of the cooker. Tom turned to look. Orris, very carefully, unwrapped two of them, trying to avoid the escaping steam getting his fingernails.

Orris said: "Now, at this point, my lovely assistant will bring me a newspaper from the cupboard in front of him . . ." Tom put it on the floor where Orris indicated, and Orris took the tail of one of the fish, shook it slightly, and the skeleton lifted away. He laid it on the newspaper and repeated the process with the second fish. In the foil lay four neat fillets. "There you are. Normally, if you were worth looking at, I'd re-wrap them and they'd go back in the oven until the great moment. Then perhaps splash a drop of the special amontillado shipped in from my uncle's hacienda, unless she happens to be doing Hispanics."

"Or intelligent," Tom said. He went downstairs to the dustbin outside the back door. The dark woods waved over his head. When he came back, Orris was cooking a packet of frozen peas which he had kept up against the window glass to keep as frozen as possible. He transferred the fish to plates warmed in the bathroom sink and opened the third foil packet. In it were soft slices of potato, and melted cheese.

"Cheese ends," Orris said. "Impressive?"

"Amazing," Tom said, eating the fish, which was delicate and rich and quite delicious. "Does it work? I mean, does it have a devastating effect on girls?"

Orris scratched his ear. "Well, I can't say it's actually aphrodisiac. More soporific." He looked thoughtfully at his plate.

There was a moon, and Tom drove down to the sea and passed Zoe, walking along carrying a suit. Tom pulled up alongside and hooted mutedly, but Zoe kept her eyes to the front and walked faster. Tom tried again, and then had to pull out sharply to miss a parked car. He drove a hundred metres ahead, then got out and shouted at her.

"Sorry, Tom," Zoe said. "I thought you were a kerb crawler."

"Well, thanks."

Zoe got in, cradling the suit on her knees.

"What's that?" Tom said, trying to get the car to start again. It was obviously upset by the sudden stop.

"It's Alf's," Zoe said.

"But it's a suit," Tom said.

"Well, it's still Alf's," Zoe said, slightly offended. "It belonged to Rosie's brother, and I've been altering it. It's for the Rag Dinner Dance on Saturday. You know, the Superior Restaurant. Are you going?"

Tom, not wishing to admit that he'd forgotten about it

and that he didn't have anyone to go with anyway, just said, "No," airily.

"Well, it looks a bit stuffy," Zoe said, "but we thought it would do Alf good. Get him to posh himself up. I just hope he doesn't get us thrown out."

Tom marked his disenchantment with the Rag from about that point.

Everyone else seemed to be out doing things every day, but when he went to watch people climbing the high street with crampons and petons and ropes, he didn't find it funny, and when he watched people drinking yards of ale, he thought, among all the laughing and cheering, that it was disgusting. The ultimate insult was when he met A.B., wearing a college scarf, who sold him a Rag magazine which he thought was smutty rather than funny.

The flat was generally empty. Now that Cal and Vince had gone the house seemed curiously quiet. Liam was either working or with his invisible girlfriend; Alf was doing extra hours at Carlo's, apart from the hours put in eating spaghetti, and Robbie had revealed himself as a master cushion-stuffer and spent a lot of time down at the Hall.

Tom, consequently, and with a certain dour satisfaction, turned back to work and he was looking at his books one evening when Zoe came bouncing up the stairs.

"Hi, Tom, seen the lad?"

"He's down at Carlo's. An evening barkeeping, I think."

Zoe came across the room and opened Tom's dictionary.

"Better check the psyche," she said.

Tom watched her.

"Go/said the bird/human kind cannot bear very much reality.
– Eliot.

Hmn.

You are a philosopher, Dr Johnson. I have tried too in my time to be a philosopher; but, I don't know how, cheerfulness is always breaking in. – Oliver Edwards.

Better. Hey, what's this?

> *Only to kiss that air/That lately kissed thee.*

Who's that?"

"Somebody called Herrick. Nice isn't it. The last one's best. It's from a poem called '*Nobody loses all the time*', about this guy who every type of farm he tries goes wrong, and then he dies."

> "*and down went/my uncle/Sol/and started a worm farm.*"

Zoe shook her head. "I'm beginning to wish I hadn't looked. Maybe there's hope for you yet." She patted him on the head and went out.

Tom watched the gas fire for a minute or two, and then looked back at his own writing.

Sue and Zoe were beginning to think that it was rather too much. Now that Zoe's room was half-empty with Mary gone, it was rapidly filling to the ceiling with the white sacks of foam that were to be the typewriter keys. Robbie and Liz would come back from lectures and have long giggly fights with the foam on the pretence of stuffing things, and then come back and do the same after the disco. A lot of sewing went on in the utility room, and Sue went out for most evenings with either Michael (to serious things), or Fred (to lighter things), and only once had forcibly to eject Robbie. There was an air of frenzy about the place, rather, as Zoe said, as if they were all standing around a big fire to keep the winter and the dark and the gloom away.

By Saturday, they were exhausted.

Sue went round to Toby and Penny's and walked in on a meditation session being conducted by a monk, who, apart from the cowl and rope, could have passed for a Rugby-playing truck driver.

Sue slid onto the sofa. The silence was, after a week in Hall, absolutely blissful.

The monk said: "In some views, meditation is a sort of prayer. You can either simply, or complicatedly, be at one with the universe or you can direct your thoughts AT somebody."

A girl sitting in front of Sue raised an indicative finger. "But surely that doesn't do anything directly," she said. "That would be very crude thinking." There was a faint hint of challenge.

"That's a debatable point," the monk said, "but the least that you can say is that if you really pray for someone, really concentrate and think about them, then you're very likely to end up doing whatever you can. So, if you'd like to focus on an object, or a person, we could pray."

Sue looked across the room at the dark windows reflecting the light. What a year for poor Jo. Sue thought very hard about her and fixed her very clearly in her mind and began to seriously wonder what she could do for her, almost to compensate for this amazing year she herself was having. Perhaps that's praying, she thought, but she didn't close her eyes.

Chapter Twenty-two
RAG DAY

Just to make things worse, Tom thought, it was a beautiful day, pretending to be spring, with bright sunshine and the sky very high and very pale.

Tom had woken up to find the flat completely empty and he had gone down to the bus station for breakfast to cheer himself up before going to load the float and be surrounded by jollity.

He walked across town where students were everywhere, wearing scarves very conspicuously and waving collecting tins. There were three bands playing on corners and buskers and pavement artists and a string quartet playing in one of the arcades. Tom turned, with some relief and still feeling very unfestive, into the backstreet behind the Hall.

At the end of the road, there was a high wooden gate and, inside, a lorry, hired with a very taciturn driver, who was reading the kind of newspaper that Robbie read when Liz wasn't looking.

Robbie and Orris, not looking at all friendly, had one end of the frame of the typewriter, and were pushing it up onto the back of the lorry among cabbage-leaves. It was being guided by Fred and Michael, who didn't seem to like each other either, but who were being rather quieter about it.

Tom, feeling superfluous, was about to walk on when a parade of large white sacks came out of the rear door of the Hall and Sue, behind the first one, saw him.

"Tom, I wondered where you were. Come and carry a cushion."

"Yeh, go and carry a cushion," Robbie said, trying to push the beam up. "We can manage. Don't mind us."

Tom got underneath the beam and heaved. Orris seemed to have made the thing out of railway sleepers.

But, after some cushion-carrying and bolster-moving, and the illicit borrowing of a good many bedspreads, what emerged, if it didn't exactly look like a typewriter, could not have been mistaken for anything else.

Orris caught him as they were about to leave. "Next job," he said. "You look like a likely lad."

"But I hate the ruddy Rag," Tom said. "All this jollity."

"Shut up," Orris said, amiably. "Next thing is the barbecue. Trish is organising it and somehow she knew we were here, so get fell in."

They walked around the side of the Hall, where the windows were barred and pipes ran down and moss grew on the stone path, came back into the sunshine and crossed the promenade. On the beach, just below the Hall, on the stony shelf above high tide, what looked like a reconstruction of trench warfare was being enacted, under the stern direction of Trish. Tom, before he could think of a protest, was told off to help in digging trenches and humping logs and iron grids off a truck parked on the wide pavement. He was beginning to feel like a general labourer and it wasn't entirely clear where the fun of it all actually lay.

"Am I supposed to be enjoying this?" he said to Trish.

"You mean you're not?" Trish said, clearly deciding that Tom must be joking. Tom gave up.

He went to Nick's Café for lunch and, in the afternoon went to finish the barbecue. Orris and Trish were being helped by Joy.

"We'll get a good view of the procession," Trish said. "It ends here." And while they were chopping the last of the wood, the noise level towards the town rose and the first floats came onto the promenade, showered from the flats along the seafront with water and other things. Tom, Orris, Trish, and

Joy climbed onto the promenade-edge, standing outside the railings.

People were dancing along each side of the procession, wearing anything but what could be readily identified as clothing. The Parachute Club had a float with wings, and the Anti-Nuclear group had a blackened lorry. It wasn't getting many laughs, but its accompanying skeletons with collecting tins seemed to be doing very well.

"They used to have a Rag Queen," Joy said, "but there were so many protests that they stopped doing it."

"Sexist," Orris said.

"Right," Trish said. "One year, apparently, they had a rival Rag Queen, in drag, and a female Rag King, and that kind of killed it."

The huge typewriter was on the fifth float with Sue and Annie and Zoe bouncing on the keys and a bottle of correcting fluid throwing back whatever was thrown with great energy. And the framework hadn't fallen off.

The lorries turned in front of the Hall. Joy and Trish climbed the railings and went to stand near the Hall doorway.

On the next float was Karen, sitting behind a very wet jazz band. Tom swallowed.

"Don't look like that," Orris said. "Not allowed on Rag day." Karen was sitting between two men who had their arms around her.

"Isn't she fantastic?" Tom said.

"No," Orris said pedantically. "Quite solid. And she's over there and you're over here and that's that, so stop being such a pain."

"Less than the dust beneath her chariot wheels," Tom said.

"Quite," Orris said. "Now shut up."

The procession was breaking up into a shambles of lorries and people.

"Just look forward to tomorrow," Orris said. "Stripping the float. Cutting open all the bags. Taking the foam back."

"Thanks."

They walked along the beach, parallel to the sea. Orris was carrying a plastic bag.

"What's that," Tom said. "Mince? That's a bit down market, isn't it?"

"It was going to be lobster," Orris said. "You're supposed to kill them by dropping them into boiling water." He shook his head. "I tried it last month. Steeled myself to do it, and the thing screamed at me. It was only the air escaping but it still sounded horrific."

"So it's back to mince."

Orris threw the plastic bag up and caught it. The sea slid up along the beach. Parallel to them, on the prom, were the backs of crowds of people watching the trucks go by and the bands and the singing and cheering. "Don't knock mince. You just beat it up and then roast it in a lump. Dead easy."

"It says in the cookery book," Tom said, "that you ought to add onions."

"There you are," Orris said, "proves my point. Whoever wrote that never lived in a bedsit or had a girlfriend with a nose. Avoid onions. They stink the place out and you can't get the smell off your hands. There you are, her head resting on your arm, stroking her hair, dead romantic, and she starts sniffing."

They went back to Orris's flat through the thinning crowds and played chess, and Orris checkmated himself a couple of times.

"I'll have to chuck you out now. I want to get ready for the Fancy Dress Dance."

"Not the Dinner Dance, surely," Tom said. "Bit posh for you, isn't it?"

"I know that's fancy dress," Orris said, "but I can't afford it. No. There's a dance at the Union. Where have you been all week?"

Tom, who regarded such a dance with deep distrust, because it conjured up vistas of embarrassment from being a small child and forced to participate, said, "What are you going as?"

Orris held up a pair of long striped underwear.

Tom merely looked.

"Why not?" Orris said.

"You'll get arrested."

"Nonsense. I'm going as a pirate."

Tom said, "I'll see you later," and went out into the chilled evening, starting to feel a little more human about the whole thing.

In the flat, Robbie and Liam and Alf were all, for a wonder, dressed and politely allowing each other turns at the mirror. Robbie and Liam were in dinner jackets, and Alf's suit made him virtually unrecognisable.

Robbie caught Tom's incredulous look.

"It's all Zoe's doing," he said. "We're having her canonised tomorrow. It's better than water into wine."

"Very odd," Alf said. "I'm away to Carlo's to get some shoes." He padded out in his socks.

"So it's the big dinner, then," Tom said, trying to appear unmoved.

"That's right. A bit of class, my son," Robbie said. "We may see you at the barbecue afterwards."

"We'll just drop by in the limo and see what you peasants are up to," Liam said.

The doorbell rang.

"There's the taxi," Robbie said.

"Taxi?" Tom said.

"If a thing's worth doing," Liam said. "Have a nice miserable evening." They went cheerily down the stairs.

Tom stood in the empty flat for a minute, wondering why he was incapable of organising himself. Nobody to go anywhere with. No fancy dress. No formal dress. Serves you right for being bloody-minded, he thought, and felt slightly better for thinking it.

But he washed and put on his best collection of clothes,

and went down to Nick's Café. Nick gave him soup and cleared up around him and then politely threw him out and closed up.

Tom went despondently into the town and began to circumnavigate all the pubs where there might be a familiar face. It was a technique he had perfected; you opened the door, looked round, and went back onto the street. Or, you could work your way across the bar and go out by the far door, possibly calling at the GENTS. In this way, you saw lots of people revelling, but didn't actually have to join in. The total effect was of great individuality and terminal depression.

He finally went to Carlo's, although he thought that the ebullience of Carlo's personality might be even worse, but Carlo wasn't behind the bar. Tom had a drink, thinking how sobering having a drink on your own is. He walked down to the prom. In the distance he could see the first glow of the barbecue, but obviously nothing was happening yet. He walked across the campus to the Union.

The bar was crowded. Across the wide corridor, there was music coming from the great hall. Tom paid, and showed his Union Card and went in.

The hall was virtually empty, with just the support band practising under the lasers. He came out and squeezed himself in one end of the bar and had another drink. The only effect seemed to be that his stomach was uncomfortably full.

Over the bar there was a large sign that said that nobody would be admitted to the dance after 10:30, and nobody who looked inebriated would be admitted at all. Tom had another drink and some peanuts and read a newspaper that someone had left behind the corner upright, and tried to ignore the conspicuous jollity while trying to look abstracted, mysterious, and Byronic, in case Karen came in.

After a while the crowd thinned and Tom slid off his stool and went back into the dance. It was crowded with people, and people dancing, and the band was winding itself up, and he circulated the room, trying to look as though he were looking for someone. That didn't work and so he decided to cut his losses and have a final drink and be really virtuous and be the only person in the town to be working.

When he got to the door, though, there was an argument going on. The dance now had two large students on entrance duty, and in front of one of them, gesticulating, was Orris.

It took Tom a fraction of a second to recognise him, because, far from wearing long striped underwear, he was dressed in a kilt and a tweed jacket, with large hairy socks and what looked like an elk's foot sticking out of one of them. The only thing that spoiled the Highland effect was that his face was covered in burned cork. He was, clearly, not being let in and Tom had to admit to himself that the doorman had a good point.

"There wasn't enough notice," Orris was saying. "I've got a ticket. I should be allowed in. And it's a damn good costume."

He bent down and pulled at the elk's foot, which turned out to have a large blade attached to it. "Complete with dirk." He waved it around, and several people stood back. "Give me one good reason why I shouldn't go in?" His voice might have been mistaken for one of sweet reason, had he not been waving the knife around. The doorman who, Tom thought, must have been a shrewd judge of character or have no nerves, said, "You're drunk. Push off."

Orris turned round. The duty constable, who had been standing outside on the steps of the Union, had come into the foyer. Orris, still holding the knife, walked across to him. Tom slid between the doormen and walked cautiously after him.

The policeman looked at Orris carefully.

Orris stood in front of him and explained his case with what Tom thought was admirable lucidity. The policeman didn't change his expression. He leaned slightly forward.

"I understand your problem, sir," he said, "but the rules are the rules and," he went on, dropping his voice, "I'd go home and have a rest now, and I'd just put that thing away before I'm forced to nick you for carrying a dangerous weapon."

Orris looked at the knife in surprise and shoved it back into his sock. Tom stepped forward and nodded to the policeman as if to indicate that he was Orris's keeper, and steered him across the foyer.

By the entrance was a long trestle table with piles of torches made of cardboard tubes and with cotton-wool heads, soaked in paraffin.

Orris refused to pass the table without buying one.

"But the procession doesn't start until eleven." Tom said.

"Somebody's got to start it," Orris said.

They walked down towards the prom, carrying the unlit torches.

"Why the black face?" Tom said.

"I'm a mult-racial Scot," Orris said.

"It looks like a good way to be beaten up," Tom said.

"Actually," Orris said, lighting his torch with some difficulty and carrying it ostentatiously over his head, "I started out as a pirate and I figured that a pirate ought to be smeared with soot. So I did that, and I called in at the corner pub down the road for a quick one, and the landlord asked me to leave. So I came back and I borrowed the skirt off the girl downstairs, and I sort of forgot to get rid of the cork."

Tom, wondering what he had been reduced to and thinking that at least it would soon be over and he could have a sausage at the barbecue, walked on, a little morosely. At the corner of the promenade, he could see the flames from the barbecue trench and, winking along the arc of the bay, bobbing flames of torches. It really looked very pretty.

Tom looked round to make this observation to Orris, but there was no Orris. Tom backtracked, and there was an open doorway and somewhere in the depths of a hallway, a flicker of flame. Tom sprinted into the house and dragged Orris out.

"You really will get arrested," he said.

"Seemed a good place to go," Orris said.

They went on towards the barbecue, with specks of light following them as people came down along the prom. There was a crowd in the space between prom and water.

"I hope we built it above high-tide level," Tom said.

"Not as much as I do. Trish would kill me."

"Still living in hope, eh?" Tom said. He lit his torch from the remains of Orris's. Most of the people walking were couples. Tom felt a trifle conspicuous.

People danced by them and there was some fairly merry singing, and then a very concerted and beautifully modulated barber's shop quartet came by.

At the barbecue, Trish and Joy and their assistants, in white aprons, were turning chops and sausages and hamburgers on the grids set in the sand. Torches were stuck in the woodwork around and two guitarists competed at each side. Trish handed Orris and Tom rolls from a large plastic sack.

"Help yourselves," she said, with a rare display of bonhomie. "Free for the workers."

Tom, feeling slightly more an insider, took a hamburger. There were tubes of mustard perched on the dark wood groins. Orris threw the end of his torch, arcing the flame out to sea, and then went over to one of the guitarists.

Tom stuck his torch in the pebbles and ate, but his mood of euphoria was slightly punctured by the arrival of a row of taxis, which disburthened Robbie and Liz, and Fred and Sue, and Zoe and Alf, with others in dinner jackets. Tom stepped back out of the torchlight. The girls all looked elegant beyond words and Liz was wearing, more or less, the sort of dress which explained Robbie's fascination. They walked down to the barbecue.

"What was it like?" Joy said. "You look happy with it."

"Magic," Robbie said. "Flunkies, silver, the lot."

"Food," said Alf.

"You won't want a sausage, then."

"Several," Robbie said. "It was yer *nouvelle cuisine.*
Looked very pretty, but three mouthfuls and that's it."

Tom climbed over the woodwork into the dark and
worked his way along the beach, feeling as if he could be seen
until he came to a set of steps, worn by the sea. The
streetlights just lit the top of each step. He climbed onto the
promenade and waited, watching until Orris emerged from
the barbecue crowd.

The fire-glow lit the beach and the sky with such an odd
light that everything seaward looked as though it was part of a
very cheap film-set, made of dark-blue cardboard. In the
darkness, the sea endlessly shifted and rolled the pebbles.

When Orris eventually came past him, he was seeming
the worse for wear and Tom laboriously helped him back up
to his flat. Orris collapsed on the bed and Tom had just got to
the door, when Orris said, calmly, "I think we might have
a problem here. I thought my foot was a bit squelchy." He
rolled down his sock. The dirk, thrust down the sock, had
missed the scabbard and scabbarded itself in his calf. There
was a long bloody wound.

"A great anaesthetic, alcohol," Orris said.

Tom got him outside and half-carried him up to the
hospital. The nurses on reception at Casualty greeted them
with such blank expressions that Tom felt exceedingly
embarrassed, and sat next to Orris hoping that he wouldn't
be identified.

After a while, Orris was taken into a cubicle by another
very straight-faced nurse, who clearly didn't share the sort of
tolerance shown by Vince's policemen for the *jeux d'esprit* of
the middle classes, and to judge from the sounds, some of the
effect of the anaesthetic must have worn off.

Tom sat and waited on the hard plastic chairs, and read
the magazines, the like of which he hadn't seen for a long
time. The fluorescent light had a curious effect in the room,
making the night seem darker and colder even though it
wasn't a friendly light. Around him there were drunks and

accidents, and fights. He kept reading, pushing away the thought that these were the sad and unfortunate and there was no reason on earth why he should be here at all.

After a while he went to see where Orris had got to. Orris, it seemed, had been taken down into the town with an ambulance full of walking wounded some time ago. Tom was feeling too numb to react to this and he walked out of the hospital and down the hill.

It was a clear night, not cold, but late, now, and there were only a few homegoing couples. He passed Karen's house and paused for a minute under the street-lamp and looked at the telephone box and felt rather old for a minute. Then he tucked his scarf in tightly and went home to the flat.

Chapter Twenty-three
END OF TERM

———————————●———————————

Into March, the weather became imperceptibly more civilised and there were mornings when Sue stopped in her morning run and simply looked out over the sea, which drifted in perfect layers of light, from reds to greens. Up on the cliffs, the world of the University seemed very small and fragile.

The end of term seemed to come very quickly. Sue got three As for her last three assignments, and had lost by a very small margin in the semi-finals of the open badminton tournament. About the only blemish on the term was a large fine for three library books which she'd forgotten to take back. Jojo, her traction over, was out of hospital and recuperating at home, and had taken to sending Sue postcards signed with different male names, every day. She still went into the **APATHY** offices occasionally (usually when the Word Processor had done something awful), and twice she had jogged past Toby and Penny and they'd invited her in for herb tea.

It was even peaceful in Hall. Liz, for a change, had settled down to work – after an interview with the Senior Tutor in which he had said threatening things about her grant – and still went to see Mrs Prothero every week. She even restricted Robbie's visits, although, as Sue could now retreat to Zoe's room, even this scarcely upset the even tenor of their lives.

Annie had a birthday, and they had a party in the utility room. The warden had come along to ask them to keep the noise down, which was rather embarrassing because Joy was there too. And Zoe and Alf continued on their unstable way.

On the last morning, Liz was being taken to the station for the early train by Robbie, and Alf and Zoe were getting a lift home together. Annie had already gone.

Sue, waiting in the Hall, until it was time for for the afternoon train, met Joy in the corridor. "The cleaner found this," she said, holding up Zoe's wallet. "Has she gone?"

"She might still be at Alf's," Sue said. "I'll take it round."

It was a beautiful spring day, with a clean wind off the sea. Tom opened the door and smiled at her.

"Sorry, they've gone," he said. "Come in, though. They might come back. They generally do. Have a coffee." Sue followed him upstairs. On the landing, all the doors were open, and the windows were open.

"I've just finished moving into the small bedroom," Tom said. He indicated. The small room, which had the plank wall dividing it from the kitchen, had a bed and a small table and chair, and a sink, and a bookshelf, and a small wardrobe. The vacuum cleaner stood in the hall. "I've got to stay on for a few days." Sue nodded. "My folks are on holiday," Tom went on, as if this behaviour required a more detailed explanation. "They keep a shop, and my aunt and uncle come and run it for a couple of weeks. But they don't, well, I don't think I count in their plans." This was rather a long speech, and Tom began to feel as though he was justifying himself and his parents to the point of gibbering. He moved the vacuum cleaner, for something to do.

Sue looked into the bedroom and then into the kitchen, where the usual tide of grease and stale bread was just winning against more hygienic elements.

"It's very clean," she said, indicating the bedroom. "I mean, compared." Her tone showed a very slight new respect for Tom.

"Well, what do you expect after a term of Liam being in there," Tom said. "I can't take the credit. I thought I'd clean out the kitchen, though. I haven't really done much to it, this term."

He put coffee into mugs.

Sue said, "That's what I like about you. You're always so honest."

Tom was about to consider this, when the bell rang downstairs. Tom said, "Help yourself. It's probably Zoe." He went down the stairs and along the hall. The shadow in the glass didn't look a lot like Zoe.

It was a grey sort of man who looked as though he had a secret sorrow.

"Top flat?" he said. Tom nodded. "I'm the Lodgings Inspector," the man said. "We've had complaints. Can I come up." Even though he was a diminutive figure, this wasn't really a request.

Tom led the way, wondering. On the landing, he stopped and rested his arm on the vacuum cleaner in what he hoped was the manner of an interrupted cleaner.

The man looked into the bedroom, then the living room, then the kitchen. Sue, who looked eminently respectable, smiled at him. He managed half a smile.

"Complaints," the man said, looking past Sue at the rest of the kitchen.

"I'm not surprised," Sue said.

"Terrible, isn't it," Tom said. He stood back. "My room –" he said. The man looked in at the contrast.

"And you're –"

"Tom Rowlands," Tom said.

The man looked down at his clipboard. "Ah. I've heard about you." Sue raised an eyebrow. "It must be terrible, living with this lot," the man said.

Tom nodded. "I've just started to clean it up, now they've gone," he said.

"I wish you luck," the man said. "You can tell them they'll all be getting letters at the beginning of term." He took another look into the kitchen and nodded at Sue and then went down the stairs.

Nobody said anything until the front door had shut. "They'll kill me when they get back," Tom said.

SUMMER TERM

... of important days
Examinations, when man was weighed
As in the balance! of excessive hopes,
Tremblings withal and commendable fears,
Small jealousies, and triumphs good or bad,
I make short mention...
—Wordsworth (The Prelude)

If the careless writer of a novel closes his book without
marrying, or putting to death, or somehow disposing, not only
of his principal personages, but of all who have acted a part
in the drama above the degree of a candle-snuffer, he creates
an unsatisfied want in the minds of his readers... and they
hardly part friends.
—Robert Bage (Hermsprong, or Man as he is Not, 1796)

Chapter Twenty-four
PRE-EXAMS

———————————————●———————————————

In the third term, after an Easter spent catching up on all the work he thought he had done already, the lectures dwindled away and Tom was left with a prospect of two virtually empty weeks before exams came upon him.

"I seem to remember sitting in the library a lot," he said to Liam, who had moved the collapsed bed into the other corner of the living room and who worked there at odd times of the day.

"Doesn't mean a thing," Liam said, unhelpfully. Tom had the impression that Liam had already worked out the answers to all the exam questions.

That was the night that Vince and Cal had returned, amid a great deal of cheerful banging and whooping, and mutterings from the landlord. Tom, rather to his surprise, was very glad to see Vince, whose days on the rubbish tip seemed merely to have consolidated his ape-like mien. But, after that first night, a rather unnerving silence had settled on the first-floor flat.

One lunchtime, Tom was having lasagne with Alf and Zoe in 'The Lion and the Unicorn' and Tom consulted Carlo on the matter.

"I mean," Tom said. "Does Vince have a fearsome father who's put his foot down?"

"Rather difficult to imagine Vince having a father," Zoe said. "Like Grendel having a mother."

Carlo was moved to a smile. "It's called bloody-mindedness," he said. "Everyone expects them to be thrown out, so they're damned if they are going to be thrown out."

Alf looked at the lasagne on his fork. "Something in that," he said. "But I think it might be that Cal's parents live on a council estate in a mining village with no pit and this is his chance to get out of it. And when it comes to the pinch, he's not going to blow it. Simple."

Tom nodded. "What about Vince?"

"He's his mate," Alf said. "They do things together."

Carlo started to clear away their dishes. "If you ask me," he said, "Vince despises the system so much that he's going to beat it with one hand tied behind his back. Even if he had to tie it there himself."

But, most of the time Tom spent in his single room at the small table beside the window that looked out onto the jumble of roofs where the cats fought every now and then. This meant that he didn't have to fight for a desk in the library, which was packed with silence.

He wobbled between highs of great confidence and sloughs of profound alarm as he worked back and forth through his six ring-binders, one for each of his courses, and distilled what seemed to be very little wisdom onto file cards.

The April mornings suddenly seemed high and bright and April sliding into May meant warm winds off the sea and the library windows open. He worked late at night, too, watching the cats, and the sun reluctantly going down, and ignoring the occasional crashes and raised voices from the rest of the flat.

Orris, for whom imminent Final Examinations didn't seem to be a problem, occasionally came round to the flat and dragged Tom out for a drink just before the pubs shut, but usually he didn't go.

"It's a nice life," Tom said, "and I don't want to lose it."

"You won't," Orris said. "Getting here's the difficult bit."

"I don't think I'll risk it," Tom said, and Orris went away.

There was a great trade in lecture notes. Tom lent one

set to the best-looking girl in his seminar group, not with the best of motives, but she merely passed them back with thanks and said she couldn't read most of them.

And then, one late May day, the weather, clearly in league with the University system, turned hot. Tom, perspiring in the small room and wondering how to get the air to move in through the window, began, subversively, to wonder whether a blameless life shifting dustbins or lying on the beach might not be preferable to this; he took a break and went down to Nick's Café to buy a sandwich.

"Hot," Tom said.

"Exam weather," Nick said. "Always like this. It gets stifling during exam fortnight and, the day they end, it'll rain. You see."

There was now an upright piano at the far end of the café, and sheet music pinned all along the walls. Michael was playing, rather softly, and watching the people walking by, brown in the sun.

"Good, isn't he," Tom said. He had no idea whether he was or not but it sounded wonderful.

"Brilliant," Nick said. "I wish he'd smile, though."

Tom considered going down to talk to Michael but he couldn't think of anything to say.

Nick put away some cups under the counter. "I just hope he doesn't go and fail," he said. Tom picked up his cheese sandwich. "I've told him," Nick said. He shook his head.

Tom came out under the new sign ('The Clef Stick') and took his cheese sandwich down to the prom and sat on the railings. The sun was hot and the beach was crowded with holiday makers. The children's paddling pool was open and being splashed in, and the ice-cream and hot-dog vans were open.

Tom sat and chewed and thought what a rather good world it was, outside his head. The sea, he was distracted to notice, actually sparkled. He remembered the expression

from book after book, but here it actually was, as if fragments
of light were breaking away and floating on each wave and
blinking and sinking.

Alf and Zoe came along the wide beach below him,
holding hands. Zoe was eating ice-cream. They stopped and
looked up at him and Tom raised his hand and blessed them,
just in case.

"Great place to be a sociologist," Alf said. "Look at
them. There's the into-the-library-the-moment-it-opens-
and-twitch-a-lot mob, and there's the if-I-don't-know-it-
now-I-never-will mob."

"There's a sub-species," Zoe said, "like Liz. I-haven't-
got-a-chance-but-who-cares."

Tom, sitting on the railings, felt Olympian. "Which one
are you, Alf?"

"I'm the insane but quietly confident type," Alf said.

"It's amazingly quiet in Hall," Zoe said. "How's the
flat?" Alf looked at the sea. Tom looked at the sea. Zoe said,
"I see Vince and Cal are back."

"They're no problem," Tom said. "They seem to be
working like stink. Robbie provides most of the entertainment."

"Liam calls him an emotional switchback," Alf said.

"I think he's a godsend," Tom said. "Light relief." He
brushed cheese from his fingers. "Every now and then
somebody translates all my books into Swahili overnight, so
having Robbie around gives you a sense of proportion." He
thought, but he didn't quite dare say, that what he wanted
most at those times was his late lamented teddy bear, but that
wasn't something you lightly admitted to the likes of Alf.

"Well, he sure as hell hasn't got one," Alf said. "He
spends all the days lying on the beach with Liz and most of
the nights in a blind panic. He's driving Liam mad."

"What about you two?" Zoe said.

"I've got the single room," Tom said, "and Alf'll sleep

through anything." Tom climbed down onto the beach. "Liam's in the living room and Robbie ends up working in the kitchen. He makes himself endless cups of coffee."

They went back to work.

Tom didn't find it odd to be working in this way because all the people who had otherwise been rational and approachable started to become reclusive (except Alf and Zoe).

That evening, Zoe came round to the flat and worked with Alf, and then made coffee.

They stood in the kitchen. It was very quiet.

"Unnerving, isn't it?" Liam said.

"You should worry," she said. "Toby says that in the USA, in the pre-med schools, they tear out pages from library books so that nobody else'll be able to read them."

Robbie said: "What's pre-med?"

Tom said: "Who's Toby?"

Robbie's behaviour became more and more eccentric. Two days before exams began, he woke everyone up by banging his way out of the flat at one in the morning and was apprehended outside the Hall by the combined might of the porter, the warden, and a passing police patrol. The warden, who said she had quite enough to cope with without gratuitous idiots, banned him from the vicinity. The police, who took him home, seemed to think it was funny.

The only people who were apparently enjoying themselves were second-year students, who, by and large, didn't have exams. Tom watched them on the beach and then went back to work, feeling increasingly as though his eyes should be, or could be, propped open by matchsticks.

And then it was the last week before the exams and Tom settled into a routine.

He got up early, before the others had emerged, walked on the beach and threw stones at the sea and then went back to his room. Sometimes he spent an hour or two in the Architecture library and *then* went back to his room.

And, quite often, in the early mornings, he met Sue who would be running. And, quite often, she stopped and told him the news of the Hall.

Zoe walked the corridors late at night, reciting poetry, and Liz muttered strange French oaths in her sleep. People had been known to burst into tears and the warden had held a meeting and warned against drugs – even caffeine tablets – and told awful stories about people working all night and then going to sleep in the middle of exams.

"How about you?" Tom said.

"I'm not worried," Sue said. She looked healthy and untroubled by the world of mortals, Tom thought. Most unfair. "Really," she said. "I'm pretty sure I know it and I usually do well in exams. I can't see the point of panicking." She flipped a stone at the sea. It hopped down the pebbles and splashed into the edge of the water. "You?"

"Oh, that's easy," Tom said, half wishing that he'd bought a tracksuit and then thinking that he'd probably just make a fool of himself beside Sue. Orris was an awful example. "I'm not too bright," he said. "So I just play exactly by the rules. If they say do that, I do that, and I generally pass. So I'm just grinding it all in." The sea sloughed against the stones, warmly.

Sue smiled at him. "There you go, honest again. See you tomorrow morning?"

"Might do," Tom said. "It's my first exam."

"Break a leg," Sue said. She unsquatted, and, with slim, or thin, brown legs, climbed up the dipped steps and ran off along the prom. Tom watched her out of sight and into sight, and, to his surprise, when she reached the bandstand, she turned and jogged backwards, and waved.

Chapter Twenty-five
EXAMS

As it so happened, Tom didn't see her the next morning.

He had got up early and had read, in bed, a quantity of totally incomprehensible notes. Timing himself carefully, he went out into the kitchen. Liam was standing there, holding a saucepan.

"I'll kill him," Liam said. "I will, so help me. No jury would convict."

Tom looked into the pan. "I don't know how he does that with scrambled eggs."

Liam shook his head. "Not Alf. I don't mean Alf. Alf's all right."

"You've been overworking," Tom said, filling the kettle.

"No," Liam said. "He's anarchic and smelly and that blanket he sleeps in should be painlessly destroyed, and he's got the wrong politics and he makes a foul mess when he scrambles eggs. But beside Robbie, he's a saint."

"Lie down and tell Uncle Tom," Tom said.

Liam took a pace up the kitchen and down the kitchen, and went on with the air of someone who has survived a particularly harrowing experience.

"Well, first he decides that he's going to stay up all night. Then at 1 a.m. he decides to play darts with himself against the back of the living room door. So I get up and address a few civil words to him, and he bursts into tears and starts to tell me about the blasted Liz for about the ten millionth time."

"What about Liz?"

"You don't want to know. She's packed him in again."

"Oh, nothing new," said Tom. He spread some Hall butter on a slice of Hall bread.

"So then he decides he's going to bed and after about ten minutes, just when I'm dozing off, he has a nightmare or something and starts shouting that he'll never be able to do it and he'll have to work at the Town Hall."

"Hardly surprising if you look at his tan."

"Then he gets up and goes into the kitchen and by the sound of it smashes up all the crockery and dismantles the cupboards. Didn't you hear any of this?"

"No," Tom said.

Liam looked at him murderously. "Then I just get to sleep, and he wakes me up to tell me he's going to fail and how Liz doesn't love him and how he'll fail and never see her again."

"Probably the best way of seeing her again," Tom said. "I shouldn't think she'll pass either."

"Look," Liam said. "This was three in the morning. He wasn't very coherent. Anyway, he's raving on, and you can tell what it was like because Alf got up." Liam seemed to feel better at the thought. "He came into the living room and he told Robbie, in what I have to say was very concise language, just what he'd do to him if he got woken up again. So Robbie went to bed, and about thirty seconds later, Alf gets up and starts smashing eggs and whistling." Tom poured Liam a coffee in his private mug. "I've got as much chance of passing this exam —"

"Where's Robbie now, then?" Tom said,.

"You must be deaf," Liam said. "Didn't you hear him just now, singing in the bath? He's decided that he's going to get a first class degree and Liz loves him after all." Liam morosely took down his personal packet of cornflakes, poured some into a bowl and added milk from his private bottle. "Honestly, I'm catatonic. Whatever possessed me to get into this shambles, I'll never know."

"Don't take on," Tom said.

"I'll be one of those pathetic ones who sit there just copying the question out over and over again for three hours."

"We'll make it," Tom said. "Just imagine if you were Vince."

Liam thought, and drank his coffee, and shook himself. "OK," he said. "Beside that feat of imagination, any exam would be easy."

By far the worst bit of exams was waiting outside the exam room for them to begin.

All over the University, any sizable room had been laid out for exams and Sue, despite her stoicism, was juggling descriptions and categories in her head as she walked down to the University with Annie.

They stood outside the laboratories, which had also been laid out as examination rooms, talking, for some reason, in muted voices. Lecturers came and went and walked into the exam rooms, being cheerful and encouraging. Nobody looked cheered or encouraged by any of this.

On the second day, a girl fainted, and on the third, another girl arrived having been knocked off her bike on the way to the exam room.

Annie, who had no intention of failing anything, looked on dispassionately.

"The percentage fail rate," she said, "is under four percent. You look at the number of obvious wrecks around here, and you can't see why you should worry."

"I think it's barbaric," Sue said. "It's like the old mill towns. All those women hunched up over the looms, and overseers walking around with whips."

But it was Zoe who had the most interesting things to report. Many of the first year exams were bunched together into the Assembly Hall, a rather pastel-atmosphered vault in the Old College Building. There were the same small groups of worried students, some smoking and talking mutedly, with the occasional lecturer stalking between them. A few people were still reading their notes, their lips moving.

The porter ordered them in and they left their books and coats and bags at the back of the hall and some sat down and then got up again to get their pens.

The exam papers were on the desks and the students sat and read them and filled in their registration slips, and panicked because they couldn't remember their University number, or the date, or their name.

The invigilator intoned the rules and looked at the clock and said, "You may now begin," as if there was a choice.

Zoe, sitting in Nick's Café, drinking a milk-shake, and reporting all this, said:

"And then we all started writing and about twenty minutes after we started, in come Vince and Cal. They got very coldly directed to their seats and then about half an hour later, the invigilator shouted, 'Put that cigarette out!' You might have guessed. And then, about an hour after we started, Liz got up and walked out."

"I still think it's barbaric," Sue said.

"Did she say anything?" Annie said.

"She said she'd written everything she could think of," Sue said.

"I still think it's daft to walk out," Zoe said. "You might think of something afterwards."

"Toby says it's barbaric, too," Sue said.

After three days, the tension was so heavy in Hall that she went round to Toby and Penny's. The atmosphere there was as calm as ever, and Sue sat on the window seat and read for an hour. Toby came in and painted, looking out of the window, and transferring the delicate blue of the sky onto a delicate canvas. Down on the beach, there were summer visitors and second-year students and others. For once, there was no sign of Liz or Robbie. The Yoga-sitter came in and played the guitar for a while, and Sue decided that she needed some tension, after all, and went back to Hall.

Liz was lying on the bed with her eyes shut.

"I hear you walked out again," Sue said.

"It's ᴏᴋ," Liz said without opening her eyes. "I'm allowed to fail two of them. I'll re-sit in September."

"So you're going to pass the others?" Sue said.

"Sure," Liz said, "no problem." She opened her eyes and, for the first time that Sue could remember, actually looked worried. "I think."

Chapter Twenty-six
POST-EXAMS

It was hot. Sue looked at her pale toes and wondered where the weather had been for the last six weeks.

The last time she remembered looking it had been cold, and now it was just June, and the sky was bright and translucent, and the sea had fluffy waves and it was all really rather remarkable. She sat on the beach, with her back against the promenade steps, and let the wind blow into her hair. The sea. She closed her eyes and opened them. Tom was coming down the steps. He saw her and hesitated, and smiled, and sat down beside her.

"Hi."

"Hi," said Sue. "Have you finished?"

"Half an hour ago," Tom said. "We all had plans to meet in the pub and have a great celebration, but somehow everyone's drifted away. I thought I'd have a walk before I go to bed. Do you mind?"

"It's a free beach," Sue said. She stopped and said, rather quickly for her, "No, I didn't mean it that way."

Tom sat down. "Still working?" He indicated the pad on her knee.

"No. I'm just writing to my sister. I haven't for ages."

"Any progress? Zoe told me about her."

"Pretty good," Sue said. She looked out at the sea. "She's finished her traction, and they're doing the final tests and then she should be all right again. But it's been nine months, poor thing. Makes me feel guilty being here."

Tom nodded. "When are you going home?"

"I don't know," Sue said. "I suppose I could stay until

the results come out, but that's nearly a fortnight. I should really get home and see Jo. My sister."

"Bit awkward, isn't it," Tom said. "They keep telling us to get on with next year's work, but there doesn't seem to be a lot of point until I know whether I've passed."

"You've passed," Sue said.

"So have you. Get on with it, then." Tom smiled at her. "How about the rest of you?"

"I don't know. We're not often in the same exam room, so our paths don't cross. Robbie seems to be in a bad way."

Sue nodded. "And Liz. She walked out of some exams early. She says she doesn't care."

Tom pursed his lips.

"Amazing, isn't it. My brain's still running. Must be on overload. I'll leave you to your letter."

Sue nearly said, "Don't go," and Tom said, "I'll see you before you go," and Sue said, "Probably," and Tom went up the steps.

Sue took her pen from the spine of the pad and looked at it.

She wrote, 'Dear Jojo,' and then held the pen between her fingers and looked out at the calm sea, frowning.

Dear Jojo,

Well, sprightly sis, this is last letter of the term, because I'll probably be home the day after tomorrow. I'm just recovering from the exams. I really can't remember anything much about them, except that I answered the requisite number of questions and I only went totally blank once.

We didn't have much drama, either, except Liz. She walked out of at least two exams. One bloke actually did go to sleep in the exam, just in front of me. Had his head down on the desk, writing, one minute, and then I looked up and he was obviously asleep. The girl across the aisle put her hand up and the invigilators came, and eventually they had to virtually carry him out. And a few people left early. I can't understand that. I mean, surely sitting there writing something is better than not being there at all.

The best bit was when one student asked the invigilators to stop chatting. Toby does some invigilating, and he says it's the most tedious thing you can do. They walk around having competitions to see who they think is the best-looking girl (they're mostly MCPS), and things like that.

(But Annie said that I've got to stress that 96% of people pass and 99.9% don't go to sleep or break down and blow up, So As Not To Be Discouraging For When You Go. Anyway, all the work you've done this year, it should be a doddle.)

Sue looked along the promenade, and at the pebbles and the sea and the sun and the sky. She wrote:

But it's been a fantastic year. The only thing that hasn't happened (sorry) is being carried off on a white horse by some prince charming (OK, if you prefer, that I haven't carried off a prince charming). They're mostly OK, but nothing to my taste, my dear.

Sue looked at her pen, and then looked out to sea and then, with her head on one side, looked up the steps to the promenade, very thoughtfully.

Chapter Twenty-seven
BEGINNINGS

The next day, it was even hotter, with a warm wind blowing off the sea and Tom, after sleeping for sixteen hours, woke up late in the morning feeling that there was nothing but freedom around and that life had begun again.

Orris, who had never slept for more than six hours in his life, (his mother, he informed Tom, had never much liked him, as a result) had finished his final Final Exam the evening before, and had been swimming for most of the morning. They walked on the promenade, looking at the sea, and Orris took him into 'The Red Lion' because when the back and the front doors were open, as they were, you could sit at the bar and eat egg and chips and drink cider and look down at the sea and people on the promenade.

Some of the students had already gone home, either to get jobs or to get back to their girl/boyfriends, but the rest seemed to be caught in a timeless inertia. Everybody was supposed to be working, anyway.

Orris played himself at darts and the warm air moved softly and sweetly around the bar. There was a half-tyre around the fluffed-out dartboard, and a black rubber mat with worn-off distances and chalk dust and beer smells.

Tom sat and ate and drank and looked and felt quite contented and quite directionless and thought how fine it all was.

In the afternoon, they took a random book each from Orris's curious bookshelf and went up through the woods at the back of his house to the cliff and lay and read them. The short grass with the occasional tall strands was close to Tom's

eyes and out to sea there were sails. And it seemed to Tom
that he had never read better and happier books and there
could scarcely be a better and nicer world. Even Orris, not
noted for being elevated by things of the spirit, was reading
Chesterton, propped up in the lee of a wall, and visibly
turning browner and blonder. The warmth of the world
seemed to come up out of the ground. Tom stood up and
looked inland; miles of wonderful country.

"I'm feeling guilty again," Tom said. "All that poverty
and misery and grot all over the world and here we are." He
waved a hand to indicate what they were.

"Trust you," Orris said, not looking up. "What a waste
of time. Look, if I feel guilty, I don't enjoy this, and if I don't
enjoy it, then even the nice things in life become miserable
and that's insane."

They drifted down into the early evening town where
the streets were more or less emptied and somehow tentative,
with newspapers in the gutters and dustiness in the air. The
shops were closing and it was as if the air and the people had
both thinned out together.

It seemed a great waste to go inside at all and so they
nibbled away at a cider here and some chips there, sitting in
pub doorways and on benches under the full trees, and they
sat by the beach and ate candyfloss and the translucent light
changed and paled into greens and yellows and pinks and
other unlikely colours. At one point they took on the locals in
'The Red Lion' at darts and beat them three times in a row.

"It's Zen," said Orris. "You let the hand and the eye do
the work and leave the mind out of it."

Tom found that he was doing that quite naturally, while
Orris, as usual, was doing the opposite of his own advice and
playing fiercely, putting all his compact weight behind the
darts so that they had to be prised out of the board.

After the third game, they decided that they were getting
a bit too good for their popularity rating with the locals, and

so they lost gracefully. The consumable air was still drifting in and out of the bar and they decided that a hill would be a good thing to climb, and they walked onto the pavement and met Sue, who was looking rather less than her usual composed self.

"Have you seen Liz?"

They shook their heads.

"What's happened?" Tom said.

"She's had one of her glooms," Sue said, "and she's gone off. Robbie's been more nasty than usual, apparently, and she upped and went."

"Hasn't she done that before?" Tom said.

"She just looked very odd," Sue said.

"We could get the car and drive round and look for her," Tom said.

"I'm not driving anywhere with you," Orris said. "You're awash with cider." In the half-dark, Tom could only see the blur of his fair hair, and then his white teeth.

"No need," Sue said. "I'll find her, I should think."

They turned onto the main street and walked into Liz, who was shambling along in a rather striking imitation of Mary. Tom thought, surely nobody can be sad on a night like this. Aren't people stupid?

He said: "Look, why don't we go somewhere, anyway. A drive might cheer you up. It's a great night for driving." He paused. "Can you drive? Anybody?"

"I can," Sue said.

They walked round to the car and Tom slid the window down and unlocked the doors. Liz silently got into the back with a very cheerful Orris.

"Don't know what sort of therapist he'll be," Tom said quietly over the roof to Sue. Sue sat and adjusted the driver's seat and Tom slid into the passenger seat and reached across her to switch on the light switch, feeling very conscious of her brown legs.

The engine, just to be perverse, Tom thought, started at once, and Sue let the clutch in and eased the car out from between the parked cars.

"It's obviously taken to you," Tom said, thinking that she was a better driver than he was.

They drove up out of the town and onto the top of the cliffs, heading west. After a mile or so, at the first crossroads, she slowed the car.

"Shall we go down to the little beach?"

"Remember last time?"

"Not likely to forget. Poor Mary."

The road narrowed under the coppices and the moon came out from the high cloud and Sue steered firmly down the bends. Tom looked into the back. Liz was sitting as far from Orris as she could and Orris was slumped cheerfully in the corner. He grinned and raised a hand.

The lane came out onto the shingle bar, with the stream running under the wooden footbridge and spreading out onto the sand. Tom, despite the silence in the back, felt marvellous. The air was still quite intoxicating.

Sue swung the car round, turned off the lights and the engine, and pulled on the handbrake. The silence fell over them and they sat silently for a moment. The sky shaded down in layers of blue to the dark sea and the line of the horizon. Then they got out and Liz stalked away across the beach and Orris, circumscribing small circles and hopping like a demented gnome, followed her.

Tom leaned on the top of the passenger door and looked over at Sue.

"Is it the sand you can smell or the grass?"

"The sea, I think," Sue said. "I can't believe that this is the same planet as last term."

"It isn't," Tom said. "We're on the other side of exams." He breathed in. "Makes you feel like hugging it, doesn't it."

Sue nodded and then said, "Yes," in case he couldn't see

her. There was a sweep of beach and dark sea and an incredible sky. Something was sawing thinly in the grass.

"Have you heard anything from Mary?" Tom said.

"No," Sue said. "I don't think I expect to. The chaplain called in to see her, he was up that way, but nobody answered the door."

"Only time I've ever seen Alf really shocked," Tom said. "Poor Mary."

"It's been pretty good, though," Sue said. "I mean, the year, for things like that. You hear about all these disasters, but that's the only person we know –"

The end of her sentence was covered by a scream from along the beach and Tom was so quick off the mark that he was twenty metres down the sand before Sue caught him up.

There was a lot of undifferentiated splashing and squealing and, out of the sea in the moonlight, rose Orris with Liz in his arms. He took two steps and disappeared in a huge splash and in among the squeals, there was, definitely, laughter. Then there was more swashing and Liz staggered to her feet with Orris in her arms. She took three steps and dumped him in the shallows.

"Who is this wonder-man who can make Liz laugh?" Sue said.

Orris sprinted out of the sea, slopping and splashing water around him, and grabbed two sticks of driftwood from the high-tide line and threw one to Tom and, by the simple process of attempting to beat him around the head, forced him into a lunatic stick fight up and over the bridge and through the stream. Tom finally ran out of breath from having to really defend himself, and prostrated himself on the driest bit of sand he could see in the moonlight, and Orris put a foot on his chest.

"And now, my lord, may I have the hand of your daughter."

"Don't you want the rest?"

"Nope. I'm kinky for hands."

Then Liz and Orris were stomping in the shallows, and
Sue came and sat next to Tom.

"That's amazing."

"He has curious effects on people," Tom said,
guardedly.

"Still, he cares, doesn't he," Sue said. Tom hadn't
considered that. Orris, he would have said, cared primarily
for Orris but he didn't say it. Sue said, "You do, too."

Tom said, after a faintly delirious moment, "Well,
thanks."

Sue said, "Isn't this amazing," and Tom turned his head
and her face was very close, really, and it was very easy just to
move his chin forward slightly and Sue moved slightly
towards him and their lips brushed each other. Sue rested her
hand on his on the sand, and, despite the splashing of Orris
and Liz's laughter and the swash of the sea, the night seemed
to go very quiet.

Sue sat on the window seat of her room, looking down at the
lights, floating over the sea in little oily puddles. And she
wrote:

Dearest Jojo,

It's midnight, and I just thought I'd mention it, because
something's happened that you want to stay up till midnight
to tell somebody about.

OK, you guessed. I forgot my white horse, but otherwise,
is good. It's so magical out there with the dark sky and the
sea and it's all warm. Remember saying that going to
university was like fantasy? Well, here it is, and it turns out
to be Tom, who's been around all the time, plugging away in
the background. Nothing looks really real. I don't feel like
going to bed at all, just wandering around. I feel like one of
those Romances we used to read, where the heroine was
suddenly aware of the breeze in the trees and the bright

faces of the flowers turning up to the sun and all that kind of garbage. Well, I'm aware of the fact that I'm very tired and very nice and loved, but it comes to much the same thing so I think I'll sit up a bit longer.

Tom slid his key into the lock of number 21 and took it out again. He didn't feel like going to bed, and it didn't even feel much like night. It was warm and half-dark and there was lovely air flowing down the street. He turned and walked back down towards the promenade.

Liz and Orris had been dropped off at Orris's house, still soaking wet and giggling at each other. There had been occasional silences in the back, but Tom hadn't looked round. In fact he hadn't looked anywhere much except at the road blurring away under the headlights, not wanting to stare at Sue's profile which was a really nice profile.

And then Sue had parked the car in the dark street behind the Hall and there'd been a very nice five minutes in the darkness, under the roof of the car, which seemed, inexplicably, to have got lower, and then Sue had gone in and he'd walked back, swinging round lamp-posts and rather hoping that he'd be stopped by a policemen so that he could tell him how nice the world was.

He went down onto the beach and discovered a kind of undulating silence and he could hear the plop of the stones he threw, but he couldn't see where they landed. The occasional car moving around back in the town sounded rather raw.

He walked along past the Hall of Residence. There were still some lights on, perhaps Sue's, and he stopped and leaned on the railings and looked up at them. But he didn't feel like causing disturbances, although, for the first time, he had an idea of how Robbie felt. That thought led to wondering what Robbie would say if he knew where Liz was, and then as to what Liz was doing. Eating scrambled eggs, possibly.

In the moonlight, it was easy to pick a way up the side of the hill and he walked up the short grass, just feeling the world. He looked down on the chaotic roofscape of the Hall, very black-shadowed, and thought, for some reason, of the fine hair at the back of Sue's neck. He walked and sat and walked, and contemplated climbing down the cliff but decided that this was a particularly good time to stay alive, if at all possible. After all, if he fell off and his body was washed up on the beach, nobody would know what a *happy* body it was.

The early dawn changed the colour of the sky, and Tom worked his way down into the woods, with their deep shadows, and past the back of Orris's house and along a path that followed the back of the terrace and into the town. He walked slowly down to the cattle market and the very first sun was lifting a mist between the empty metal cattle-pens. But the greatest café in the universe was open for business.

He sat in a corner seat and ate mushrooms and burnt bacon and drank tea and then ate toast and marmalade and drank more tea, and read a copy of the tabloid paper that was lying on the counter. He spent quite a long, reflective time looking at the undressed lady of the day and wondering whether she was of the same species as the girl he'd kissed in the car. It didn't seem very possible.

By the time he'd finished eating, he had the faint feeling that his chin was being held to his ears by invisible straps. But thinking about everything, everything felt good, if a little grey. Tom looked at the streaky wet glass, and thought: Susan Annette Marriot; very distinguished. In fact, she was downright terrifying. For a moment, he could only think, I'm panic-stricken. Obviously she'd mistaken him for somebody else and what would he do when she found out? And what would he do with her anyway? What was he expected to do?

But things must be different, he thought, because that doesn't seem to matter too much. I can just panic at quiet moments when nobody's looking and make the most of it until she *does* find out.

He pushed the plate away and walked back through the town and let himself in to the flat, slipping quietly up the stairs past the sleeping bedroom and sending out a bit of ethereal love to the brown limbs and Sue who lived in them, in the grey morning.

Chapter Twenty-eight
IDYLLS AND OTHERS

●

Tom woke up towards midday, terrified that he'd dreamed it all, but it didn't quite feel like that, and so he still washed and dressed very carefully and then walked very circumspectly down to Hall, expecting the worst possible things. He stopped and looked at ordinary shops and houses and pavements and the sea, all the way, just so as he didn't think too much about where he was going.

Zoe and Alf passed him on the opposite pavement and went into a extravagant routine of cheering and dancing, and when he came in sight of the end of the prom, Sue was not only standing waiting for him, but actually walked and then ran a few steps to meet him.

And so they decided to stay on for the ten days until the exam results came out.

Over the next few days, Tom started to use his sunglasses merely to shield his eyes from the sun. Previously, he'd used them largely because there were so many girls around with so few clothes on, that he found it less embarrassing to stare at them through blanked eyes.

"Do you mind if I stare at you?" Tom said to Sue, after thinking about it for a while. "I don't mean stare, exactly. I mean, you're...I mean, I give up." He gave up.

"Bit strange if you didn't," Sue said.

The days began to take on new patterns. Tom would call at the Hall and they'd go swimming or walking. Sometimes, rather to Tom's chagrin, Sue seemed just as pleased to go to play tennis with Annie, or to have tea with her tutor, and he had to stop himself saying anything.

Robbie wasn't helpful. "They're all the same," he said, causing Tom to wish that the tide had been in that time when Robbie'd jumped off the prom. "Don't think you've got her sole attention. And don't you dare complain or she'll think you're wingeing."

Tom found, reluctantly, enough truth in this to make him pause. Fortunately, Zoe came by while he was sitting waiting for Sue in the bandstand when there was a warm, misty rain drifting in from the sea.

"Good, is it?" Zoe said.

"Incredible," Tom said.

Zoe looked at him. "Can I give you a bit of advice, out of my superior wisdom?"

"Anything," Tom said. It was easy to be honest with Zoe. "I'm way out of my depth."

Zoe smiled. "Don't be greedy, then," she said. "Sue's probably just as scared as you are, and she's got a lot going for her and she doesn't want to lose any of it. So don't crowd her and don't take it too seriously."

"Is that all?" Tom said.

"I might as well talk to the bandstand," Zoe said. She patted him on the head. "Just remember that she's real." She walked off along the wet paving stones, and Tom, watching her, felt even more out of his depth than before.

But he tried, very hard.

He and Sue sat on the hills a lot, and drove to quiet beaches, and found out things about each other, like the fact that Tom missed his grandfather and Sue's grandfather had carried his pillow with him all through the war. Or that Tom had once broken his wrist by falling from a haystack and hitting it on a cart-shaft, or that Sue had once broken her thumb by falling on the pavement outside her primary school, and now one thumb was bigger than the other (oddly, the one that had been broken).

One Thursday, when the car had decided to boil in an unpicturesque side-road, they had sat on a gate, looking over a wheatfield, and talked and talked about anything at all. Houses, homes, mothers and fathers and aunts. Working for farmers, going to Israel. And next year Sue and Zoe, and perhaps Liz if she got back, would take a flat together, with a room to put Sue's computer in.

"I met the chaplain the other day," Sue said. "He'd had a very peculiar rude mind-your-own business letter from Mary's father."

"So he must have been hiding behind the curtains."

"Mary's having treatment. She won't be coming back."

"Is there any treatment for a father like that?"

And Sue talked about Toby and Penny and the sanctuary from all the madness, and Tom nodded and smiled and said that it sounded marvellous, all the time feeling hideously jealous. Only the dark and green trees around the cornfield forced him to be reasonable.

They filled up the radiator a little too soon, despite all the talk, and there was a deep gurgle and hot rusty water shot upwards. So they talked some more, about what they were going to do in the summer. Sue was planning a trip to Italy, and maybe Greece, with Zoe. Tom's stomach sank, despite another major attempt at being rational.

"What're you going to do?"

"Back to the shop, I suppose. Earn some loot. Bit of harvesting."

Sue looked at the cornfield. "Sounds nice."

"Well, that depends. When you've done a field, all the rabbits gradually get forced into the centre and the farmers have shotguns on the tractors and the combines and when the rabbits break out –" He stopped.

Sue looked at him. "Do you shoot them?"

"Well, they generally let me have a gun. Absolutely illegal, but they don't see it that way. It's not particularly for fun. Rabbits are just vermin you can eat and there's none of this nonsense about giving them a fair chance." He looked back to where the car was steaming gently under the arch of trees in the gateway. "I did shoot one once. Pure fluke." He remembered it in his mind. The flat report and the slight punch on the shoulder. "Horrible really. After that I always aimed to miss. Mind you, with me that's probably more of a risk for the rabbits." He looked over the field. "Tell the truth, I was always slightly worried in case the gun burst. And the son of the farmer always used to carry his gun as if he were John Wayne, swinging it. Very stupid."

There was a pause. Sue put her hand on Tom's on the gate. After a while she said, "Have you seen Robbie lately?"

"Only a couple of times," Tom said. "Our paths don't seem to cross much these days."

"He's made it up with Liz," Sue said. "I don't understand them. Do you?" Tom, who didn't understand himself, shook his head. Sue said: "I wonder what happened that night with Orris?"

"Better not to ask," Tom said.

They looked at the empty cornfield.

"Looks empty, doesn't it," Tom said, thinking of rabbits.

"It's not," Sue said. "I could spend a lifetime telling you what's in there."

Tom started to say, "ok, then," but thought better of it. The temptation to just hang on to her was terribly strong. He wondered whether he'd ever get over being frightened of her. He took a big risk and put his arm round her, and, after a fraction of hesitation, Sue relaxed up to him. This didn't help Tom a great deal, but at least her hair was against his face.

Sue sat up. "We're in great danger of getting sloppy," she said.

Tom was slightly offended. "You mean it isn't romantic?"

Sue said, "You know, I think we read too many books." They slid off the gate and walked along the headlands beside the corn. "I always get embarrassed reading about people – well, you know –"

"But this is real," Tom said.

"Isn't it just," Sue said, and kissed him.

They reached the corner of the field and turned back.

"Books do that to you," Tom said. "I mean, it's the end of the year, so I keep expecting everything to end neatly. As if having terms means that you divide life up like a book, into sections, and sections have endings and endings are usually happy."

"I know what you mean," said Sue. "It's like wanting to get all the loose ends tied up before we leave."

Tom thought for a moment about what might be happening to Karen, for example.

"But it's all so untidy," Sue said.

"I wonder what happened to A. B.," Tom said aloud.

"Who's A. B?"

Tom explained about A. B., editing out his own connivance at some of the meannesses.

Sue said, "You don't then."

"Don't what?"

"Wonder what happened to him." They refilled the radiator and drove slowly back towards the town. On the way, they debated ideas such as that all world leaders should discuss defence and armaments stark naked to put the discussions in their right perspective, and by the time they came over the hill and looked down on the sea, even the rest of the world (which was on the whole misguided and unlucky) seemed to have possibilities.

They stopped in the layby at the top of the hill.

"Sure this isn't sloppy?" Tom said.

"What?" Sue said.

"Well," Tom said. "It's the sort of stuff you get in the sort of books my granny reads."

"No it isn't," Sue said. "I don't think you've got eyes like passionate coals or whatever it is. They're just nice sensible eyes."

"Oh," Tom said, "OK."

One afternoon, when it was raining, they called at number 21 to pick up Tom's squash kit. Robbie was sitting at the dining table, writing.

"Hate to tell you, but it's all over," Sue said. "You can stop writing now. Finish the sentence."

"Doing my accounts," Robbie said. "I'm trying to convince my father that my overdraft is due entirely to spending on books and file-cards."

"How're you doing?"

"You write fiction for the paper," Robbie said. "You have a go."

Tom picked up his holdall and the hardly-used racket, and they drove across the town to the old Union squash courts. Apart from the fact that the wiper-rubbers had nearly perished away, the car seemed intent on showing off.

As there was nobody in the white corridor, they kissed each other and Tom went into the changing room and tried to make himself look as athletic as possible, although the mirror was rather discouraging.

He came up the sweaty stairway to the echoing observation balcony, and watched the two games, one each side of the wall. In one court, two men; in the other, two women. They all seemed intent on hitting the ball as hard and straight and repetitively as possible. And they all looked sweaty and unattractive.

Sue came up the steps. She looked exceedingly neat with exceedingly long legs. She looked over at the men.

"Rotten, aren't they?"

"You ain't seen nothing yet."

She put her brown arm over Tom's shoulders, and they waited until the half-hour and the change-over time, and then went downstairs and rapped on the door with Tom's racket handle. The girls came out and they went into a curious space where their legs seemed to have got shorter until they moved them.

The game was distinguished by a lot of laughing and by

the remarkable feat by Tom of getting the ball out through the grid over the extractor fan, which led to the unusual sight of two people in squash kit searching in the rain on the lawns outside for a squash ball.

"Any fool can get them stuck on the beams."

"Nuts, really."

Tom found that he was playing squash like Orris – as if it were snooker. Sue, who might normally have been irritated, was so intrigued by the difference of the game, that she forgot to try to win so much and they kept forgetting the score.

After the game, they went into the snack bar, famous for its variegated soup, and drank a curious orange substance, which had the advantage of being cold.

"It says 'Orange' on the bottle," the snack bar lady said, rather defensively.

Orris came in carrying his squash racket. He nodded rather absently at Sue and bought a glass of orange liquid, and tasted it, and left it on the bar. The snack bar lady looked at him suspiciously.

"Anything wrong with it?"

Orris picked it up again. "No, no. Fine." He sipped the liquid. The snack bar lady went behind her screen.

There was a silence. Orris was trying, obviously, to be nonchalant.

Tom said, "Waiting for someone?"

Orris said, "Well, you know," and that seemed to be about that.

But when they were getting into the car, outside in the small car-park (which had a collapsed collapsible pole as a barrier), Trish walked past, and nodded and went into the sports hall.

Tom smiled to himself and they drove away, passing Penny walking along the tree-lined street carrying a holdall. Sue waved and Tom said, "Who's that?"

*   *   *   *

The day before the exam results came out, Zoe called in at the flat.

The kitchen window was open (that is, it was, once open, impossible to shut) onto a bright and warm wafting day.

Tom was wrapping small aluminium-foil parcels.

"A picnic."

Tom nodded. This was an Orris-style picnic, as impressive as possible, although there wasn't much money left, and Tom didn't think that his father would be as gullible as Robbie's seemed to be.

There was cold roast-beef which, on Orris's advice, had been cooked for most of the night, and an iceberg lettuce and mustard and some mineral water and apples and white Stilton and brown buns. Zoe looked on approvingly.

"I think she likes you anyway," she said.

"Amazing, isn't it," Tom said. "Do you understand it?"

Zoe shook her head. "Beats me."

"How am I doing?" Tom said.

Zoe tapped his shoulder. "Just great. Keep at it."

Tom said, "Alf's not around."

"I know," Zoe said. "I just popped in to say goodbye."

"Where are you going?" said Tom, surprised. "Results come out tomorrow."

Zoe said: "If I haven't passed, then I can't pass. Simple as that."

"I feel just the same," Tom said. "What're you doing for the summer?"

"I'm lifeguarding at a pool at home. Alf's staying on here to barkeep for Carlo; he fixed it up today. And Sue and I are probably going to Italy later. Maybe as far as Greece. You know?"

Tom's stomach rolled over again at the thought of Sue going away anywhere. He folded the foil and looked up. Zoe had gone, but she came back into the kitchen, carrying his dictionary.

"Just thought I'd check the state of mind.

> *Fair tresses men's imperial race ensnare*
> *And beauty draws us with a single hair.*

I know that. Pope, OK. What's this:

> *As a perfume doth remain/in the folds where it hath*
> *lain/so the thought of you remaining/deeply folded in my*
> *brain/will not leave me: all things leave me/you remain.*

Who's A. Symons? You're going soggy, Tom. And this one:
bit sexist, isn't it."
    "I think it's beautiful."

> *"She is all states and all Princes I;*
> *Nothing else is.*

It's that MCP Donne, again, isn't it. Still he was nice to Mrs
Donne." Zoe left the book on the shelf beside the door. "Have
a good summer."
    "Thanks."
    Tom watched her go down the stairs, and then packed all
his perfect picnic into carrier bags with expensive logos on
them, and took them out to the car.
    It stood on the slope, glowing in the sun. Objectively, he
thought, this is not much of a car. But at least it doesn't
pretend to be the thing it is not. There's no go-faster stripes
on it, and it's not boy-racer or spoiled boy-racer, or any of
that. And the plugs are clean.
    He drove along the promenade with all the windows
open. Sue was waiting on the Hall steps in the sun, looking
rather worried about something.
    Tom swung the Ford neatly round in the turning circle,
and, as far as the car was capable of it, swept up to the door.
He leaned across and opened the passenger door and Sue got
in.
    Tom, whose sensitivity to doom would, he decided, have

detected a small nuclear leak in Afghanistan, decided to ignore the obvious in the hope that it would go away.

"Hi. Where shall we go?"

Sue looked through the windscreen

"How about the station?"

Tom panicked again and had to laboriously reason out that Sue didn't have a bag with her, so she couldn't be leaving.

"The station?"

Sue looked at him with some sympathy.

"Actually, it's Jo." She kept looking at him for a reaction. "She rang up this morning to say she'd be arriving on the 12.32. It's a surprise."

"Right," Tom said.

"You're supposed to say, 'Good.'"

"Good," Tom said.

Sue put her hand on the dashboard, and then transferred it to Tom's shoulder, and then leaned across and kissed him. "I know it's a bit of a bore," she said, almost apologetically, and the apologetic tone seemed to seep away, "but it's great. No more hospital, no more traction – you will like her, won't you?" Tom made a heroic effort, thinking, nothing to it. Good old Zoe.

"You're miffed, aren't you?" Sue said.

Tom let the clutch in, and drove along the prom, thinking, well, of course, the answer is 'No,' and the truth is I've gone to all this trouble making a picnic and we were going to go and sit somewhere very private and eat and things and now the blasted sister has turned up.

He said, "No, of course not," and a very clear picture of his mother and father standing at the top of the stairs out of the shop, shouting at each other, came into his mind, and he said, because Sue was still looking at him, "I mean yes. I mean. I was planning" (and to his relief, he began to find it funny in the middle of speaking) "wicked things on a beach, and I want you all to myself, so of course I'm miffed."

Sue looked relieved. "Good," she said. "I am a bit, but you'll have to share her. Love me, love my sister." Tom opened his mouth and Sue put her hand over it and said, "That's a figure of speech."

And so they turned into the station forecourt and Tom found a parking space straight away, for a miracle, and they went through between the bookstall and the ticket office and the plastic buffet and stood on the wide platform. Tom began to feel left out before Jo arrived.

The train slid into the platform, and Tom stepped back a pace to let Sue meet Jo, and then stepped back even more to let her have even more room.

Jo turned out to be a darker and smaller and generally bouncier version of Sue, which Tom found continually distracting; and she didn't limp. She fixed him with a devastatingly analytic eye, which Tom worried about because it might be catching among sisters, and he confined himself to monosyllables, partly to be on the safe side and partly because he was too terrified to try sentences.

They came out of the station. There was a parking ticket on the windscreen and leaning over and looking at it with great interest were Vince and Cal. Tom closed his eyes. This is not how to make a good impression about university life.

"Welah," Cal said. "Sorry about this. I tried to chat up the traffic warden, but it didn't work." He looked at Jojo. "We were just leaving. Mind, I could think of staying."

"Have a nice vac," Tom, said, trying not to grit his teeth.

Vince grinned at him and shambled into the station. Cal bowed and followed.

"Friends of yours?" Jo said, sweetly.

Tom drove them back to the Hall, ignoring as far as he could Jo's comments from the back about real cars, and went and sat on the beach for a couple of hours, or days, while they did whatever sisters did.

The only people he knew on the beach would have to be

Robbie and Liz who were chasing each other in the shallows.

Tom tried to appear invisible and put his sunglasses on.
It didn't work.

"Nose out of joint, eh?" Robbie said.

Tom decided that Robbie was too large to be easily
beaten into the sand.

"Don't worry," Liz said, very pleasantly. "She's got to
be nice to Jo, but she wants to be nice to you."

Tom looked at Liz with a rather new view and decided
that it was too easy to judge people by their externals. Not
that much of Liz's externals weren't on view. At least it was a
nice thought, even if it wasn't entirely convincing.

But they took the picnic to the top of the cliffs and Jo said
nice things about it, but it was difficult to say anything much
except, "See you tomorrow," when Sue had to get out of the
car first to let Jo out of the back.

"Tomorrow's the day, then," Jo said. Tom nodded.
"We'll get the champagne ready."

Tom went early into the School of Architecture, and walked
along the long corridor to the notice-boards. It seemed like
several years ago since he'd stood by them wondering where
the School of Architecture actually was, and now he knew.

There was a narrow piece of paper with very dark official
printing on it.

PASS LIST. YEAR 1.

He ran his finger down it, read his name, and then did it
all again, so there would be no mistake. There was no-one in
the corridor, so Tom jumped once off the ground with his
arms out, in silence, and then composed himself and went to
tell Sue. And, of course, Jo.

But Jo turned out to be surprisingly amenable and took
herself off to the shops (apparently a luxury after lying on her
back for months), and so, that afternoon, after several hours
of walking in the deep lanes, mostly, as far as Tom was

concerned, several centimetres above the ground, they came down through the old woods behind Orris's house and Orris was leaning out of the window, apparently having just got up. Tom felt faintly guilty that he hadn't asked what had happened to him.

"I take it you both passed," Orris said.

"Yup," Tom said. "You?"

"Indeed," Orris said. "*Cum laude*, as they say. I'm doing research next year. What about the others?"

"All passed," Tom said. "Even Vince. Amazing."

"Except Liz. She's got to re-sit two papers, the ones she walked out of."

"Ah yes, Liz," Orris said.

Sue and Tom waited. Orris coughed.

"You're no doubt wondering," he said. Tom and Sue waited, standing, holding hands under the trees. The hill sloped up so steeply that they were almost level with his windowsill. "Bit of a disaster, actually," Orris said. "Very delightful lady; ate well, said all the right things and we played chess while her clothes dried and she wore my sweaters and things. And it got to be after midnight and we decided that it was really a bit too late to walk across to Hall."

Tom and Sue waited.

Orris coughed. "So she stayed."

"Disgraceful," Tom said, imagining it, and hoping for details.

"Well," Orris said, cheerfully. "That's what I thought. Great. There's only one bed, nowhere else to sleep. I thought, this is it. She went off to the bathroom, and came back with all her clothes on and got into bed and went to sleep. I mean, what can you do? I don't know why girls' mothers are so concerned about their virtue. Girls are very difficult to unwrap at the best of times. So I spent the night in the chair."

"Did you give her scrambled eggs for breakfast?" Tom said.

"Certainly. Best of friends."

"She seems to be best of friends with Robbie, now," Tom said. "They're going on holiday together when Robbie's done his stint at the morgue." Orris looked rather relieved. "What are you doing for the vac?"

"Staying here," Orris said. "Working as relief lab assistant. I thought I'd make some wine. Things like that. Then I'm hitching to Turkey. Something like that." He looked up at the blue sky as if he was really rather satisfied with it.

"You know," he said. "I'm the first person in any known branch of our family to get a degree."

No response seemed to be required. He looked down at them. "Tom. Before you disappear, the flat upstairs is going free next year. It's got a bedroom and a big kitchen. If I take it, how about you take over my room and we could share the kitchen and the rent?"

Chapter Twenty-nine
GOING DOWN

They stood on the platform. The train was having its doors slammed and seemed about to move. Jo, grinning, had taken her case and gone to sit away in the carriage. There was a pause, until the door had slid shut.

"I'll write every day," Sue said. "Phone." She said: "I never thought I'd say anything as stupid as that."

"You must be used to it," Tom said. "Writing, I mean."

"It's all totally out of character," Sue said. She kissed him.

"Never had this urge before?" Tom said.

"Don't worry," Sue said. "Never." She got into the train and Tom pushed her suitcases in after her. She shoved them behind her, and Tom shut the door and then opened it and slammed it. Sue leaned on the windowsill, and leaned down to kiss him, and the train jerked away, and Tom ran sideways and kissed her anyway.

And then he stood and waved and Jo's head and arm appeared, waving wildly and then was pulled in, and Sue leaned out and waved and waved until the train had pulled out from under the station canopy and round the curve, and then Tom, waving still, didn't quite know what to do with his hand, and the station filled up with emptiness.

He stood there, thinking, is this the most important thing that's happened to me this year? Or ever, even. A year of good university education and all I really know is that I want to get to see Sue again. He looked round. He was the only person on the platform. He looked at the empty rails, and then turned round and walked out to the car.

That was it. Tom went straight back to the flat, and picked up his bags and suitcases, which were stacked on the bed. The flat was stripped, looking only a little more scarred than when they'd first been there. He considered several people he might say goodbye to, like Robbie, but he didn't feel like looking for him.

Alf had already gone and he'd only said goodbye because Zoe, grinning behind him, had pushed him into the room. Alf said, "Bye, then," and that was about that. Scarcely oozing with sentiment.

Liam was just finishing his packing, and Tom waited and gave him a lift to the station.

"Robbie was really hurt by that nasty letter from the Lodgings Officer," Liam said.

"Well, we all got one," Tom said, keeping his face straight.

"See you in October."

"See you."

Tom drove out of the town, still too busy watching the temperature gauge to remember that this was a momentous moment, the end of something. When he did remember, he decided that it wasn't at all momentous. The only real interest was the next thing, which was getting home and going to see Sue.

Well, not quite the next thing. The next thing was stopping ten miles on because the rear nearside tyre was flat.

Tom got out of the car, looked at the tyre, and patted the car's roof.

"Well, I suppose it was a bit much to expect you to get home," he said, and opened the boot to look for the spare.

A PAUSE